FORBIDDEN TEMPTATION

FORBIDDEN #3

R.L. KENDERSON

FORBIDDEN TEMPTATION

ONE

MACKENZIE SWANSON WAS DRIVING AS if her life depended on it.

Maybe because it did.

She looked in the rearview mirror to make sure she wasn't being followed and then glanced down at the passed out cat-shifter lying in the front seat with his head on her lap. *What in the hell am I going to do? And why am I stuck with Sawyer again? Why couldn't I have been kidnapped with some sex god instead?* Thankfully, she didn't have to pretend to be his wife anymore.

To say they had a complicated past would be an understatement.

But she needed to put that aside for now because it wasn't important. Kenzie and Sawyer had just escaped from their kidnappers after being abducted and locked up for ten days—or maybe it was eleven. All the days had started to run together after a while. Now, they were on the run. If she didn't need Sawyer's help to get back home, she'd probably tell him that they'd be better off parting ways.

They'd finally escaped their kidnappers, but they had been shot at. They were driving a stolen vehicle with a possible GPS tracker. They had no cell phone, money, or IDs, and they had no idea where they were. The icing on the cake was that Sawyer had been drugged and smacked in the head, and he was now unconscious.

Kenzie was trying really hard not to panic, but without her cell phone, she didn't know anyone's number. *Stupid electronic age.* She had her fingers crossed that Sawyer would know someone's number. Knowing him, he probably had every number memorized, and for privacy, he hadn't even thought of putting their numbers into his phone. She snorted. He probably deleted his call history after every call, too.

Because of Sawyer's uptight ways, his very nature gave Kenzie hope that they would be on their way home soon. After Sawyer woke up, they would find a public phone somewhere, and he could call someone to pick them up.

First though, they needed to ditch the car that she was driving. Not only was Kenzie worried about it having a GPS tracker, but it also had bullet holes from when they had been shot at. She was driving a cop magnet. That might sound good to anyone else, but how would she explain to the cops that Sawyer and she had been accidentally kidnapped? Being mistaken for the Minnesota Pride alpha's son and a vampire princess wasn't information she could volunteer. Of course, she wouldn't have to give them all the details, but she was pretty sure they would still investigate. When she had been gifted the knowledge of vampires and shifters, she had promised to keep the secrets.

Right now, she needed to find someplace safe to go until Sawyer woke up, so she could make sure he was okay and then ditch the car. But where in the hell was somewhere safe? She had no idea where they were. She didn't even know if they were in Minnesota anymore. When they had been kidnapped, she had been unconscious for part of the trip, so she didn't know how long they had driven or what direction they had headed before they had made it to the house where Sawyer and she had been held captive.

At the moment, they were in the middle of BFE, out in the country on some lonely two-lane highway, with a fourth of a tank of gas. Oh, yeah, and it was November. They needed to find somewhere to go and soon, or they could add freezing to death as another thing to worry about.

Shit, shit, shit. They were so screwed.

Kenzie wasn't a very emotional girl. She didn't cry at sad movies or books, and when boyfriends had broken up with her, she'd either blow it off or get pissed. But frustration was a whole other thing. If she was really and truly frustrated, that was when the tears would come. Currently, she was frustrated, and she could feel the burn at the back of her eyes, which only made her more upset. Crying wasn't going to save them.

After about five minutes of taking calming breaths, she saw a sign for the next town—Hudson, Wisconsin. Had they finally caught a break? Her whole body sagged with relief. Maybe Sawyer and she had finally run into some good luck because her brother lived in Hudson. She could simply go to Bastian's house, dump the stolen car, wait for Sawyer to wake up, and use her brother's cell to call whomever Sawyer thought of first. Then, *bam*, they'd be rescued. Their ordeal was almost over.

After she made it to Bastian's street, she drove around the block a few times to make sure that she hadn't missed someone following them before she approached the house and went up the driveway. She sprinted from the car to open the garage door with the keypad on the side of the house. The garage was empty, but she had expected that since her brother should be at work. Then, she quickly pulled the car inside and closed the door.

Turning off the engine, she sighed. Step one of the plan—finding someplace safe—was done, but step two—getting Sawyer into the house—was going to be difficult. Sawyer was over six feet and had to weigh over two hundred pounds. She was five-four and weighed one hundred ten pounds. She couldn't get him inside even if she dragged him. He'd been drugged and knocked out, and she had no idea if she would be able to wake him. It wouldn't be ideal, but if he remained unconscious, she would have to leave him on the garage floor while she got rid of the car. He hadn't moved since they got away, so the floor was looking like it might be her only option.

She stared down at Sawyer, asleep in her lap. He looked so peaceful, and she felt a little bad that she would have to wake him. She brushed his tawny hair off his face and neck before picking his head up and softly setting it down on the edge of the driver's seat.

She climbed out of the vehicle and opened the door to the house, so there wouldn't be anything in their path from the car to the house once she woke him.

She opened the passenger door and poked his leg. "Sawyer. Sawyer."

Nothing.

This time, she shook his arm. "Sawyer."

Still nothing.

She leaned in and shook his shoulders.

Nothing again.

Finally, she reached into the car and lightly smacked him on the face while trying not to fall on top of him. "*Sawyer, wake up.*"

"Mmm."

"Sawyer, you need to wake up, so I can help you into the house. It's cold out here."

No response.

She went back around to the driver's side since his head was lying on the driver's seat. She sat down on the outside half and gave him a few more pats on the face since that had seemed to get a response out of him. "Sawyer, you need to get up. Now."

"Mmm," he muttered again. This time, he turned his head toward her and mumbled a word that sounded like *make* or *Nate*.

"*You big oaf, will you please get up?*" she hissed.

He opened his eyes.

Finally. Apparently, calling him names had worked.

She leaned her head over, so he could see her better. He looked at her with his amber eyes and smiled, as in an everything-is-hunky-dory-and-life-is-good kind of smile. Sawyer rarely smiled and never a smile filled with such happiness and contentment. And he certainly didn't smile at her.

Something wasn't right.

She tried to see his pupils since he had been drugged and knocked out, but the garage was too dark to assess them.

"Hey there, big guy. Can you get up for me, so we can go into the house?"

"Sure," he said with a dopey smile, still lying there without even attempting to get up.

Sure? Now, she knew something was wrong.

This was not the Sawyer that she knew. Sawyer was not passive. Sawyer was not cheerful. And Sawyer certainly did not agree with anything she said.

The sooner she got him into the house, the better.

"Okay, big boy, let's get you up."

She exited to go to Sawyer's side of the vehicle again. As she walked around to the open passenger door, he stared at her the whole time through the windshield, almost as if he were in a daze. He was starting to creep her out a little because he was never like this.

When she reached him, she got his legs out of the car and grabbed his hands. "I'm going to help you sit up. On the count of three, you push, and I'll pull, okay?"

"Okay," he answered.

She wasn't sure if he'd even heard what she said.

"Okay." She nodded. "One, two, three, and go!"

She yanked on his arms, hard, and it appeared that Sawyer was trying to help, but holy shit was the man heavy. She got him into a sitting position, and his feet were on the ground, but it hadn't been easy. It took another ten minutes to get him into the house, and despite the cold garage, she had started to break a sweat.

"Let's go to the couch," she told him.

Thankfully, it was cleared off. Her brother was a bachelor, and even though he was in his early thirties, he still lived like he was ten years younger. After she helped Sawyer get to the couch, she looked around and noticed the place was remarkably clean. She hoped it didn't mean what she thought it meant.

She went over to the thermostat and saw that the temperature was turned down to sixty-two degrees. That wasn't good either. She turned the heat up to seventy before she used the bathroom. She prayed her brother's girlfriend, Anna, had left some feminine products there.

Kenzie was in luck. She was relieved to get rid of her makeshift pad. Thank God that she was on birth control, that her periods were really light and would only last a few days, and that she was already on day three.

After she was done with the bathroom, she rummaged around her brother's coat closet for a warm coat, hat, and gloves. Once she found a spot to leave the car, she'd have to walk home. To say she wasn't looking forward to freezing her ass off while wondering if someone was out there, planning to kill her, would be an understatement.

She looked back at Sawyer and tried to ignore her irritation. She knew it wasn't his fault that he'd been drugged and injured, but it wasn't fair that she would have to do this all on her own either. She could really use his help right now.

After finding everything she needed, she returned to his side to check on him before she left. His eyes were closed, but he didn't seem to be sleeping, so she nudged him.

He opened his eyes and looked at her. She could see his pupils now, and they didn't appear to be dilated. That was a good sign, yet something was up. Even injured, she couldn't believe he wasn't taking charge, getting things done, and bossing her around.

She'd have to worry about it later though. If she had to deal with one more piece of bad news right now, she might explode. "I need to go and get rid of the car, but I'll be back as soon as possible."

She put on her brother's winter gear while Sawyer watched.

"Do you think you'll be okay while I'm gone?"

No reply.

He just blinked and stared at her hands while she put on the gloves.

"Sawyer, did you hear what I said? I need to get rid of the car. Are you going to be okay?"

He slowly raised his head and looked into her eyes. His brow furrowed, he asked, "Who's Sawyer?"

☾

"Are you *fucking* kidding me? This cannot be happening right now," the sexy blonde human in front of him screeched. She pointed a finger at him. "You're Sawyer!"

Me? "Me?"

She grabbed on to the side of the bulky hat she was wearing, pulled it down over her face, and screamed into it. He winced because, even though the sound was muffled, it hurt his sensitive ears, and his head was pounding with one fierce headache.

After she was done yelling, she reached up to the top of her head and yanked the hat completely off. Her brown eyes flashed with a mix of annoyance and disbelief. "This can't be happening. I needed you so that you could call someone and get us out of this mess. Now, you're telling me that you've lost your memory? We are so screwed." She closed her eyes and took a deep breath before opening them again to look at him. "What's the last thing you remember?"

She was obviously upset, and he didn't like seeing her that way, so he tried to recall…anything.

"Uh…waking up in the car and you bringing me inside." He looked around. "We don't live here, right?" He picked up on the scent of a human male and the fainter scent of another human female, but it didn't smell like either the blonde or him, so he didn't think that this was their home, but he wanted to be sure.

She looked at him like he was crazy. "No, we don't live here. *We*"—she gestured between the two of them—"don't live anywhere. This is my brother's house."

He was confused because he recognized what his body was telling him.

"Sawyer, what else do you remember?"

He sniffed the air around them.

She sighed. "Sawyer?"

He sniffed his upper arm.

"Sawyer?" She snapped her fingers in front of his face. "Sawyer!"

Sawyer? Oh, yeah, that was him. He met her chestnut eyes. "What?"

"What do you remember?"

"Like I said, you waking me in the car, coming inside, and telling me my name is Sawyer. What's your name?"

"Kenzie."

"Kenzie," he repeated. He liked the sound of it on his tongue. "Kenzie, is there any way I can get something for my head? It's killing me."

"Oh, shit. Yes. Sorry," she said. She threw her hat on the couch and took off her gloves as well.

Then, she ran into the other room. By what little he could see of it, it was the kitchen.

She returned with a bottle of water and some medication. "So, your head really hurts?" she asked as she passed him the H_2O and pills.

He sat up and immediately got light-headed. He waited for the dizziness to pass and swallowed the tablets down. "Yeah."

She took the seat next to him. "Okay, so you don't remember anything before now. But do you *know* anything?"

He set the bottle of water on the table next to the couch. "What do you mean by, know anything?"

She bit her lip. "Um…do you know what you are?" She touched her chest. "Do you know what I am? Do you know that we're different?"

"Do you mean, do I know that I'm a cat-shifter and that you're a human?"

"Yes." She sighed with relief. "Thank God you remember something."

He was glad that he'd done something to make her happy. He liked her happy. He grabbed her hand, brought the back of it to his lips and nose, and inhaled, trying to determine if he was right about his earlier assessment.

"Uh…what are you doing?"

"I'm smelling you." He turned her hand around so that he could sniff her palm.

"I can see that. *Why* are you smelling me?"

Because her lemony aroma had only a trace of his earthy scent on top of it. "I'm just trying to confirm what you are to me." He was definitely confused now because his scent was deep in her pores yet not as strong as it should be. Something didn't add up because either—

She yanked her hand away. "What in the hell are you talking about?" She stood up and grabbed her hat and gloves. "You know what? Don't even tell me. I don't have time for this right now. I need to go and dump the car." She pointed a finger at him. "You stay here. Do not go anywhere. Don't even go outside. I have enough to deal with, without having to look for a cat-shifter with amnesia. I'll be back as soon as I can."

It raised his hackles a little that she was talking to him like he was a child, but he could see that she was under a lot of stress at the moment, so he didn't push her. They could discuss things after she returned. He really needed to find out what had happened before he lost his memory.

He wished that he could help her more right now, but with his headache and vertigo problem, he knew it would be better if he stayed back. "I understand that you are worried right now and you need to take care of some business, but we really need to talk when you get back. You need to tell me everything that you know."

She put on her hat and gloves. "I agree. We can talk as soon as I get back."

"Sorry you have to do this by yourself." He shook his head. "*I* should be the one doing it."

A small smile reached her lips. "There's a bit of the Sawyer I know and hate."

Hate? She had to be joking because how could she hate—

Before he realized that she'd even left, the door slammed, knocking the rest of his thought right out of his head.

TWO

SAWYER—HE wondered what his last name was—slowly rose from the couch. Even with his gentle movements, his head began to spin. He paused once, standing still to let the stars clear from his vision. Deciding that he might be better off on four legs rather than two, he stripped off his clothes and changed into his cat.

He still didn't feel good, but his cat form would make it easier to scope out his surroundings. The blonde—Kenzie—had said it was her brother's place, but he still wanted to make sure that he would be ready for anything. He couldn't just take someone's word that this was a safe place.

On the main floor, there was the living room, kitchen, dining room, an office, and a half-bathroom. So far, the whole place had an empty vibe, as if no one had been there for a while. No dirty dishes were lying around, the office's desk was tidy and empty of a computer or paperwork, and the bathroom had a freshly cleaned smell.

Sawyer made his way upstairs and found the master bedroom and bath, two extra bedrooms—one with a bed and the other used as storage—and a third bathroom. Everything smelled clean upstairs, too, as if a cleaning lady had come and gone, and no one had touched anything since. The house was obviously lived in...just vacant.

Feeling that everything was safe for now, Sawyer eyed the shower through the open door of the bathroom. A shower, food, and a nap sounded great, and since he was already upstairs, he might as well start with a shower.

He put his paws up onto the counter and was met with the sight of a tawny-colored big cat with matching eyes. As a cat, he was about the size of a jaguar but had the coat of a cougar. He braced his paws on the counter and shifted into his human form.

He immediately cringed. He looked like shit. His shoulder-length hair was ratty, and his eyes were bloodshot. He leaned over to get a closer look. Thankfully, his pupils weren't dilated, so it looked like he didn't have a concussion. He stepped back to balance on his feet and to make sure he wouldn't pass out in the shower.

He had a good amount of muscle mass, but his ribs were showing. He'd lost weight.

He frowned. How did he know that he'd lost weight? Was he starting to remember?

He looked himself up and down, hoping something else would come to him, but he was coming up blank. Disappointed by the lack of memory, he got in the shower and turned it on.

He took his time, enjoying the warm water, and his thoughts turned to Kenzie. Something was going on there, something to do with the two of them, and he needed to fix it. Once Kenzie returned, he was going to make sure that there was no mistaking where the two of them stood.

After he was finished washing, he shut off the water and grabbed one of the towels hanging on the towel rack. He dried his hair and body and hung the towel back up.

He exited the bathroom and made his way downstairs. He needed some sustenance. Looking for something easy, he decided on having the frozen meals in the freezer. There were five of them, and he was so hungry that he ate all five. He would figure out a way to pay back Kenzie's brother. He didn't know how, but he would figure it out later.

After he had stuffed his belly full, he was hit with an overwhelming wave of fatigue. He lugged his tired body upstairs to the second bedroom and flopped down on the bed. He didn't even take the time to pull the comforter and sheets down before he fell asleep.

☾

Kenzie breathed warmth onto her hands through her thin gloves. It was so cold outside, and she still had two blocks to go before she would be back at her brother's house.

At least she had successfully gotten rid of the stolen car. She'd remembered to wipe it down with a rag from her brother's garage. Hopefully, there would be nothing that could lead the vehicle back to them if the police were the ones to find it. She wasn't too worried about the stolen part of the equation because the only reason that they had taken it was to escape their kidnappers. But if she explained this, the cops would wonder why no one had reported her or Sawyer missing.

She stopped in her tracks. At least, she hoped no one had reported her missing. She'd totally forgotten about her job. She'd never missed work without calling in. They were probably wondering where she was. Had they called the police and sent someone to her apartment? Had the cops started investigating her disappearance, and she would be the reason that the shifters' cover was blown?

She started sprinting back toward the house. She was only a couple of houses down from her brother's when she saw a black SUV one block up. Her heart began to race, and her breathing became shallow. The worst part was that she froze on the spot. If it were the kidnappers, she was out in the open, like a sitting duck. Just when she thought that she might faint from lack of oxygen, the SUV turned left on the street in front of her.

She had no idea how much longer she stood there until some sense came back to her. Her heart rate slowed, and she took a couple of deep breaths. Realizing that she was still standing in the same spot, she resumed her steps and made it the rest of the way to Bastian's house. She opened the garage door with the code again, hurried inside, and closed the big door. Once in the house, she rested her back against the door and counted to ten.

She needed to remember that she was safe now. She was away from the abductors. She was in her brother's house, a familiar place. The kidnappers didn't even know who she really was. When Sawyer and she had been taken, they had thought that she was her best friend, Naya, and that Sawyer was Naya's mate, Vaughn. They weren't going to look for her at Bastian's house. And now that she had gotten rid of the captors' vehicle, there was nothing to trace back to her.

Even if they found their car, they sure weren't going to go to the police and tell them it had been stolen. *"Yes, officer, my car was stolen by the people I kidnapped."*

She snorted. *Yeah, right. Like that would happen.*

She was safe. Sawyer was safe. Nothing bad was going to happen to them now.

Her biggest worry was going to be how to let Vance Llewelyn, Sawyer's alpha, know that they were safe. But even if she had to wait for Sawyer to regain his memory, they would be fine. She felt bad that the other cat-shifters would be worried about them, but she only had so much to work with.

Pep talk finished, she opened her eyes and went to see how Sawyer was doing. The first thing she noticed was that the couch was empty. He'd better not left when she'd told him to stay there. The next thing she saw was the pile of clothes next to the couch. She went over to inspect them and saw that they were the clothes Sawyer had been wearing earlier.

What the hell? Why were they lying on the floor?

She threw off her winter gear and went in search of the missing amnesic cat-shifter.

He wasn't anywhere downstairs, so she headed for the second floor. She found him in her brother's guest bedroom, facedown, sleeping on the bed. He was butt-ass naked. And what an ass it was, along with the rest of him. Muscular back and thighs did not have a single mark on them. She had seen some of the other cat-shifters' tattoos, but it figured that Sawyer would keep his body free of any markings. She loved tattoos, but Sawyer's unmarred skin was beautiful, too.

She felt a little dirty for looking at him, but she had never seen his bare butt before. She'd briefly been naked with Sawyer once, but it had been anything but romantic or sexual.

It had been the first day in their captivity, and the only reason that they had been naked was so that they could talk privately in the shower. At the time, they hadn't known if the room they were trapped in was wired for sound, and they had needed the water to drown out their voices. They had both been under stress, and she had made sure to keep her eyes on his face, no matter how much she had wanted to look down and see what the man carried in his pants.

He was such a confident asshole that she was certain that he had to be hung like a fricking horse, and she'd be lying if she said that she had never thought about seeing it, touching it, licking it, or feeling it inside her. Sawyer and she might get along as well as a valley girl would in a third-world country, but he had been the main source of her spank bank lately. Sometimes, it'd only take her a few minutes to come just from imagining the angry sex that they would have.

Deciding that she'd done enough gawking, she went to the linen closet in the hallway and grabbed an extra blanket. She went back to the bedroom and placed it over Sawyer. She'd let him sleep for now. He probably needed it. Hopefully, the rest would refresh his memory.

She went downstairs and grabbed his clothes. They were the only ones that he had, so she might as well wash them while he was sleeping. Her brother wouldn't have anything for Sawyer to wear. Bastian was five-six and a beanpole. His clothes would fit Kenzie better than Sawyer, which was good for her but bad for Sawyer. With any luck, they wouldn't be here for long. Even with Sawyer's memory loss, there had to be a way to get ahold of the cat-shifters. She just needed to brainstorm.

In the basement, she threw Sawyer's clothes into the washing machine. She looked down at the oversized outfit she was wearing. Thankfully, their kidnappers had been too stupid to realize that all the clothes they had provided for Naya were too big on her.

Idiots.

Wanting to wash away the memory of being held captive, she threw her stuff in there, too.

She started the washer and sprinted up the two flights of stairs, naked. She peeked into the bedroom just to make sure Sawyer was still sleeping. Relieved to see that he was, she got in the shower and began to scrub the last week and a half off her skin. While she let the water run down her body, she began to come up with some other ideas for how they could get out of there. She just needed her brother to get home.

When she was done with her shower, she dried off with a towel, wrapped it around herself, and went searching for clothes in her brother's room. She found her brother's plain V-neck T-shirt and gray zip-up hoodie and a pair of black yoga pants that had to belong to her brother's girlfriend. Anna and Kenzie didn't really care for each other, and Kenzie could just picture Anna curling her lip at the thought of Kenzie borrowing her clothes. But Anna wasn't there, and they were very close in size. What Anna didn't know wouldn't kill her. Kenzie also found a package of briefs that her brother hadn't opened yet, and she was relieved that she wouldn't have to borrow anyone's underwear. The only thing left was a bra, but her boobs were so small that she didn't really need one. This was one of the few times that being a member of the Itty Bitty Titty Committee came in handy.

The sun had started to set while Kenzie was in the shower, and even though it was a little early for dinner, she decided to go in search of something to cook. They'd been living on protein and granola bars while they were kidnapped, and the thought of real food made her stomach rumble.

Before she went in the kitchen, she checked on something in her brother's office. Her findings, or rather the lack thereof, were a major disappointment. She wasn't ready to lose hope yet, so she pushed away all thoughts, except for food.

Once in the kitchen, she noticed a dirty fork in the sink. It looked like Sawyer had already eaten. There were no other dirty dishes, so she checked the garbage. *Is that five microwave meals?*

She looked in the freezer. Sawyer had cleaned her brother out. Well, at least she didn't have to worry about feeding him. She could let him sleep, which was good.

She knew they had things to talk about, but after everything she had been through recently, all she wanted to do was eat, go to bed, and worry about her problems later. They could discuss everything the next day. It didn't look like they were going anywhere anyway.

Kenzie made herself a grilled cheese sandwich from the bread she had removed from the freezer and thawed in the microwave. Then, she sat in the living room and watched TV. She needed some mindless entertainment for half an hour or so. Once she was done eating, she cleaned up her dishes and then went downstairs to throw Sawyer's clothes in the dryer.

With no other excuses to keep her mind off of it, she looked at the time and told herself she had to face the fact that her brother wasn't coming home tonight. It was getting late, and he still hadn't arrived. Sure, he could've grabbed drinks or dinner with friends, but there were other signs as well. His house was incredibly clean, which meant his cleaning lady had been there and her brother hadn't been back to disturb anything. His thermostat had been turned down very low to conserve energy while he was away. And the worst part was that his computer was missing.

No phone. No computer. No hope. Her brother was clearly out of town for the time being. *What a shitty ending to a shitty day—no, make that a shitty week.*

Kenzie sighed and dragged herself upstairs to bed. She turned on the hall light to peek in on Sawyer one last time. He hadn't moved, but she made sure his torso was moving up and down to confirm that he was still breathing. Convinced that Sawyer wasn't dead, she ambled to Bastian's room and climbed into his bed.

Promising herself and the universe that she would face all her problems tomorrow, she closed her eyes and was asleep within minutes.

THREE

THE NEXT DAY, Kenzie awoke to see that the alarm clock next to her brother's bed read well past noon. She rolled over onto her back and stretched. She must have been more tired than she'd thought if she'd slept that late. She wasn't really a morning person, but she had gone to bed really early the night before.

Suddenly, Kenzie realized that while she had slept a long time, Sawyer had slept even longer. She hoped he was okay. She jumped out of bed and ran to the other room. He had rolled onto his side. She took this as a good sign since he had moved sometime during the night. People in a comatose state didn't move. At least she didn't think they did.

She frowned. Maybe she should check to make sure he was okay.

"Sawyer?" she whispered once she reached his side.

No response.

She had assumed that he hadn't woken up in the car the day before because of his head injury, but maybe he was a heavy sleeper.

22

She shook his shoulder and spoke his name a little louder, "Sawyer?"

Nothing.

It'd worked the first time, so she patted his cheek and practically yelled his name, "Sawyer!"

"What?" he grumbled, keeping his eyes closed.

"Are you okay? You've been sleeping for, like, twenty hours." She wasn't sure on the exact time, but that had to be about right.

"Yes. Just healing."

She waited for him to say more, but his chest was already rising and falling to the rhythm of someone in a deep slumber.

She shrugged and went downstairs to find coffee and food. After she had her fill of caffeine and dry cereal, she sat down in the living room to brainstorm, but she didn't get very far because she woke up, drooling on the couch.

Great. She had fallen asleep. That shouldn't even be possible.

She should have been so rested from all the sleep she had gotten last night that she shouldn't have needed to sleep for a day, but instead, she had taken a nap. Now, a whole day had passed since they got there, and they weren't any closer to getting home.

One thing was for sure. She and Sawyer needed to talk. It was necessary that he knew what had happened. He'd been sleeping for twenty-four hours now. He could get up whether he wanted to or not.

She supposed, in exchange, she could make him dinner. That way, they could talk while they ate.

She found beef in the freezer and spaghetti sauce and

noodles in the cupboard. She even found an onion in the crisper. Spaghetti was something easy to make, and it would fill them up. Well, it would fill her up. Sawyer ate a lot, going by the amount of frozen meals he'd eaten the night before. They would just have to find something else if Sawyer was still hungry after all the food was gone.

She fried the beef, added the spaghetti sauce, put the noodles on the stove, and decided it was time to wake up Sawyer. First, she grabbed his clean clothes out of the dryer. Then, she went up to the second floor and turned the light on in the hall to help her see. She entered the guest bedroom and saw Sawyer was once again sleeping on his stomach.

She threw his clothes on the opposite side of the bed. Then, she sat on the edge of the bed and touched his shoulder. "Sawyer? It's time to get up."

Nothing.

She sighed. *This again?* She might as well smack his cheek and skip all the steps in between.

But before she did that, Kenzie hesitantly touched Sawyer's shoulder again. When he didn't stir, she moved her hand down and over his back. She only wanted to touch him for a second or two.

Sawyer had a little bit of a problem with control and giving it to others. The two of them had never had sex, but they'd had a couple of bouts of angry third base. Technically, Sawyer had gotten to third base. Kenzie had never even gotten to put her hands on him. The first time, she'd been so overwhelmed and caught off guard that she didn't even try. She'd been too busy coming to even try to touch him. But going by the second time, when he'd held her hands away from him, he hadn't permitted it anyway.

So, now, she was going to enjoy the fact that he was sleeping, and she could touch him. Just a little. She trailed her fingers down to where the blanket covered his butt and then started the trip back up to his shoulder. He was softer than she had thought he—

Kenzie yelped as Sawyer whipped an arm up and pulled her underneath him. He buried his nose in her neck and wrapped his arms around her, squeezing her tight. Then, he didn't move.

He had fallen back asleep, if his deep breathing was any indication.

It took some maneuvering, but she freed her arms from Sawyer's hold and pushed on his shoulders. "Sawyer, you need to wake up and get off me." She pushed again, but it was like trying to move a rock. She tried to kick her feet out, which ended up being a bad idea because Sawyer landed right between her legs.

The man was hard and definitely not small.

Crap. What was she going to do now?

Drastic times called for drastic measures, so she reached up for a chunk of Sawyer's hair and pulled his head up. "Sawyer, if you don't get off me, I'm going to rip off little Sawyer and shove him in your ear."

His eyes slowly blinked open. Threatening a man's body parts worked every time.

Sawyer smiled. "Hi, mate."

Mate? Oh God. Not only had he lost his memory, but he now also thought that he was Australian.

She sighed. "Sawyer, we're not mates. Can you please get off me?"

He frowned. "Yes, we are. You can't lie to me."

She rolled her eyes. They were more like frenemies than friends, but it would just be easier to agree with him. "Fine, we're *mates*." She emphasized *mates* with an Australian accent, so he would realize how ridiculous he sounded. "Now, will you please get off me?"

"No." He kissed her.

God, he tasted good, and even though she should stop, she kissed him back.

He grabbed her hair in much the same way that she had done to him, but instead of trying to wake her up, he used his grip to angle her head the way he wanted.

She loved a man who took charge in the bedroom, and she reached up to touch his back, his shoulders, and his chest. Apparently, Sawyer had forgotten his dislike of humans and his revulsion of her because he didn't stop her.

She knew she shouldn't keep going because, once Sawyer regained his memory, he'd be pissed, but she was greedy, and he'd started it by kissing her. She slowly moved her hand down his chest, then onto his side, and across his hip. As if he knew where she was headed, he rolled the tiniest bit to the side, and she took the opportunity to grab his cock.

He was even bigger than she had originally guessed. There was no doubt about it. The man was hung.

She touched him just like she'd always fantasized about, and he broke their kiss.

"Holy shit, that feels good," he said.

Kenzie smiled with satisfaction. Unlike some women

who only liked certain aspects of sex, Kenzie liked it all. All of it turned her on. She loved giving just as much as receiving. She liked touching a man, and she even liked giving head. But, right now, she loved the sounds that Sawyer was making. She loved that she was the one making him feel this way.

He put his mouth next to her ear. "Take off your clothes. I wanna fuck you."

Her breathing sped up more than it already had. Now, he was talking dirty to her. She *loved* dirty talk, and the fact that it was coming from Sawyer made her hot as hell. She'd never thought that she would hear him say naughty things in the bedroom. Strong and silent was his normal MO.

She really wanted him to fuck her, too, but she was starting to feel like she was taking advantage of the situation.

It was one thing to touch a guy's penis when he couldn't give full consent, but it was another thing to have sex with him. With her luck, Sawyer would cry rape once his memory returned.

She let go of his dick and tried to push him away. "We can't."

He raised himself up to look at her. "Why not? I know you want me as much as I want you." He dragged his hand down her body and cupped her between the legs. "I can smell you. I can smell how much you want me inside you."

"Goddamn it, Sawyer."

He was making it really hard to say no.

He smiled with satisfaction and used his thumb to press down on her clit.

She moaned when he started rubbing. Maybe it

wouldn't be so bad if she let him touch her for just a minute.

Sawyer reached for the top of her pants and underwear, and despite her sexual haze, she was struck with the excuse used by women across the globe.

She put her hand on his, stopping him. "Wait. I have my period."

She smiled apologetically at him, but inside, she was giving herself a mental high five. Her period was pretty much over now, but he didn't need to know that.

"So?"

So? There wasn't supposed to be a *so*.

While they had been in captivity, he'd seemed to be repulsed by her period, and now, he was saying, *"So?"*

What was she supposed to say now?

Suddenly, Sawyer arched up and sniffed the air. He looked down at her, brow furrowed. "Are you cooking?"

"Oh my God. I forgot about dinner." She tried to shove him away. "I have to get the noodles off the stove."

She pushed against him again, and this time, he rolled off of her. She jumped from the bed and ran for the door.

"Kenzie?"

She paused and looked back at him.

"You go ahead and get dinner, but this isn't over. Once your period is done, you'd better be ready because I'm coming inside you."

She felt her eyes go round, and she ran out the door.

He yelled after her, "I'm going to make sure you are good and—"

She didn't hear the rest as she got too far away, which was a good thing. It was already taking everything in her not to turn around and let him have his way with her.

FOUR

SAWYER HAD LET KENZIE GO. He'd figured that they didn't need the house burning down, and truth be told, he was starving. He slowly rose from the bed, testing out his equilibrium. His nap must have helped because his dizziness and headache were gone.

He looked around and saw his clothes neatly folded on the bed. He picked them up and sniffed them to be sure they were clean. Kenzie had washed them, and the thought made him smile. Cooking for him and washing his clothes— he took that as good signs.

As he pulled on his jeans and buttoned them, he saw the time on the clock. He didn't know what time Kenzie had returned from dropping the car off somewhere, but he didn't think she would have had enough time to wash and dry his clothes while he slept.

Shit. How long have I been out?

Without bothering to put on his shirt, he made his way to the kitchen.

When he reached the main floor, he paused when he

saw Kenzie in the kitchen. She wasn't classically beautiful. She was kind of plain, her lips were thin, she had barely any curves to speak of, and she had no boobs, but his dick wanted her anyway. His cat wanted her. His cat had chosen her. And who was he to argue with nature?

As he neared, he could see that her face was flushed, and while it could be the heat from cooking, he liked to think that he was the reason her cheeks were pink.

She looked up when he entered the room. "Go ahead, and sit down. I'll bring your plate over."

"Thanks. How long was I out?"

"A day."

"No wonder I feel better."

"Do you remember me trying to wake you?"

He frowned. "No."

"You told me you were healing."

"Yeah, sleep helps us heal faster. My headache and dizziness are gone."

She looked at him with hope. "Did the sleep help your memory at all?"

He regrettably shook his head. "Sorry."

She nodded as if she understood.

After they were both seated and their dinner was on the table, he spent the first few minutes shoving food down his throat. He couldn't believe how hungry he was.

When he felt semi-full, he asked Kenzie, "Why don't you tell me how we ended up here?"

She sat forward in her seat. "Where to start?" She twirled her food for a second. "Okay, you are part of the Minnesota Pride, and you're a sentinel for your alpha, Vance Llewelyn." She paused. "Does that ring any bells?"

He shook his head. "No."

She looked disappointed but continued, "Vance's son, Vaughn, is the next alpha. He's one of your fellow sentinels and your friend. Vaughn is mated to my best friend, Naya. Naya is also the daughter of the king and queen of the vampires. Both Vaughn and Naya are kind of important to the nonhuman world."

Sawyer held up his hand. "Hold on a minute. You're saying a cat-shifter is mated to a vampire?"

"Yes."

He was stunned. "How did that happen?"

Kenzie smiled. "Well..." she started but then stopped. She lost her smile and sat forward in her seat. "Are you telling me that you remember something? You remember that vampires and cat-shifters are enemies?"

She looked so hopeful that he hated to let her down.

"Yes, but that's not uncommon with amnesia. The part of the memory that deals with facts and concepts about the outside world isn't usually affected. So, yes, I know that vampires and shifters don't get along. I also know that cat-shifters live in prides and in secret from humans, present company excluded, but I don't remember my alpha or my role in my pride."

She sat back in her seat. He'd disappointed her again.

"Sorry it's not what you were hoping, but maybe the more you tell me, the more likely I will remember something."

She picked at her food. "I suppose you're right."

He hoped that he was. "So, tell me how a vampire and shifter ended up mated to each other."

She smiled again, which was good. "They met in a

nightclub, and they started as a one-night stand. The night they met is the night that I met you actually."

"Really?"

"Really."

"So, were you and I a one-night stand also?"

She looked at him like he had sprouted horns. "Sawyer, you couldn't get away from me fast enough." She shook her head and laughed as if the whole situation was funny. "Now, I know for sure that you've lost your memory."

Sawyer wasn't laughing, and he didn't think it was funny.

Seemingly unaware that he didn't like this news, she continued, "Naya and Vaughn had a one-night stand, and then Naya got pregnant, found out that shifters existed, and gave up the throne to her cousin. Now, she and Vaughn are mated and just bought a house. You and I were at their new house, getting it ready for them to move in, while Naya and Vaughn were at an appointment for the babies…" She trailed off.

"What's wrong?"

"I just realized Naya and Vaughn had found out if the babies were boys or girls the night we were kidnapped." She set her fork down as a look of sadness crossed her face. "I don't even know what she's having."

Sawyer reached over and squeezed her hand. "Kenzie, I'm going to make sure that you get home and find out about your friend's babies." He didn't know how he would do that yet, but he was going to try his best.

She looked up at him and slipped her hand out from under his. "Thanks."

She didn't sound like she believed him, but he didn't press the issue.

"Why don't you continue with what happened that night?"

"Some men broke into the house and kidnapped you and me. They shot you with a tranquilizer, and they knocked me out, but before they did, one of them had called me princess, so I knew that they thought we were Vaughn and Naya. Because both of us were unconscious while they transported us, neither of us knew how long we had been in the back of the van. Of course, now, I know we're in Wisconsin." She looked at him. "We're in Wisconsin, by the way. I just remembered that you were passed out when I saw the sign, and you had no idea where my brother lives."

"Good to know." Sawyer felt himself tensing up. The thought of these men putting their hands on Kenzie was starting to piss him off.

"They kept us locked in a room with a bathroom in the basement. They had video cameras, so they could watch us, but after some testing, you and I discovered that they couldn't hear us. We pretended to be Vaughn and Naya, so they wouldn't realize that they had grabbed the wrong people.

"We finally escaped when I got my period. We pretended that I was miscarrying and needed to go to the hospital. It worked, but in the process, they managed to drug you, and then you got cracked in the head. Thankfully, we were already in their car. They must have ditched the van that they'd kidnapped us in. I drove like a bat out of hell until I saw a sign for Hudson, Wisconsin, and I brought us here. When they'd kidnapped us, they had taken our phones along with your wallet and ID. My purse is probably still sitting on the counter at Naya and Vaughn's house.

"We are very lucky that my brother lives here. I figured, once you woke up and my brother got home, we could call someone to come and get us. I hadn't taken the time to learn anyone's number in years, thanks to cell phones, but I had hoped that you would know someone we could call."

"Did they—" Sawyer cleared his throat as he clenched and unclenched his hands under the table. "Did they touch you at all?"

"Did they touch me at all? You mean, did they try anything sexual with me? Oh, no. They stayed as far away from us as possible."

Even though the situation was still upsetting, he was relieved to know that Kenzie had gone untouched.

"I don't think they knew that you were a shifter, but they knew something was up with you. They were prepared for someone strong. The door to the room that we were in was made of steel. That was probably the reason that they drugged you. They didn't even open the door to give us food. They shoved stupid granola bars through a hole in the door."

"That would explain my hunger."

"Speaking of food, why don't we finish up and then you can ask me anything else you can think of?"

The two of them finished their spaghetti and cleaned their dishes.

Sawyer looked at the clock, noting the time and the fact that he had slept a whole day, and thought he should bring up his earlier suspicions. "Kenzie, what time does your brother usually get home from work? I have to tell you, after you left to get rid of the car, I looked around the place, and it felt like no one had been here for a few days. He didn't come home last night, did he?"

Kenzie leaned back against the counter. "No," she said with a humorless laugh. "It would seem that my brother is out of town." She rubbed her eyes. "You and me—we have all the luck." She scoffed. "Every plan I've come up with to get us home has been a bust. I thought we could call for help." She threw her arm out. "You don't remember anything, but it's not like we have a phone anyway. I thought maybe I could email Naya in hopes that she would check her email, but my brother always takes his computer with him on business trips." She threw her other arm out. "Even though I'm worried our kidnappers are out there, watching for us, I thought my brother could drive us back to the Twin Cities while we hid in his backseat or something, but he's not here, and neither is his car. We can't even drive ourselves." Now, both arms came out, flying wildly. "We are so fucking screwed."

Sawyer stepped forward and engulfed her, pulling her arms around him.

She buried her face in his chest. "Why us?"

Sawyer ran his hand down her hair. "I don't know, baby." He pulled her back, so he could look her in the eyes. "But I'm going to do everything I can to make sure that we get home. Right now though, I need you to remember that we are safe. I'm not going to let anyone hurt you. Okay?"

"Okay." She turned her head to the side. "Why are you being so nice to me?"

What an odd question. She was obviously confused.

"Kenzie, you're my mate. Why wouldn't I be nice to you?"

She rolled her eyes. "Um, Sawyer, I hate to break it to you, but you're not Australian. You can call me your friend."

Now, he was the confused one. *What does Australia have to do with anything?* Then, he put two and two together.

He laughed. "No, Kenzie, not my mate, as in my friend. My mate, as in my partner." As a human, maybe she wasn't used to the term. "You know…you're my wife."

☾

In shock, Kenzie stepped away from Sawyer.

His words, calling her his wife, stirred something deep inside her.

A longing she hadn't known that she had.

More like, a longing that she had denied since the moment she met him.

One thing was for sure. She had to shut this down before things went any farther.

Before they got more complicated.

Before they got in too deep.

Before Sawyer regained his memory and broke her heart.

Her chest ached just from her thinking about it.

"Sawyer, I'm not your mate," she gently spoke the words. "You don't even like me. In fact, I'm pretty sure you hate me."

His mouth was set in a grim line, and his eyes were hard. This was how he usually looked at her. "I don't understand."

She sighed. "Honestly, I don't understand a lot either.

All I know is that you don't really care for humans—me, in particular. I don't know if it's because we have this chemistry—which I'm sure you would deny if you were your usual self—and you resent me for it or if it's something else, but you've hated me from the beginning. And since you're mostly an asshole to me, you're not my favorite person either. We mostly try to avoid each other."

Sawyer stepped forward with determination.

She didn't know what he was going to do, and she intuitively took a step back and ran into the counter.

"What I don't understand," he said as he reached up and pulled both sides of her sweatshirt and T-shirt away from her neck, "is, if you're not my mate, then why the fuck do you wear my mark? Why the fuck do you smell like me?"

She tried to shrug him off, but he didn't let go.

"I don't know, okay?" She threw her hands up in the air. "I have no idea why you do anything that you do."

He stepped closer. "Did I mark you during sex?"

She purposely shot him an are-you-stupid look. "You're not listening. You don't like me. We've never had sex."

Some of the anger left his face, and he looked off to the side. "Ah…that explains some things."

"What? What does it explain?"

"Why my scent on you is not as strong as it should be." He met her eyes again. "If we didn't have sex, then when did I mark you? How many times?"

"Um…three times." She hesitated to tell him what had led to him biting her because this new Sawyer wasn't going to like it. "The first time was when we were at the same nightclub where we had met, and I was hitting on one of your coworkers and friends."

Sawyer let go of her shirts and brought his hands down to her hips as the fire returned to his golden eyes.

"He turned me down," she quickly added, "but you were still super ticked off. I basically told you that you had no hold over me and that I could fuck whomever I wanted." As she spoke, she felt his fingers tighten around her. She needed to hurry this story up. "This obviously upset you—which was my goal, I admit—and you dragged me into the restroom where you…you know…got me off and bit me. Then, you told me that nobody would touch me now, and you just turned around and left."

Sawyer swallowed. "And the second time?"

"Naya and Vaughn had a meeting with their parents, so everyone came, including your alpha's nephew. He basically called me your whore because I smelled like you, I guess."

Yikes. If she'd thought that Sawyer was mad before, the anger that crossed his face now almost scared her.

"I overheard you tell him that I wasn't your piece of ass and that I belonged to you, so he needed to leave me alone. Then, just to prove it, when he looked at us later, you bit me again. And that was it."

Sawyer took a deep breath. "And the third time?"

"Uh, it was the other day while we were being held captive. I may or may not have said something to piss you off again, and you were about to dump me in the shower and turn the water on me. But since I was supposed to be your pregnant wife and the cameras were on us, you started kissing me instead. Things got a little heated, there was some heavy petting, and you bit me again."

She decided to leave out the fact that she had pushed him

away before she came. Just like the first time, he had only tried to use her body and an orgasm as a way to control her, and she hadn't wanted to let him have that power over her.

"I'm not really sure why you bit me the last time, but you can see that, while two of those times were sexual, it really wasn't because you wanted me."

Sawyer didn't say anything. He seemed to be deep in thought.

She put her hands on his chest. "Sawyer?"

He met her eyes.

"You okay? Do you understand better now?"

"Fuck no." He moved his hands from the outside of her clothes to underneath and rubbed her bare hips. "So far, I've discovered that I'm a dick and that I want to kick a couple of people's asses."

She smiled briefly. "Well, if that's an apology, I'll accept it. As far as the asses you want to kick, like I said, your friend turned me down, and you already put the alpha's nephew in his place. Plus, that was months ago. It's over with." She drew her hands from his chest and squeezed his arms. "Does that help?"

"No. But I'll get over it."

"Are we good now? You get where we stand? You understand now that I'm not your mate?"

Sawyer shook his head and pulled her close. He leaned down and put his mouth next to her ear. "I heard every word you said, and I believe you, but I also know what my nose, my body, and my instincts are telling me. Shifters don't just go around marking anyone and everyone. They mark their mates. So, while it seems like I might have had my head up my ass, I don't anymore. You are my mate, Kenzie."

She gasped and opened her mouth to protest.

"And before you go denying it, your body doesn't lie. My scent is inside you. This means that you opened yourself up and let me in. You accepted me just as much as I claimed you. And if you think I'm going anywhere, you're fucking crazy. I might not remember anything, but I know this. You are mine, and I am yours." He leaned down and kissed his mark on her neck. "And before we leave here, I'm going to make sure the whole world knows it. Especially you."

FIVE

PHOENIX KAPLAN WOKE UP BOUND, gagged, and really pissed off. She was going to strangle Gerald Llewelyn with her bare hands if it were the last thing she did. The fucker had pistol-whipped her and kidnapped her.

He had sure picked the wrong she-cat. She was going to make him pay.

She looked around the back of the SUV. First, she needed to get out of here though.

She looked through the windows, relieved that she could see lights. They were still in the Cities somewhere. She had no idea what the crazy cat-shifter planned to do with her, but she was going to do her best to stop him.

Not only had he abducted her, but he had also orchestrated a whole plan to kill their alpha, kidnap his children, and take over the pride. She couldn't believe that he'd thought he could actually get away with it. He should have never involved the wolf-shifters and the vampires.

Phoenix's alpha, Vance Llewelyn, had learned that his cousin, Gerald, had plotted and schemed to take over the

Minnesota Pride. Vance and Gerald had never been close, but this news had been a surprise. Vance never said it, but Phoenix thought he might have been hurt that his own flesh and blood had tried to have him murdered.

Tonight, Vance had confronted Gerald with his discovery. Everything had been going according to plan from what she could detect. Phoenix and Tegan had been stationed on the main floor while everyone else was in the basement. The two female sentinels had been able to hear the conversation below, and it had sounded like it was going well—until the gunshots. The lowlife asshole had chickened out and brought a gun. He was too weak to even use his own claws.

Tegan and she had been prepared and had met Gerald when he ran up the stairs. Unfortunately, they hadn't managed to get his gun, and he had shot Tegan before using the butt of the gun on Phoenix.

She wanted to kill Gerald just for getting the best of her.

Phoenix was attempting to get free. She tried to shift first and was unsuccessful. He must have silver on her somewhere. Going by the heaviness around her neck, he had some sort of choker on her. Silver was shifters' kryptonite, leaving them with the inability to shift even a finger.

Phoenix shivered. The fact that he had come prepared with silver, ropes, and a gag meant he had been planning to kidnap someone all along. She was pretty sure she had been a split-second decision, which left her wondering who his original target was. She had a sick feeling in her stomach that it was supposed to be Lilith, her alphena. Gerald was one sick freak.

Phoenix was grateful that Gerald had gotten her instead, and it only made her more determined to get away from him alive. Thankfully, the dumbass had the music on, so it would cover up her movements. She worked her gag off with her shoulder and took a couple of deep breaths. Next, she bent her knees and tried to reach the rope tied around her ankles. Her hands were secured behind her back, so it took quite a bit of work and some time, but she slowly managed to get her feet untied.

She sluggishly maneuvered her body to the back of the seats. It wasn't easy with all the crap Gerald had lying around his vehicle. The man was a pig. She managed to reach the lever that would lower the backseat on the driver's side, and she used her shoulder to push back against it. Once she knew the latch was free, she let go of the lever and pushed the seat the rest of the way down.

She then scooted her butt to the end of the seat, which wasn't easy with her hands behind her back. She noticed the city lights had dimmed and started to fade, indicating they were no longer on a major road, and she knew that she needed to hurry. She pulled her legs toward her body. Then, using all her momentum, she kicked the back of Gerald's seat.

"What the fuck?" he yelled from the front.

She kicked his chair again. And again and again. The SUV swerved right and then left. She hoped that someone would see the vehicle and call the police. Getting the cops involved in shifter business wasn't ideal, but if it was going to save her life, she was willing to risk it. She knew her alpha would understand. Plus, they had shifters in the police force to take care of such matters if they arose.

"You fucking bitch, I'm going to kill you!" Gerald screamed as he tried to keep the SUV on the road.

"You can try!" she yelled back as she kicked his seat again.

After a few minutes, when she felt she wasn't going to get him off the road, she side-kicked him in the head with her right leg and then side-kicked him with her left leg. The vehicle started to veer to the right, so as fast as she could, she dropped onto the floor between the seats and braced for contact.

Boom!

She had no idea what they'd hit, but she got up as fast as she could. She really needed to get her hands loose because it seemed to take forever for her to get the door open. She finally found the handle and pulled. Nothing happened.

She looked behind her. *Shit*. She'd forgotten to unlock the door. *Stupid, stupid*.

Unlocking the door and getting it open felt like it took a year, but once the door swung wide, she was out of there.

They were in a residential area, but she didn't want to stop at the first house she saw just in case Gerald awoke, so she ran down the block. She really wanted to cut through some houses, but with the snow on the ground, she was afraid she would fall, and her footprints would be obvious. She was lucky right now that the sidewalks were as shoveled as they were.

She wanted to look behind her but wouldn't dare, and with the winter wind and her deep breathing, she couldn't hear if Gerald was close. She needed to find a house with lights on. She didn't want to wait for someone to get out of bed to answer—

"Oof!"

Gerald had come out of nowhere and tackled her into

the nearest front yard. He knocked her on her stomach, and with her hands out of commission, she could barely put up a fight, but it didn't stop her from trying. The cold snow didn't help her struggling.

He pulled on her hair. "You're a fucking cunt, you know that?"

"Get off me, asshole."

He yanked harder. "I was going to fuck you and then use you as ransom for my freedom, but now, I'm going to fuck you and kill you."

The thought alone was enough to scare her, but she couldn't let him know that he had found her only weakness.

"You can try. I'm betting you can't even get your dick up," she said with a mocking laugh.

"I always knew you were a dumb bitch," was the last thing Phoenix heard before she saw Gerald's fist flying toward her face.

☾

Saxon Einar really hated getting shot. His shoulder burned where Gerald's bullet had gone through him.

Worse than being shot though was his inability to do anything. He was sitting at the shifter infirmary, waiting for one of the doctors to get their butts in gear and stitch him up already. *What a waste of time.* He should be out there, grabbing that fucker, Gerald, and finding Phoenix.

Just thinking about Gerald and Phoenix made Saxon antsy. Phoenix was like a sister to him and one of the few women that he'd ever let get close to him. If Gerald hurt her, Saxon was going to do the same thing back to him times ten. Phoenix was one tough chick, but Gerald was a man, and she was a woman. Saxon was pretty sure that was the one thing she couldn't handle.

Just when Saxon was ready to get up and find someone to help him, there was a knock on the door, and Vaughn walked into the room. His dark hair was messy, like he'd been running his fingers through it, and his blue eyes were full of worry.

"How are you doin'?" Vaughn nodded in greeting.

"Hurts like a bitch." Saxon nodded toward his shoulder. "But I'll be better once someone fixes me up."

"That's good."

"How's Zane?"

"Shot in the chest. Hit his lung. He's in surgery now."

Saxon sat back on the bed. "Aw, man. I hope he'll be okay."

"He will. They think he'll pull through just fine."

"Do his parents know?" Saxon asked.

"Yeah. My dad called them. They're on their way."

"What are we going to do about your uncle and Phoenix?"

"We're going to head out now. Check his house, Brent's mom's place, and any other place that we can think of where he might go."

Brent was Gerald's son. Gerald never married Brent's mom, but it still wouldn't hurt to see if he was there.

There was another knock.

Vaughn opened the door and spoke to the person on the other side without opening it. "Hey, baby, I was just filling Saxon in about what is going on."

"You can let Naya in," Saxon told him.

Vaughn opened the door all the way to let his mate in.

Naya, vampire princess and future alphena, entered the hospital room with grace. Despite her expanding belly, it was obvious to Saxon that she was royalty.

"Hey, Naya."

"Hi, Saxon. Are you doing okay?"

He smiled at her. "I'll live."

She laughed. "That's good."

Vaughn brushed her dark locks off her shoulder. "Did you need something, baby?"

She looked at her mate. "I just came to tell you that we're leaving. Mother and Father don't feel too comfortable here."

Saxon could only imagine. It had only been with the recent mating of Vaughn and Naya that the shifters and vampires were comingling. He imagined the king and queen of the vampires hated being in a place filled with only shifters.

"Are you going to be okay going with them tonight?" Vaughn asked her.

"I'll be fine." Naya coyly smiled up at Vaughn, her purple eyes full of mischief. "I'll miss you though."

Oh God, barf. Saxon looked away before he threw up on them.

Out of the corner of his eyes, he saw Vaughn bend down and kiss her. "I'll miss you, too. I'll come get you before sunrise. Will you be okay? You don't need to feed, do you?"

"I'll be fine. You just find them." She looked away from Vaughn. "Get well soon, Saxon."

He looked back at the couple. "Thanks, Naya."

She kissed her mate good-bye and was out the door.

Vaughn's question to Naya had triggered a memory in Saxon, so after she'd left, he asked, "Hey, man, can I ask you a question before you take off?"

"Shoot."

"It's kind of personal."

"Well, if you didn't have my attention before, you do now. What's up?"

"When Naya feeds from you, can she sense you or anything like that?"

Vaughn tilted his head to the side but didn't tell him to butt out. "She can sense my emotions more than anything, I think. She knows when I'm close, so if we're in the same room or even building, she can find me. If I'm not blocking my connection to her at all, she can sense me even farther."

Saxon nodded his head.

"Does that answer your question?"

"Yeah, I think it does."

"Why do you ask?"

Saxon shrugged. "Just curious. Thanks, man."

Vaughn paused but seemed to accept Saxon's answer because he put out his hand. "No problem. I'd better get going."

Saxon clasped hands with Vaughn, and the two leaned into each other with a guy hug.

"Keep me posted," Saxon said.

"You know I will." When Vaughn reached the door, he turned and pointed a finger at Saxon. "Keep an eye on Zane."

"You know I will," he repeated Vaughn's words back as he smiled.

"Later."

Once Vaughn was out the door, Saxon used his good arm to free his phone from his jeans. He opened his phone and flipped through his Contacts until he got to the Ds. Saxon had worked with Dante a few times before, and despite the fact that the man was a vampire and Saxon was a shifter, the two had clicked, so much so that they had exchanged numbers and made plans to get a drink together sometime after everything calmed down.

Saxon had no idea what Dante would think of this request though. He hoped he wouldn't be overstepping as he clicked on Dante's number and hit Send.

☾

Dante Leonidas snatched up his ringing cell phone and saw Saxon's name.

He and the other Guardians had been on standby when they'd found out their king, queen, and princess had gone to Vance Llewelyn's meeting. He'd been shocked when the king and queen had insisted they were safe with the shifters and that the Guardians didn't need to be in attendance. But that didn't mean Dante was going to neglect his job. The Guardians had been stationed in their vehicles in various locations around the Llewelyn home, prepared to help if they were called. With news that everything was now over, Hunter—his partner tonight—and he were on their way back to the compound.

"Hello?"

"Hey, Dante. Did you hear what happened?" Saxon asked, skipping over any pleasantries.

"Yes, I heard shots were fired and that a couple of you are in the hospital. You are all lucky the royal family made it out alive." Dante liked Saxon, but he was angry that the people he was in charge of protecting had been in danger.

"Nah, not lucky. Once the gun came out, Vaughn took them to the other room. He would never let anything happen to them."

"I think you and I might have to agree to disagree on whether or not they were in danger. Lennox and Lexine are escorting them home, so at least we know they are safe now."

"Good to hear."

"Who was shot?" Dante asked.

"Zane was shot in the chest."

Dante hadn't met that particular cat-shifter.

"And I was shot in the shoulder."

"*You* were shot? Jeez, why didn't you tell me to shut up and quit complaining?"

Saxon laughed. "I understand what it's like not to be there to protect the ones you are supposed to be protecting."

Dante supposed he did. Only recently, the daughter of Saxon's alpha had been in an altercation where she was almost kidnapped. Luckily, she had been rescued by the now alpha of the wolf-shifters.

"Listen, that's not why I was calling though." Saxon's voice had lost all amusement.

"Okay. What is going on?"

"Um…well…"

"Saxon, spit it out."

"Can you find someone if you've fed from them?"

Suddenly, dread filled Dante's stomach. "Why are you asking?"

"I don't know if they told you, but Gerald grabbed Phoenix when he escaped."

Dante swore.

"And I could be mistaken, but I'm pretty sure you fed from her."

"You're not wrong," Dante answered. He glanced away from the road to see if Hunter was following the conversation.

"Is there any way you can sense her through her blood? Can you find her? She..." Saxon cleared his throat. "She has a few issues, and I have no idea what Gerald will do to her. He tries to hide it, but I've seen the sick lust on his face. I'm afraid he..."

Dante gripped the steering wheel so hard that he feared he would break it. "You don't need to spell it out." And Dante didn't need Saxon to expand on Phoenix's issues either.

When he'd met the female, he'd known there was a reason she would hide her shapely body under hideously baggy clothes. Right now, the thought of someone hurting her further than she'd already been hurt upset him way more than he'd ever thought it would.

"So, is there anything you can do?"

"It's not like it is in the movies. I don't have a way to find her just anywhere. I have to be close enough to sense her." One thing he did have going for him was the fact that Phoenix didn't know how to block him like other vampires did. "But I will do anything I can to find her. I don't want her hurt any more than you do."

"Oh, thank God."

The relief in Saxon's voice over Phoenix was apparent, and Dante had to wonder if the two of them had some sort of romantic entanglement. On the heels of that thought was a horrible feeling of jealousy that he had no business feeling. "Just tell me where you need me, and I'll be there."

"Thanks, man. I'll text you the details."

"You're welcome. I'll talk to you later."

"Later."

Dante ended the call and looked at Hunter.

"Sounds like we're going in search of a female cat-shifter," Hunter said.

"You okay with that, or do you want me to drop you off?"

Not everyone was super happy about the new alliance between the shifters and the vampires.

"Bring it on. An asshole is an asshole, no matter the species. No woman deserves that."

Dante smiled his thanks. "I always knew there was a reason that I hired you."

SIX

KENZIE AWOKE from a deep slumber to the feeling of cat whiskers rubbing against her hand.

Without moving from sleeping on her stomach, she murmured into her pillow, "Go away, Abby. There is a reason I bought you an automatic feeder and fountain. Leave me alone."

Crabby Abby was the cat that she had inherited when her grandmother passed away. As with a lot of cats, Crabby Abby thought Kenzie lived in *her* house, not the other way around, and every morning, bright and early, she expected to be fed. This was why Kenzie had bought the automatic cat feeder and pet fountain.

Falling back asleep, she was awoken again by the feeling of cat whiskers. This time, it was accompanied by a deep and odd noise, something like a cross between a meow and a roar. That did not sound like Crabby Abby. Next, her hand was nudged by a cat head that was way too big to be her cat.

She shot up onto her elbows, remembering that she wasn't at home and recalling everything that had transpired recently. She slowly moved her head to the side and saw the huge animal sitting on the bed, staring at her.

She screamed and moved away, only to fall ass-first onto the floor. She jumped up, ready to run or fend off the big cat, when it attacked her.

Where the hell did it come from?

The cat didn't move from the bed.

Glancing behind her, Kenzie saw the bedroom was open. "Sawyer!" she yelled for help as she backed out of the room.

The cat meowed but didn't follow her.

"Sawyer!"

Meow.

As the rest of sleep drained from her and a light bulb turned on, Kenzie got it. "Sawyer?"

Meow, came from the bedroom.

"Sawyer, if that is you, please come out into the hall."

A second later, the big cat emerged from the bedroom and sat down. He had the same coloring as Sawyer and Sawyer's yellow-orange eyes.

Kenzie felt like a fool. Of course this was Sawyer. Had she really thought some big cat was loose and broke into her brother's house? She blamed it on being only half awake rather than a lack of intelligence.

"You tell anyone about this, and I will cut your balls off," she told him.

The cat stood and backed up a few feet.

"I'm glad we understand each other."

Meow.

"What are you doing, Sawyer?"

He tilted his head to the side.

This had to be about last night. "You can turn back now. If this is for last night, you got me. The joke is over now."

After Sawyer had told her that he was going to mark her and make sure everyone knew that she was his, she had pushed him away and explained to him that she couldn't deal with that right now. She had told him she was tired, gone up to bed, and locked the door.

Then, she had lain there for hours, just thinking. She had heard him moving around the house and thought he would try to talk to her, but he didn't even knock on her door.

She had eventually fallen asleep and had woken up several hours later to go to the bathroom. The house had been quiet, so she had left the bedroom to see what Sawyer was doing. He had been sleeping peacefully in the guest bedroom.

She had felt a mix of relief and disappointment that he had given up so easily.

She must have forgotten to close and lock the bedroom door when she had gone back to bed, and Sawyer had used it as an opportunity to play a prank on her. She had to admit that he'd gotten her good. She'd been scared out of her mind when she first woke up.

But, instead of shifting back into his human self, Sawyer walked past her, making sure to rub her legs with his body as he passed, and went down the stairs.

Kenzie spun around and chased after him. "Sawyer, this isn't funny anymore." She finally caught up to him in the kitchen where he sat down next to the bowls sitting on the floor. "You don't seriously expect me to feed you, do you?

Besides, those are dog dishes. They belong to my brother's girlfriend's stupid yappy dog."

Kenzie had no problem with dogs. In fact, she liked them a lot. She just didn't like Anna's dog. Truth be told, the dog didn't like her either.

Sawyer didn't move or make a sound.

Kenzie rolled her eyes. "Well, I'm going to make coffee and find some breakfast like a normal human. You can just starve, I guess."

She got busy with filling the coffee pot with coffee and water and then dug in the cupboard for something to eat. She poured a bowl with cereal and milk and started eating. She turned to lean against the counter to see Sawyer staring at her. He tilted his head to the side, and she had to admit that he looked kind of cute.

"Fine," Kenzie said as she grabbed the box from the counter. She set her bowl down and filled one of the dog dishes with cereal. "Are you happy now?" She picked up the other dish and filled it with water from the sink. "You don't get any milk though. I know it's bad for cats, and I don't know how this"—she moved her hand around in a circle—"works with you being part human. But until you tell me otherwise, no milk for you."

Sawyer rubbed up against her again and went to town on the food and water.

She kind of felt bad for him. Cats needed protein to survive. They were carnivores. Again, she didn't know how that worked with his human half, but she didn't want anything bad happening to him. She looked in the fridge for something else she could make for him, completely forgetting about her own food.

Sawyer curled up on the floor in front of the couch with a full stomach.

Kenzie followed him in and sat on the couch. "Man, Sawyer, you purr loud."

What could he say? He was one content cat.

His plan to have Kenzie warm up to him was working. After she had pushed him away the night before and locked her bedroom door, he had known that he needed a new plan of action. She was wary of him. He understood this from the little she had told him about himself, and it was going to take some convincing for her to understand that he wasn't going anywhere and that he was going to try his best not to hurt her again. He did not take being mates lightly.

In the middle of the night, he'd gotten the idea that Kenzie might be more open to him in his cat form rather than his human form. Most women loved animals. At least he thought that was a correct recollection. If he could get Kenzie to trust Sawyer the Cat, then maybe she would begin to trust Sawyer the Man.

He realized that he should be more focused on getting his memory back, but all he could think about was that it wouldn't matter if his mate was rejecting him. Mate first, memory second.

"Well, since we're not going anywhere, we might as well watch TV, right? What do you like?" She looked down at him as she grabbed the remote off the end table. "Never mind. You can't answer me, and you probably don't remember anyway." She aimed the remote at the television.

He heard the thing turn on, but he didn't bother turning his head. He was much more interested in watching Kenzie.

She started flipping through channels when, all of a sudden, her face fell.

He raised his head.

"Christmas commercials," she said in a soft voice as she leaned forward while still looking at the TV. "What day is it?" She hit something on the remote and sat back in her seat with an expression of wonderment. "It's the end of November? I missed Thanksgiving, and now, it's a month until Christmas."

Sawyer stood, and Kenzie looked at him.

"Besides Naya, I wonder if anyone even missed me." She looked around the room. "Bastian's obviously out of town, which doesn't surprise me. But what about my dad and sister?" She snorted. "They probably didn't even notice."

She looked so sad, and Sawyer didn't like it, so he jumped onto the couch.

"Whoa. What are you doing?"

He answered her by lying down and putting his head in her lap.

"Uh, Sawyer?"

He shifted his head, so he could look up at her face.

"Ah," she said with a shrug, "what the hell?" She put her hand on his head and petted him.

Sawyer loved her touch on him and immediately resumed purring.

☾

Kenzie finished brushing her teeth and left the bathroom, only to stop short at the big tan cat sitting on her bed.

She shook her finger at him. "Oh, no, you are not sleeping here."

Sure, they had spent the day hanging out and getting along. It'd probably helped that Sawyer was a cat all day, but they had still enjoyed each other's company. She had ended up cooking him two more meals and feeding him. She wasn't sure what to think about that.

Sawyer responded by flopping down and rubbing his body all over the bed. He probably thought that he had won this.

An idea struck. "Fine. I'll go sleep in the other room."

She marched toward the bedroom door and was stopped short when Sawyer jumped in front of her.

He sat down and gave her the cutest look, his amber eyes looking so sad.

"You know, for a cat, you sure have some good puppy-dog eyes."

It wouldn't kill her to let Sawyer sleep with her as long as he stayed in his cat form, she supposed.

"Okay, you can sleep with me. But if you shift back into your human self, I am kicking you out." She held out her hand. "Deal?"

Sawyer put his paw in her hand, and she shook it once.

"Okay, let's go to bed."

They settled down to sleep. At first, Kenzie was on edge, thinking Sawyer would try something, but after about fifteen minutes, she could hear his deep breathing, and she relaxed. Before she knew it, she was out like a light.

SEVEN

PHOENIX CRINGED as she watched the motel door open, and Gerald entered the room after being outside to make phone calls. They hadn't made it far the night before. While Gerald's SUV had been drivable after he had crashed it, it'd made clanking noises, and he hadn't wanted to risk going too far in it and having it breakdown. This had earned her a black eye next to the one she'd already sported from when he punched her after her escape. She'd managed to peek at them the few times when she was allowed to go to the bathroom, and they hadn't looked too pretty.

He had found a cheap roadside motel room to stop and stay, and he'd immediately trussed her up to make sure she wouldn't escape again. She would have tried during the transition from the vehicle to the motel room, except he had kept his gun on her head the whole time.

He had tied a rope around her wrists and then wrapped the rope around the back of the headboard, so her arms were spread wide on the bed. This time, he had gagged her, too. Thankfully, he had tied her feet together and then to the dresser across from the bed. She didn't know if she could have stood it if she'd had her legs tied spread eagle.

So far, he hadn't raped her, but he had tried. After he had tied her up, he had stepped outside for a while to use his phone. The cunning asshole had watched her through the open window the whole time, and Phoenix hadn't been lucky enough to have someone walk by and see her tied up.

When Gerald had stepped back inside the hotel room, she had seen the sexual gleam in his eye, and she had wanted to puke. The thought of the traitorous bastard sticking his gross, nasty penis inside her had almost made her hyperventilate. The only thing stronger than her revulsion was her resolve for him not to know how much she was affected by his threats. Thank God he didn't know about her past.

Gerald came into the room and pulled down her gag. "Don't bother screaming. There is no one to hear you." Then, he used a claw to cut her shirt open and ogled her chest. "I always knew you had a great rack hidden under those ridiculous clothes."

She hated her breasts. She had developed early, and it had earned her attention that she had never wanted or asked for. It took all her concentration to pretend that she was bored and not trembling with fear and revulsion inside.

She shrugged. "Whatever. They are just boobs. Every woman has them."

He didn't even bother looking at her face when he replied, "Not everyone has what you have."

The man was practically salivating now, and it made her sick.

When he bent down and put her nipple in his mouth, she had almost passed out. She had gone back and forth between hoping she would and that she wouldn't. If she passed out, she wouldn't have to endure the torture, but if she did, he would know that this provoked her far more than she was letting on.

She didn't expect him to raise his head halfway from her and yell, "What the fuck?" He leaned back down and bit her nipple hard enough to draw blood.

She stifled her scream even though she wanted to shake him off and cover herself.

"Fucking whore."

She had no idea what he was talking about, and she didn't even get to ask when he bit her other nipple with just as much force.

This time, a whimper escaped her.

Gerald jumped from the bed and threw her shirt together over her chest. "I've been waiting for years to get my mouth on your goddamn tits, and now, you reek like a fucking vampire. You walked around all high and mighty, too good for anyone, but you spread your legs for a fucking bloodsucker. Fucking vampire whore. God, I can't even stand the smell of you."

She had never had sex with a vampire, but she had let Dante feed from her, and she had drunk some of his blood in return. Of course, there was the orgasm that he had given her during the feeding, but they had never had sex.

At this point, she would have welcomed Dante into her bed a thousand times if it meant that Gerald wouldn't touch her.

"Dante is ten times the man you are." She meant it, too.

This had earned her a slap across the face and a fat lip to go with her two black eyes and her bruised and bloody nipples before he'd put her gag back in place. But at least he hadn't touched her again. In truth, he had mostly ignored her since then, which was a huge relief. He had slept most of the day and spent a lot of the night planning who-knows-what. She couldn't imagine he had any allies left.

But now, he watched her as he approached the bed, and she knew her reprieve was over.

"Hey, vamp whore. I have to step out and take care of some business."

This would be her opportunity to get away.

He smirked. "Don't even think about it, cunt. I have someone watching the room. They won't hesitate to shoot your pretty head off if you try to leave."

With that, he spun and left the motel room. Apparently, he still had a few friends out there. Maybe he had hired humans to do his dirty work again.

Phoenix waited a few minutes until she heard his vehicle leaving before trying to break free of her binds. She might not be able to leave the room without getting her head blown off, but she didn't have to wait here like a sitting duck. She could plan her own attack against the traitor, including calling for backup. Dumbass had left the motel phone. For someone trying to take over the pride, he wasn't the brightest.

She started working on getting her hands loose, but she was completely exhausted. She hadn't slept at all the night or day before, even while Gerald had been sleeping, because she had worried that he would try something. Maybe if she rested her eyes for a minute, she'd have more energy to get free.

When she awoke, she saw that she had lost several hours. *Shit.*

Gerald could be back at any minute. She'd wasted way too much time sleeping.

Since she hadn't been able to get her hands free before, she tried a new strategy. She began working on pulling the dresser closer to the bed with her legs, and then she felt it. It was a tingle deep inside her, a hum in her blood. She actually looked around the room, expecting someone to be there, but she was alone.

The feeling grew, and soon, she was able to figure out what it was.

More importantly, *who* it was.

Dante.

❨

It was coming up on the end of the second night in the quest to find Phoenix, and Dante was feeling helpless. They had struck out the night before, and it looked like tonight was also going to be a bust. He hated that the sun restricted him. He wanted to keep searching. Dante had even lowered his blocking a little in hopes that Phoenix would feel him and, in turn, make her emotions stronger.

Right now, they were searching hotels and motels all around the Cities, but it was probably hopeless. If Dante were Gerald, he would've hightailed it out of town.

"We'll find her, man," Hunter said from beside him.

Dante had told Hunter he could work on this alone, but Hunter had insisted on helping Dante.

Truth be told, Dante appreciated any help he could get.

"Thanks, but I'm—"

"Dante, what is it?"

"I can feel her." Dante looked at Hunter with amazement. "I can actually feel her."

"Is she scared?"

Dante chuckled. "More like pissed."

"What are you waiting for? Let's go get her."

They were in an area with a cluster of cheap roadside motels, and it took Dante a couple of minutes to pinpoint Phoenix's location. He hadn't even been sure if that was where she was at first, and he hadn't wanted to assume.

The two vampires exited the vehicle and scouted the area. The only thing they found was the motel attendant playing video games at the desk and one family fast asleep on the other side of the motel. Hopefully, breaking Phoenix free would be a relatively quiet ordeal, and no cops would be called.

When he located the room Phoenix was in and noted the absence of any vehicle, he hoped it was a good sign that she was alone.

The curtains were pulled on the room, but once they got close, the vampires could smell the distinct scents of two cat-shifters.

"Ready?" Dante asked Hunter.

"Ready."

Dante kicked open the door and was greeted with the sight of Phoenix tied up on the bed. The look on her face and the feeling in his blood of her relief hit him at the same time. He smiled at her to reassure her even though he wanted to rage about her bruised face. Then, he looked down and saw her mangled shirt.

Dante saw red. He was going to kill the fucker for what he had done to her.

Dante moved to free Phoenix when he heard a vehicle outside. Hunter had closed the motel room door behind them, so Dante looked out the window.

It was Gerald.

"Hunter, untie her while I go take care of this asshole."

Phoenix tried to shout something under her gag, and Hunter yelled out his name, but Dante was on a mission.

The motel parking lot was scattered with lights, so he didn't have the cover of night to keep him cloaked. Dante had to move fast if he was going to get the jump on Gerald.

Gerald parked far away from the room, probably in case someone spotted his vehicle, before he stepped out of his SUV and grabbed stuff off his seat. Gerald had his back to Dante, so Dante calmed his raging nerves and walked quietly toward the cat-shifter. But it was as if Gerald somehow sensed Dante, and he spun around.

Not wanting to lose Gerald, Dante charged forward. He wanted to destroy the shifter, but he had promised Vance that he would bring the criminal in alive, so Dante's goal was to incapacitate him.

However, Dante never even got the chance to try.

Gerald hauled his ass back into his vehicle, started it up, and drove out of there as fast as it would take him.

The only thing Dante could do was note that Gerald was still driving his own SUV, going by the license plate, and the direction the automobile was going. He'd had almost had Gerald. It was a huge setback and a major disappointment.

"Dante! Dante!"

Dante swung around just in time to catch Phoenix, who had made a flying leap into his arms.

She wound her arms and legs around him and held on for dear life. "We have to get out of here. Gerald has someone watching the room. He'll kill you. Gerald said he had a gun," Phoenix pleaded with him.

Dante smoothed his hand down her hair. "Shh...it's okay. We scouted the area before we went to your room. There was no one. Gerald lied."

Her body relaxed in his arms. "What a dickface," she muttered.

Dante couldn't help but smile. "Let's get you out of here."

"Yes, let's."

He expected her to drop her legs and walk on her own two feet, but she turned her head and rested it on his shoulder instead.

Hunter exited the motel room and shook his head. Nothing there to help them figure out Gerald's plan.

Dante walked toward Hunter and dug his keys out of his pocket, which wasn't easy with a female cat-shifter wrapped around him. Once he reached his prize, he threw them at Hunter. "You drive."

Hunter grinned at Dante and Phoenix, and Dante scowled in return. This wasn't what it looked like. Phoenix was just grateful that they had rescued her. Relief was pretty much all he could feel from her blood.

They reached the vehicle, and figuring it was easier, Dante got in the backseat with Phoenix. "Phoenix, you need to buckle up."

She sighed but slid off his lap into the next seat. As she put on her seat belt, Dante noticed she wasn't wearing anything but her ripped shirt.

Dante leaned forward to take his jacket off. He sat back in the seat, ready to offer it to Phoenix, when she leaned over and put her head in his lap, so he draped it over her.

He fished his phone out of his pocket and dialed Vance.

"Vance speaking."

"Hey, it's Dante. I got Phoenix."

"Is she okay?"

"A little beat up but okay."

The cat-shifter sighed with relief. "Gerald?"

"He got away." Dante gave Vance their location and the direction Gerald had headed. "Sorry that we didn't get him."

"Don't beat yourself up. He's not your responsibility." Another sigh. "He's mine. I'm just glad you found Phoenix."

Dante glanced into the front of the SUV. "Look, we have just enough time to get Phoenix to you before the sun comes up. Do you have a place where we can crash for the day when we get there?" They wouldn't have enough time to get home from Vance's after they dropped Phoenix off.

Phoenix twisted her head and looked up at Dante. "I want to go home with you."

"Hold on, Vance." Dante moved the phone away from his mouth. "What?" he asked her just to make sure that he had heard her correctly.

"I want to go home with you."

Dante began to feel panic coming from her, so he didn't push. "Um, Vance, Phoenix wants to come back to the compound with me."

"Okay. I guess as long as she's protected. With Gerald still on the loose, she's probably safer with you."

Phoenix, upon hearing Vance through the phone, rolled back over and visibly relaxed.

"Thanks, Vance. Keep us updated."

"Will do. Thanks, Dante."

Dante hung up the phone and stared down at the female

in his lap. Despite their blood connection, he had no idea what was going on with her, and he was baffled that she would rather be with him than with her fellow sentinels.

In the end, it wasn't his job to figure her out. All he could do was keep her safe, and at this point, he would die before letting her get hurt.

EIGHT

KENZIE STOMPED her foot on the kitchen floor. "I am not doing this again. Change back."

Sawyer, who stood in front of her, tilted his head to the side.

"Don't play dumb with me, cat boy. I know you understand everything that I'm saying. You can change back and get your own breakfast. I am not catering to you all day again."

When she had woken up that morning to see Sawyer sleeping beside her, still in cat form, she had been relieved. And perhaps...perhaps she had been a little disappointed. Not disappointed that he was still on her bed, but disappointed that he was still a cat. But that was beside the point because she didn't want him to be naked in her bed. She didn't want him in her bed at all.

Keep telling yourself that, Kenzie.

However, now, she was done. She didn't want to wait on him like she had yesterday. He was not just a cat. He was human, too, with hands that had ten fingers and were capable of getting their own food. He should be making her breakfast this morning.

In response to her demands, Sawyer went over to the dog bowls and sat down.

Kenzie felt herself getting riled up, but she had a feeling getting angry wasn't going to get her what she wanted. If he had been the size of a regular cat, she would've thrown him outside in the snow, cold be damned. But there was no way she could lift him, so she settled for the next best thing.

"Fine. You want to stay an animal?" She walked over to the pantry to search for what she was hoping to find. A little bit of luck was on her side. She snatched the canister from the shelf and grabbed the can opener from the drawer. Once the container was open, she turned and walked over to Sawyer and his empty dish. "Then, you can eat like an animal." She dumped the can of Alpo in the bowl.

Sawyer looked up from the food to her face, and she snickered. She then spun around to grab her *human* food to take to the other room. Despite her anger, if she stayed and watched Sawyer not eat, she would start to feel sorry for him and probably share her breakfast.

However, she didn't make it far before a very human, very male, and very nude body pushed up against her, pinning her against the counter.

He pulled her hair off her shoulder and leaned in next to her ear. "I'm sorry. You and I got along so well when I was cat yesterday that I thought it would be easier this way."

She relaxed a little against him as some of the fight left her. "Well, it's not."

She felt this chest shake as the sound of a chuckle came

out of him. "You sure know how to fight dirty, giving me dog food."

She shrugged. "I couldn't find any cat food," she said, knowing it would have been equally unappetizing to him.

This time, Sawyer released a full-on laugh, but he didn't move. She knew she should push him away, but, damn it, he felt so good against her. And even though he held his lower body away from her, she just *knew* that he was hard. She was going to have to duck and run if she didn't want to see Sawyer in all his glory. She only had so much restraint.

Sawyer stopped laughing and stepped closer, letting her know she hadn't been wrong. He was fully aroused, and she felt all of him against her back.

She sucked in a breath and didn't move. Almost as if it were happening to someone else, Kenzie waited for what would happen next.

He leaned down and rubbed his mouth and nose along her neck. He paused by her ear. "Can you ever forgive me?"

At that point, she was so turned on that she had forgotten she was ever mad. "Y-yes."

"Good," he whispered. His lips moved down her neck again. When he got to her shirt, he reached up and pulled it aside.

Fully expecting the soft touch of his lips on her shoulder, she shook with arousal when he opened his mouth and sucked lightly on her skin. "Oh God."

He lifted his lips. "You can call me Sawyer."

Without giving her a chance to mock him about his cliché joke, he wrapped an arm around her waist, pulling her away from the counter. He resumed his attention to her neck and shoulder and let his other hand slip down inside her pants and underwear. He didn't even take the time to tease or prepare her. He kicked her feet apart, put his hand between her legs, and slipped two fingers inside her. As always, he knew exactly where to touch her.

She lifted her arm to grab his neck as she let go of her resolve and leaned her body back against his. "Oh God. Don't stop. Please, don't stop." She heard the words leave her mouth, and her sensible side wanted to smack some sense into herself. But the other part of her said, this wasn't sex.

She could keep the line drawn between them even if that might be a lie. Plus, it had been so long since she had come from someone touching her besides herself. There hadn't been anyone since…Sawyer.

And as he rubbed that magical part inside her, she understood why there hadn't been another man.

Kenzie was very sexual, and a big part of that was because she was able to achieve orgasm easily. She'd always felt bad for women who couldn't climax from sex—or even worse, women who had never had an orgasm at all. It was easy to like sex if you got off on it almost all the time. Because of this, it shouldn't be any wonder that it felt good when Sawyer touched her. But it was. It felt ten times as good as when anyone else had ever laid a hand on her, even serious boyfriends.

But she refused to give too much attention to this phenomenon. She was already blurring the lines of their relationship. Instead, she focused on the pressure building inside her. It felt so good, and she was oh-so close to coming, but she just needed one thing. It was as if Sawyer had trained her body like Pavlov and his dogs, and she could be irritated with him later.

But right now, in the moment, she barely panted out the words, "Bite me."

Sawyer pulled her tighter against him. "What, baby?"

"Bite me." She dug her fingernails into his neck. "Bite my neck. Please. I—"

She didn't get to finish her sentence because Sawyer did exactly as she'd commanded.

He bit down on her bare shoulder, and the pleasure and pain sent her flying over the edge.

"Oh, fuck," she called out as she came so hard that Sawyer had to hold her up or let her fall.

After her body calmed down and her senses returned, she felt Sawyer release her neck, and his fingers slowly slipped from her body. They left a wet trail on her stomach, but she didn't care. Her body was too sated to give a crap.

Sawyer twisted her around to face him. She had been prepared to tell him thank you or say something else nice to let him know that her body appreciated his attention, but she was stopped short when she saw the intensity in his eyes.

He was really the most attractive man she had ever met. He might not be the most attractive man in the world, but to her, he was.

She reached up to touch the day's growth of beard, slightly amazed that it had grown even though he was a cat. She had never seen Sawyer with anything but a clean shave, and it was just another side to his sexiness.

She knew she needed to shut down the situation, but before she could say anything, he kissed her, and all the passion that she had seen in his eyes was poured into his kiss.

He licked his way into her mouth, his hand gripped her hair, and his other arm pulled her close.

Knowing that Sawyer wanted her was the most potent aphrodisiac ever, and despite her earlier orgasm, she was ready to go again. Kenzie put her hands on his chest and brushed her fingers down over his torso and pelvis until she reached his groin. She wasted no time fisting his cock and pumping it in her hand. She wanted to touch him again before his memory returned.

His memory…

And that was the thought that jolted her, regardless of her sexual haze. And when Sawyer began to push down on her pants, that was all she needed to knock the sense back into her.

She let go of his erection, broke their kiss, and gently pushed him away.

"What's wrong?" Sawyer asked her, the confusion clearly written all over his face.

"We can't do this."

"Why not? I don't understand. You seemed pretty into it a couple of minutes ago."

She closed her eyes with regret. "I know." She opened them and looked up at him. "And I'm sorry." And she really was.

She felt bad that he had gotten her off and that she was going to leave him hanging—or more like, not hanging. But the point was that she was going to leave him with what would probably be a serious case of blue balls. What added to the guilt was that if he hadn't given her an orgasm, she probably wouldn't have stopped him, but he had given her one, and because of that, she was able to say no.

"I just…I can't do this." She stepped around him and made a beeline for the stairs.

"Kenzie…"

"I'm sorry," she said again, not looking back.

(

Sawyer watched Kenzie go, baffled and hard as a brick. If he didn't relieve himself, he would probably be hurting later.

He didn't understand what had happened. He knew that she had been into it. He knew that she'd wanted him. The scent of her arousal had filled the room, and when he'd touched her, she'd all but dripped into his hand because she was so ready for him. And when she had come…holy shit, there was no mistaking that. She hadn't faked her orgasm. He had felt it as her pussy clamped down on his fingers like a vise.

He rubbed his hands over his head in frustration. He simply didn't get it.

He dropped his arms as an alarming thought came over him. Maybe she hadn't told him everything. Maybe he had done something to hurt her that she hadn't told him about. He didn't feel like he could have been that kind of man, but then again, what did he know about his former self? Only what Kenzie had told him.

He needed to find out if anything else had happened.

Determined to have a serious talk with his mate, Sawyer practically ran for the stairs, only to stop short when his still erect dick bounced against his stomach.

He looked down at his penis. "Perhaps you're the one to blame for all this."

Whoever's fault it was, he certainly couldn't go marching up to Kenzie, naked and at full mast. He needed to take care of his erection and find some clothes before he dared approach her. He supposed getting clean wouldn't hurt either, and with that thought, he headed for the shower.

NINE

PHOENIX PACED the room that she'd been given at the Guardians' compound. It was the same room she had stayed in previously, but the familiarity with her surroundings didn't help her discomfort or rage.

She should have never come here. She should have insisted that Dante take her home. She should be out there right now, helping everyone find Gerald. She *deserved* to be out there. It was her right to be the one to track down that asshole and cut his balls off. But that wasn't going to happen if she was here.

Stupid moment of weakness.

When Dante had burst through the door of the motel room, not only had she seen the relief and anger on his face, she had also *felt* it. Knowing those emotions were for her... had done something to her. Then, when Dante had taken off after Gerald without any backup, she'd been scared for him. Finding out that Dante was safe and that there was no sniper had filled her with such relief. Those three things along with Gerald's treatment of her were the reasons she had insisted on coming home with Dante.

Stupid, stupid feelings.

It wasn't that she didn't care about anyone, but Phoenix never let emotions interfere with the mission or her goals. Despite what had happened back at the motel, she should have sucked it up and gone back home. Now, she was stuck here. The vampires couldn't go out in the daylight, and she wasn't going to make one of her fellow sentinels stop their work to pick her up, especially when they were down two. Dante had told her that Saxon and Zane had been shot and were at the shifter infirmary.

There was a knock at the door, and Phoenix scrambled to find something to cover herself.

After they had arrived at the compound, Lexine had brought Phoenix some clothes to wear. Phoenix had quickly washed any trace of Gerald and the motel off of her, but after she had dried herself off, she'd discovered that there was no way she would be able to wear the bra Lexine had given her. The pressure on her sore nipples was too much.

So, Phoenix had decided to just put on the sweater she'd been given, sans bra, but it'd rub her breasts anytime she moved. She'd been topless ever since. There was no way she could or would answer the door that way.

Stupid fucking Gerald.

Even if she had gone back home, she'd have had to do some fancy first aid before she'd be able to put something against her chest.

"Phoenix, open up. It's me," Dante said through the wood.

With no other options, she grabbed the shirt she'd been

kidnapped and rescued in. Because it had been cut down the middle, she could cover herself and hold it away from her body at the same time.

She slowly opened the door, just enough for her head to poke through. "Yes?"

"Are you going to come eat? Didn't Lexine tell you that we have food?"

Eating sounded wonderful. Gerald had barely fed her anything the whole time they were in the motel. But there was no way she could go downstairs as she was. She hoped Dante hadn't seen the hunger on her face.

She smiled poorly at Dante. "I'm not hungry. I think I'm going to go and take a nap."

Dante looked her up and down, studying her. "You don't look tired. You look pissed."

"I'm pissed because you won't let me sleep."

He gave her a look that said, *Really?*

She sighed. "I'm fine. Really."

"You sure you're not hungry?"

"Yes," she said at the same time her stupid stomach growled.

Dante straightened. "Phoenix, don't lie to me."

"Seriously, I'll be fine." She managed to almost sound convincing.

"Fucking hell, woman," he said as he pushed her door open.

His movements left her no choice but to step back and let him in.

"Dante, I said, I'll be fine." This time, there was no *almost*. She *definitely* sounded like she meant it. *Good.*

Maybe he'd take the hint and leave her alone.

But Dante wasn't listening to her. He was looking at the discarded bra and sweater she had left on the bed. "Why aren't you wearing the clothes Lexine gave you?" he said as he turned to her.

"I am. I'm wearing the jeans."

It was the truth, and hopefully, he would look down instead of up where her hands were clutching her ripped shirt.

It worked because Dante was staring at her legs.

She knew the jeans were tight on her, compared to her normal ones, but she didn't think she looked that bad.

Dante's gaze moved from her feet to her thighs and then up to her torso. "Why are you wearing your torn shirt?"

She fought to come up with a good reason as to why she was still wearing her top. "Uh…"

"And why are you holding it away from your body?"

Again, she didn't have a good answer, but it seemed as if Dante wasn't going to wait for an answer anyway.

He marched over to her and yanked her shirt out of her hands.

"No, wait," she said.

But Dante didn't listen.

He pulled her shirt apart and stared down at her chewed up areolas.

Phoenix's first instinct was to cover herself. She was embarrassed, fearful, and nervous. Embarrassed because Gerald had gotten the best of her, fearful that Dante was going to look at her large breasts and assume that she wanted to have sex like so many males before him even if that thought was irrational, and nervous because she cared about what Dante thought.

But when she saw his almost clinical assessment of her chest, most of her fear faded away.

Dante's cinnamon smell deepened. "I'm going to fucking kill him."

With that statement, most of her embarrassment was gone. He didn't seem to think she was a fool for Gerald taking advantage of her.

She grabbed her shirt out of his hands, stepped away from him, and pulled it back around her body. "I appreciate that, but I would prefer that *I* get to be the one to fucking kill him."

She was left with nervousness, and Dante staring down at her now covered upper body didn't help. She didn't care for the fact that Dante was concerned about Gerald hurting her. She opened her mouth to tell him to leave when she noticed that he was bleeding.

He was biting his bottom lip so hard that his fangs were buried in it.

"Dante?"

He didn't seem to hear her.

She stepped forward and shook his arm. "Dante, you're bleeding."

"Huh?" He looked up at her, and his eyes focused on her face.

She pointed to his mouth. "Your lip. It's bleeding."

He reached up and touched the blood before looking at it. "Oh." He licked the blood off his finger and then swiped his tongue over his bottom lip a few times.

There was no bleeding, and barely any marks were left from his fangs.

She stepped even closer. The only thing that she was

feeling now was amazement as an outrageous idea formed. She couldn't believe she was even thinking it. "I want you to heal me."

"Excuse me?" Dante said.

"I know your saliva heals wounds. That's how you seal the person's puncture wounds when you've finished feeding from them. I want you to heal me." She jerked her chin down toward her chest.

He looked down at her chest again, and this time, he was the one who took a step back. "That is not going to happen."

"Why not? Dante, I can't walk around here, topless, and it hurts to have anything touch me there. Plus, the sooner you heal me, the sooner I can get out there and hunt down that piece of shit."

He ran his hand down his face and sighed. "Phoenix, I can't do that to you. I can't be another person who..." He trailed off.

"Who what?" she challenged.

Dante's dark chocolate eyes met hers, but he didn't continue.

"*Please.*" She stressed how much she wanted this.

"Okay. Fine. As long as you don't tell anyone about this."

She raised her brow. "Isn't that my line?"

"Whatever. Let's just do this."

Phoenix slowly released one side of her shirt and let it fall to her side. She didn't know whether to clench her eyes shut or keep them open and observe every move that Dante made.

He stepped forward as he licked his thumb and lightly swept it around her nipple.

She shivered.

He swallowed hard.

She let the other side of her shirt slide down, and Dante repeated the process.

She stared down at her breasts. They looked the same. "It's not working."

"Fuck," Dante muttered.

"Why isn't it working?"

Dante looked around. Then, he grabbed her hand and led her over to the bed. "It's not working because I have to put my mouth directly on you. It works better when it comes straight from the source. Are you sure you still want this?"

"Yes," she answered without any hesitation.

He pushed her down until she sat. Phoenix watched as Dante got down onto his knees and knelt before her. He moved her legs apart and scooted closer. He picked up her hand and slid it to the back of his head, through his deep brown locks. "I want you to keep your hand on my hair," he said as he squeezed her fingers. "If you need me to stop, you pull on my hair, okay?"

"Okay."

He looked down. "I can't believe I'm doing this," he said under his breath.

She wondered what he'd meant by that. She didn't know what to think of Dante. He'd never hit on her or shown sexual interest, yet the time he'd fed from her, there was no mistaking the hard-on he had pressed up against her or the orgasm that had followed. And it was true that she had been avoiding Dante since then. She hadn't really seen him until he'd rescued her, and so far, he'd been acting like the feeding never happened.

Since he was clearly speaking to himself, Phoenix didn't bother answering. Instead, she looked down to where his gaze had landed. Her shirt was wide open. She was shocked that she hadn't bothered to close it as he'd moved her to the bed, and she was even more shocked that she hadn't noticed. And her nipples were hard bright red pebbles. She didn't feel cold. In fact, she was hot and grateful she wasn't wearing the thick sweater lying on the bed.

Her eyes followed Dante as he slowly lowered his mouth to one of her breasts. She cringed and forced herself not to pull back as she fought the images of other men putting their mouths on her private area.

She managed to stay still and breathed in the scent of Dante. He smelled almost like cinnamon, and it was such a comforting aroma. As she watched him and breathed in his spicy scent, making her brain recognize that this was him and no one else, she lost her anxiety and relaxed.

Dante gently licked his way around her areola. His tongue was warm and smooth, and the unexpected pleasure from this caused Phoenix to moan and curl her fingers in his hair.

Dante jerked back. "What? Are you okay?" he asked, clearly worried that he had done something wrong.

She hadn't anticipated it feeling good. She just thought it might feel…not bad. This was a first for her. She had tried letting ex-boyfriends touch her breasts in the past, but she had never enjoyed it.

She cleared her throat. "No, I'm fine. Please keep going."

He studied her for a second before he continued. He moved to her other breast and swirled his tongue around it. Then, he moved to the nipple he had started with and stroked his tongue over it a few more times. At one point, she assumed her nipple was probably almost healed, going by the tingling she felt there and the lack of soreness, but when Dante moved to pull back, she tightly clutched his hair, and he did the most startling thing.

He pulled her nipple into his mouth and sucked.

It was fucking heaven.

Phoenix was very good at guarding her emotions and feelings, even going so far as to train her body not to give off much scent, but when Dante did this, it was nearly impossible for her to hide her arousal. There was no way she fully succeeded at this feat because she felt the wetness between her legs. Thankfully, jeans were thick. If he kept this up, soon, she probably wouldn't care.

Dante moved to her other breast and drew this one into his mouth as well.

Phoenix's neck forgot to support her head for a moment. It felt so good. Then, she cursed herself and yanked her eyes back up. She wanted to see what Dante was doing to her. She wanted to memorize it.

Before she knew it, he abruptly stopped and shoved himself back. "There. You're healed." He stood up and nodded, unable to meet her eyes. "I'll see you at the final dinner." He spun around and sprinted out the door.

Phoenix didn't stop him or go after him. There was no need. She had gotten what she had asked for. And a little bit more.

She looked down at herself and hesitantly touched her breasts. She was indeed mended.

Perhaps in more ways than one.

☾

Dante ran away from the room as fast as he could.

When he'd approached Phoenix earlier, what had just happened between them was the furthest thing from what he had thought would happen.

Holy shit.

He stopped running and slowed down to walk the rest of the way to the dining room. He needed the time to compose himself.

Sure, he had been and still was truly angry at the sight of Phoenix's chewed up nipples, but the sight of her breasts had nearly brought him to his knees. The female had amazing tits. There was no other way to describe them. They were large and perfectly shaped, and as far as he was concerned, it was a sin to keep them hidden. He had the fucking hard-on from hell to attest to that.

Knowing a little of what Phoenix had experienced in her life, he understood that she didn't want the attention, and that brought his rage back up to the surface again.

She didn't deserve anything that had happened to her. She might not be his favorite person, but he knew that at least.

Pretty soon, he reached the dining room. Everyone looked up as he entered, and he knew right away that he couldn't stay and make small talk. And he certainly couldn't face Phoenix when she came in to eat.

He grabbed some food to go before heading for his office. "I have some work to do. I'll see you all later."

Thankfully, Dante would do this every once in a while, so no one suspected that he was ducking out for any other reason than the one he'd given them.

Once in his office, Dante practically threw the food on his desk. He slammed his body down in his chair and blew out the breath he'd been holding.

He needed to forget about Phoenix and her damn gorgeous tits. Just because she had let him heal her didn't mean she would ever let him near them again. Besides, he didn't need to go near them. Getting involved with that she-cat was a complication neither of them wanted or needed. He had a group of vampires to lead, and despite what had just happened in that bedroom, Phoenix was closed off and cold.

Yes, it would be better to just forget that had ever happened.

Now, he just had to convince his fucking dick.

TEN

KENZIE CLUTCHED the pillow in her lap and contemplated her next step. The reality of the situation was that she would be stuck in this house with Sawyer for the next few days. Her brother's trips never lasted for more than a week, and they were already starting on their third day there, so they had four more days at the most. She could do this. Four days wasn't forever.

If only she had someone to talk to about stuff. Situations always seemed brighter after she vented. But she couldn't vent her problem to said problem. That never worked out well. Therefore, she—no, *they* needed a distraction. They needed to do something that would take their minds off of ripping each other's clothes off and get Sawyer's mind off this whole mate business. If Memory Sawyer could meet Amnesia Sawyer, she was pretty sure he would literally punch some sense into himself.

She laughed out loud at the thought of the two Sawyers meeting.

"What's so funny?"

Kenzie jumped. She hadn't heard the door open or Sawyer enter.

"Sorry. I didn't mean to scare you."

"That's okay."

"So, what were you laughing about?"

She looked him up and down. "Just thinking about what it would be like if the *now* you met your former self, your *memory* self."

He tilted his head to the side. "Why is that funny?"

She shook her head and smiled. "Too hard to explain, but trust me, it is." She swung her legs off the bed, remembering that she needed to be on guard against this man. "Did you need something?"

He looked down at his feet for a moment before meeting her eyes. "I just wanted to apologize about what happened downstairs. I didn't mean to push you or make you uncomfortable. This is all very difficult for me."

Kenzie immediately felt bad for him. She was being a little selfish in this situation. At least she still had her memory. She stood and walked over to him, making sure not to get too close or to touch him. She had sympathy for the man, but she wasn't going to sleep with him. "I'm sorry, Sawyer. I forget that this all must be really hard for you."

He sauntered over to the window and looked outside. "It isn't easy. That's for sure. My instincts are telling me one thing, but you're telling me another. I feel a little like I'm being pulled in half here."

She huffed out a big breath. This wasn't fair. It was difficult to keep her distance when all she wanted to do was comfort him.

She walked over to Sawyer to stand beside him and look

out the window. She held up her hand behind him for a second before she decided it would be okay to touch his back. "I know I already said it, but I really am sorry. I don't mean to confuse you or hurt you in any way. I'm simply doing what I feel is best for me. If—no, *when* you get your memory back, I know you'll understand. In fact, you'll probably thank me."

He turned his head toward her and gave her a look full of skepticism.

She couldn't help but smile. "Trust me."

"You already said that."

"Said what?"

"To trust you."

I did?

Oh, he was referring to when she had talked about him meeting himself.

"Well, I might not give in to your manly charms, but I wouldn't do anything to wrong you either. Despite our normal dislike of each other, I don't think either of us *hates* the other. We just don't get along." She turned to face him. "I would never want harm to come to you. I'd probably laugh if you tripped and fell, if I'm being honest"—she laughed—"but I would never stick out my foot and cause you to trip. Does that make sense?"

He turned to her and shrugged. "Sure."

He smiled, but it didn't quite reach his eyes, so Kenzie gave in to temptation and hugged him. She braced herself in case Sawyer made a move on her, but all he did was hug her back, and she relaxed.

It felt good to be in his arms, and despite it being a friendly hug, Kenzie knew she couldn't get used to this either. As much as she liked Amnesia Sawyer, the sooner Memory Sawyer returned, the sooner everything could get back to normal. And since Memory Sawyer would recall everything that had happened when he was Amnesia Sawyer, she could rub it in his face about how right she was about everything.

"What are you smiling about down there?"

She pulled away enough to look up at him. "I'll tell you later."

He raised one eyebrow.

"I promise."

She looked out the window to see that it was snowing, and she got an idea. "Why don't we go outside? I'm pretty sure no one is watching the house, but we'll go in the back-yard. The fence, the cloudy sky, and the snow will do a good job of hiding us from the neighbors. Wouldn't want anyone calling the police and telling them we broke into my broth-er's house."

Sawyer's face grew serious. "Why don't we ask a neighbor to use their phone?"

"And who are we going to call? I don't have anyone's number. The only number I have memorized is the local Chinese food place by my apartment, and that's because it's an easy number. And cell phones aren't listed in the phone book. Plus, I'm pretty sure you and your fellow sentinels use burner phones anyway. I was kind of relying on you to remember their numbers, stud."

He looked chagrined. "Sorry."

"Don't be. It's not your fault. We'll get out of here even-tually. Let's go outside. We can build snowmen, make snow angels, and have a snowball fight."

He shrugged. "Why not?"

She stepped away and took off. "I'll race you to the door," she called out behind her.

The sound of Sawyer's laughter followed her down the stairs.

☾

Saxon sat back in his seat and rubbed the area around the wound on his shoulder. He hated this.

He was sitting in a meeting with his fellow cat-shifters and the wolf-shifters, talking about how to catch Gerald, and he felt worthless. They were all making plans and setting up shifts while he would have to sit at home and do nothing but heal. Like he'd said, he hated this.

"Saxon."

He swung his head to look at Vance. "Boss?"

"I want you to go visit Zane today. Make sure he's doing okay. Let him know what's going on here."

Saxon swallowed his protest. He had just left the infirmary. He really didn't want to go back. Worse was the look of sympathy on everyone's faces. No one wanted to be left behind.

"Sure."

Vance nodded and turned back to the group. "Everyone know what they're doing?"

After a chorus of yeses all around, the meeting broke up.

Camden slapped Saxon on the shoulder as they exited the room. "Don't worry, man. You'll be back with us in no time."

"Yeah, yeah, I know." It didn't help him feel better today though.

They all made their way outside and got in their vehicles. Saxon got in his car and headed for the infirmary. The twenty-minute drive only gave Saxon more time to stew, and by the time he arrived to visit Zane, he was on edge. He needed to make this visit short.

Saxon marched to Zane's room and knocked on the semi-open door.

"Come in."

Saxon entered. "Hey."

Zane perked up when he saw it was Saxon. "How ya feeling?"

Saxon shrugged his injured shoulder. "I'll live." He nodded toward Zane. "As will you, I've been told."

Zane chuckled. "Yeah. Hurts like a motherfucker though."

"I hear ya." Saxon pulled up a chair to sit next to Zane's bed. "Gerald is an asshole. That's for sure."

Zane gave Saxon a questioning look. "I'm guessing that's why Vance sent you. To keep me up-to-date?"

Saxon sighed. "Yeah, but there's not much to tell. Phoenix is safe with the vampires, but Gerald is still on the loose."

"Phoenix got away?"

"More like rescued."

"By the vampires?"

Saxon nodded.

"Well, that's good, I guess. Is that why she's with them?"

"Partly. She asked to go to the Guardians' compound, and Vance didn't fight her. I think he thought she had been through enough and needed some downtime before getting back out in the field."

"Do you think Gerald did anything to her?" Zane asked.

"God, I hope not."

Phoenix had been through enough during her lifetime. She didn't need Gerald adding to her trauma.

"What is Vance's plan?" Zane changed the subject.

Saxon filled Zane in on what the cat-shifters and wolf-shifters were doing to find Gerald. They had put out feelers to his friends and associates. They had been checking out places he might go, and they had set up a grid search. Also, they had let shifters in the neighboring states know to be on the lookout for Gerald.

Zane looked down at his hands. "So, the wolf-shifters were there?"

Saxon cocked his head. "Of course. Now that Damien and Payton are together, there's no way that they wouldn't be involved."

Payton, their alpha's daughter, had recently been mated to the new alpha of the Minnesota Pack.

Zane laughed awkwardly but wouldn't look up at Saxon. "Right. Of course."

"Zane."

Zane looked at him, almost embarrassed.

"Just because Damien was there doesn't mean Isabelle knows that you've been shot."

Zane cleared his throat. "Right, right. I'm sure that's it." He leaned his head back against the bed and closed his eyes.

Kidnapping Phoenix and shooting Zane and himself were not Gerald's first offenses. Before that, he had attempted to kidnap the alpha's children. Another sentinel and human friend had been mistaken for Vaughn and his mate, and Damien had intercepted Payton's abduction and rescued her. Damien had taken Payton somewhere safe, and right before his phone had died, he had called a friend to deliver a message to Vance to let him know that his daughter was safe. That friend had been Isabelle. She had gone to their alpha's home, but with Vance stashed away in a safe house, Zane had been the only one there when Isabelle arrived. With orders to keep Isabelle with him until Payton was heard from, Zane and Isabelle had slept with each other. But once Payton had been found, Isabelle had packed up and gone back home.

Saxon hadn't realized that Zane had been so affected by her.

Poor sap. Just another strong male brought down by a female.

Saxon didn't understand it. Pussy was pussy. He liked women as friends and respected them as individuals, but there was no way he was ever going to let one affect him like this.

"Do you want to talk about it?" Saxon asked.

Zane opened his eyes and stared straight ahead. "No."

Oh, thank God.

Not only did he not want to hear about how much Zane liked this female who had up and left him, but also this was definitely not Saxon's area of expertise.

They sat in silence for a little longer, and Zane's melancholy over this chick made Saxon's restlessness come back tenfold. The walls were starting to close in on him. He really needed to get out of there and blow off some steam.

"Well, I'd better go."

Zane looked at him. "Sure."

Saxon stood and almost sprinted for the door. "I'll see you later?"

"Later."

That was all Saxon needed to hear before he was out of there.

Once he got to his car, he opened his phone and pulled up his Contacts. He scrolled through until he found the one he wanted and hit Send.

"This is Rayna."

"Hey, it's me."

"Saxon? Long time no hear."

"Yeah, I've had some stuff going on. Are you busy today?"

"No more than usual."

"Do you have plans for lunch?"

"I didn't before, but I do now. I can take an early one if you want," she said.

He could hear her smiling through the phone, but he still didn't feel relieved. That would come later.

"Your place. Thirty minutes?"

"I'll be there."

He closed his phone without saying good-bye and took off for Rayna's apartment.

Once there, he knocked on her door.

It swung open a second later, and Rayna grabbed his shirt to pull him inside.

Her long blonde hair was up in some sort of bun-like thing. He grabbed for her hair tie and yanked it out as she pushed his jacket off his shoulders and then pulled on the button of his jeans. Her human eyes were bright with sexual excitement.

This was exactly what he'd come for.

No sweet words, no promises, no *I love you*, and no kissing. Just straight-up sex between two sexually charged people.

He pushed her toward the living room as she unbuttoned his shirt and kissed his chest.

When they reached his destination, he turned her around. "Hand on the back of the couch."

She bent over and arched her ass toward him.

He shoved her skirt over her hips and around her waist. "You want this, don't you?" He grabbed on to her panties and nylons and yanked them down to her ankles. He could smell how aroused she was.

"God, yes. It's been too long." Rayna looked over her shoulder. "Fuck me, Saxon."

Saxon finally smiled as he drew his already hard cock out of his underwear. "Yes, ma'am."

He grabbed her now loose hair and thrust his way inside her wet pussy.

"Oh, yeah," Rayna wailed as Saxon pounded into her.

She was one of the few women he had in his Contacts list for the sole purpose of sex. Even in this day and age with women's sexual revolution, it was still hard to find females who wanted only sex. There were a lot who thought that was all they wanted, but they'd usually end up pushing for a relationship once they'd had sex more than once.

Saxon was getting close, and he could feel Rayna getting tight around his dick, indicating she was almost there, too.

"Please come in me, Saxon. I need it. I need it."

Saxon let go of Rayna's hair and wrapped his fingers around her chin and neck. He leaned close to her ear. "You like that, don't you?"

"God, yes. Please," she begged.

What Rayna liked was the barbs in his penis. She just didn't know it. She just thought he was a sex god. Sometimes, it paid to fuck a human woman.

He shoved into her two more times before he exploded inside her.

Rayna was right on his heels and screamed as she came.

Saxon let go of her neck as he tried to catch his breath.

Slowly, his heartbeat evened out, and the barbs in his cock receded. He withdrew from Rayna's body and shoved his penis inside his pants. He pulled Rayna's skirt back down over her hips and helped her stand.

She picked up her underwear and pantyhose and went into the bathroom before coming out with them back in place. She turned around and stood on her tiptoes to kiss him on the cheek. "I don't know what it is about that dick of yours, but when you come, it gets me every time."

Saxon smiled at her. He loved being a cat-shifter. "I don't know either," he lied, "but that's why I come here."

Her lips tipped up in a satisfied smirk. "That's why we work well together, I guess." She patted his chest and took a step back as all sexual play left her. She looked down at her watch. "Well, I have just enough time to grab something to eat. You can see yourself out."

"Yep. I'm going to use your bathroom, and then I'm outta here."

She picked up her coat, put it on, and grabbed her purse

from the chair next to the couch. "Okay. Until we meet again. See you later, Saxon."

"Bye, Rayna."

Soon, she was out the door, and Saxon sighed with relief. He'd gotten what he wanted. Rayna had never failed him in the booty-call category, but he always worried that she would want more. Yet, in true Rayna fashion, she had walked out the door as soon as their business was over. Hell, she hadn't even asked him to lunch.

Saxon grinned and walked toward the bathroom. Yes, he had gotten exactly what he'd wanted.

ELEVEN

PHOENIX ROLLED over for what felt like the fiftieth time. She couldn't sleep.

She'd thought that she would pass out the minute she laid her head on the pillow, despite it being daylight outside. Not that anyone could tell with how dark the house was. The vampires had blacked out all their windows, so no sunlight could come through during the day, but she was pretty sure her body knew it was daytime, and daytime meant awake time. Who cares that she had gotten little sleep since she was kidnapped? *Stupid internal clock.*

The thing was, if she didn't get some rest, she wouldn't be of any use to anyone. She might view herself as resilient, independent, and just as tough as her male sentinels, but unlike a man, she could admit when she had a weakness even if it was only to herself. And being tired was a weakness.

She had tried everything she could think of to try to fall asleep. All her usual tricks had failed, which she didn't understand because she was exhausted.

She flipped back the covers, swung her legs off the bed, and pulled up her nearly naked, except for her underwear-clad body, to head for the bathroom. She avoided the mirror as she went to inspect the medicine cabinet. She hated looking at her nude or almost nude form, but the only thing she'd been given to sleep in was some flimsy nightgown. Lexine must have someone to impress with her lingerie. Phoenix did not, and she preferred nothing to something that was supposed to show off her assets. She knew it probably wasn't rational, but the nightgown made her feel…girlie.

She shuddered at the thought.

The medicine cabinet revealed what she had already known would be there—toothbrushes, toothpaste, floss, lotion, and painkillers. No sleep medicine. She shut the door with a sigh.

Now what?

Maybe if she found something more sensible to wear, she'd be able to fall asleep. Although being naked was a step up from wearing lingerie, it was only one step up.

She put on the jeans and sweater that she'd been given earlier and exited the room. The hall was dark and quiet, except for the LED lights illuminating from the walls. Everyone had gone to their rooms after their meal downstairs.

Phoenix made her way down the hallway, past the staircase, to the east side where all the Guardians kept their rooms. She continued until she got to the end where Dante's room was. Right before she knocked, she thought she heard a noise, but when she turned around, no one was there.

She raised her arm again and quietly rapped her knuckles against the wood.

No answer.

He was probably sleeping.

She hadn't seen Dante since he left her room. Since Dante had healed her sore nipples and she had been able to get dressed, she had gone downstairs to join the vampires in their meal earlier. When she had arrived, she'd found herself a little nervous to face him since he had sucked on her bare breasts, but then she'd been a little relieved when the others explained he had gone to do some work in his office.

She should probably be nervous now, but the desire to sleep had won the battle over nerves.

Phoenix tried the knob and was a little surprised when it turned. For some reason, she'd thought it would have been locked.

She poked her head in and whispered, "Dante," as his familiar smell washed over her.

When there was no response, she tiptoed in the room, using the small amount of light from his clock radio. She called out his name again, so she wouldn't startle him as she shut the door behind her. But when she got close to his bed, she saw it wouldn't have mattered. It was empty. She turned on the lamp next to his bed and looked around. He wasn't in the room at all.

She briefly considered trying to find him, but the compound was large, and she just plain old didn't feel like it. Instead, she walked into his closet and rummaged around his clothes until she found what she wanted—a basic white T-shirt.

She put it up to her nose and inhaled. It smelled of detergent, and even though it was clean, she could still detect Dante's cinnamon scent. This was exactly what she needed. A small part of her realized that she should focus on why she needed it, but she was too tired to care.

She shucked off her jeans and sweater, threw them into the corner of the closet, and pulled the T-shirt over her head. It reached mid-thigh on her, covering way more than that stupid nightgown had, and she smiled.

Next, after she left the closet, she circled Dante's bed, trying to figure out which side he slept on and which side he didn't, but it looked like he was a whole bed sleeper, going by the rumpled covers. She turned off the lamp, and then— in a move she would probably be shocked by tomorrow but was too weary to consider right now—she drew back the covers and slid under the side farthest from the door, bathroom, and closet.

She rolled onto her stomach and buried her face in the pillow, breathing in Dante's comforting cinnamon scent. Within thirty seconds, she was out like a light and dead to the world.

☾

Dante glanced up at the clock and threw his pen on the desk. If he wanted to be functional at all when night fell, he had better get some sleep before then. He hadn't slept much the last few days. He had promised Vance Llewelyn that the Guardians would take the night shift, so the cats could put more men out during the day to look for Gerald, and they wouldn't have to split up.

Dante stacked the papers he had in his hands into a straight pile off to the side and pushed his chair back with a sigh. He knew he was dragging his feet, but he had to face Phoenix sooner or later.

The more he had sat in his office and thought about it, the more he'd wondered if she'd be uncomfortable around him. Yes, she had been the one to ask him to use his saliva to heal her wounds, but he felt like he still should have said no.

He stood, pushed his chair under his desk, and turned the light off at the door. He exited, closed the door behind him, and took his time going to his room. Despite the quietness in the air, he expected Phoenix to jump out at him and tell him he was an asshole.

When he reached the top of the stairs leading to the bedrooms, he saw Phoenix's door was shut. He considered knocking to see if she was okay, but he couldn't see any light coming from underneath her door. It would be best to talk to her after she had gotten some sleep.

He snorted at himself. He was turning into a pussy… over a pussy…cat.

He laughed out loud at his lame joke. It was official. He needed to get some sleep. He was overtired and overthinking. Instead of turning toward Phoenix's door, he took a right.

He definitely needed sleep. First, he felt like he was being watched. Ridiculous since he was in the compound and surrounded by security. Then, he swore he smelled Phoenix as he walked toward his room, but it didn't make sense.

Now, I'm going crazy. "Dante, quit thinking about Phoenix and go to bed," he told himself.

He opened his door, and the scent of sunshine got stronger. Yep, undeniably crazy.

He closed his bedroom door, but he didn't bother turning on any lights. He hadn't changed the layout in all the years that he'd lived here, and he knew where everything was. He entered his closet long enough to strip off all his clothes and throw them in his hamper.

He got into bed, closed his eyes, and settled down to sleep when he felt movement beside him.

What the hell?

He slid his hand over and up onto what was obviously a female hip. He leaned toward her and inhaled. "Phoenix?"

"Mmm…" was the only response he got. She moved closer to him, and the next second, the rhythmic sound of deep breathing followed.

Well, that explained why he'd smelled her. At least he wasn't crazy.

He looked over at Phoenix's outline. And that solved the problem of whether or not she was uncomfortable around him.

☾

Lexine Harlow watched Dante's room from the crack in her doorway, stunned. She didn't understand why he liked that shifter. Lexine didn't have a personal problem with shifters in general. It was just this particular one. She dressed like a homeless man and had a surly attitude.

What does Dante see in her?

Lexine had seen the way that he looked at the female. Something she had never seen when he looked at her.

Lexine watched for a few more minutes, waiting for Dante to kick Phoenix out at any second. When it was apparent that it wasn't going to happen, she closed her bedroom door and leaned back against it. She took several deep breaths, trying to calm her racing thoughts.

She was hurt, angry, and shocked all at once. Lexine had been in love with Dante for five years. Five years, she had tried to gain his attention. Five years, she had waited in the shadows while he fed and fucked other females, and she never said anything.

Lexine never felt threatened by the other females, despite the rumors she'd heard. Dante never acted cocky or bragged, but Lexine had heard things. She'd heard from more than one female that Dante fucked like a god and was hung like a horse.

But since he had never brought these girls home to the compound, Lexine hadn't pushed for more. She had been biding her time until he'd realize that he was supposed to be with her.

Now, some shifter female he'd known for less than a month was in his room. In his bed.

Why? Why is life so unfair?

She was a good vampire. She was a great Guardian.

She deserved to be with Dante.

Suddenly, Lexine felt like she couldn't breathe. She sprinted from her room as silently as possible, so as not to wake anyone else. She wanted to go outside and run until her lungs burned, but since it was daylight, she went to the basement and headed for the workout room. As she walked, she pulled her blonde hair into a ponytail.

As she rounded the corner, she ran into Sterling.

"Oomph."

Sterling reached out to steady her, his gray eyes filled with concern. "Lexine, are you okay?"

"Yeah, I'm fine. What are you doing up?"

He shrugged and whipped the sweat off his short tan hair. "Couldn't sleep. You?"

"What?"

He raised his brow.

"Oh. Yeah, I couldn't sleep either." She stepped around him. "Excuse me."

"Lexine?"

She turned and noticed that Sterling had the concerned look on his face again.

"Are you sure you're okay?"

She was so upset and brimming with emotions that she considered telling Sterling everything, but she hadn't even told her twin brother, and he was the one she was closest to. She opened her mouth, but the only thing that came out was, "Yeah. Nothing that a little workout won't fix."

Sterling nodded and left Lexine alone.

Alone with nothing but her stupid broken heart.

TWELVE

KENZIE PUSHED the oven door closed with her hip as she set the baking sheet on the counter. With nothing else to do around the house, simply waiting for her brother to come home, she had decided to do a little baking. She had lucked out that her brother had all the ingredients she needed to make chocolate chip cookies. She guessed she had Anna to thank for that.

Sawyer was downstairs in the basement, shooting pool alone. She had played against him earlier, but he'd beaten her twice, and that was when she'd decided she was done. Clearly, his memory loss had not affected his pool-playing skills.

Kenzie moved the hot cookies to the cooling rack and then placed the next batch on the baking sheet before shoving it in the oven. While she waited for the cookies to cool, she went into the living room. *It's a Wonderful Life* was on TV since it was the time of year to play Christmas movies. She perched on the arm of the couch since she planned to get up again once the timer went off.

The movie was just getting to the part where George realized that he wanted to live again. She wondered what her life would be like if she experienced an alternate reality like George, like maybe one where her mother hadn't died. Perhaps her life would have gone in a different direction.

Then, her thoughts turned to Sawyer. Vaughn had once told her that something had happened to Sawyer when he was younger to make him the way he was. Vaughn had never told her what Sawyer had gone through, saying it was Sawyer's story to tell. Obviously, Sawyer wasn't talking. She had to wonder if Sawyer's life would have been better or worse if he hadn't experienced whatever he went through when he was younger that made him hate humans so much.

Kenzie straightened her spine. "Oh my God." *Alternate reality.*

She didn't need to wonder what it would be like for him to experience it. They *were* experiencing it…right now. Sawyer had no idea what had happened to him in the past. This Sawyer was basically what Sawyer would have been like if things had gone differently for him.

Instead of *It's a Wonderful Life* though, Sawyer and she were more like that movie, *The Family Man*, with Nicolas Cage. Unlike when James Stewart's character, George, got to go back to his happy family in the end, Kenzie would be like Nicolas Cage's character, Jack, where he got to see what it would be like to have a family, but in the end, he had to go back to being all alone.

Would Jack have been happier never knowing what it would have been like to get married to his college girlfriend? Or was he grateful that he'd had the chance to know how things could have been different? Going by the fact that he hunted down his old girlfriend at the end of *The Family Man*, Kenzie assumed the latter.

Sawyer was never going to change. He was always going to dislike her simply for being a human, but if she were honest with herself, she would admit that she wished things could be different.

Sawyer's amnesia was her metaphoric guardian angel. This was the only opportunity she was ever going to get to be with Sawyer, and even if it only lasted for one day, at least she wouldn't have sat back and wasted it. Yeah, he might hate her once he regained his memory, but the Memory Sawyer already did, so she would be no worse off there.

As long as she protected her heart, everything would go back to the way it was before. She would just tell him, no bite marks and no actual *sleeping* together. This would only be about sex.

Kenzie shot off the couch, quickly turned off the oven in the kitchen, and marched down the basement stairs. When she reached the bottom, she saw Sawyer sinking a ball into a corner pocket.

He was graceful, a beautiful specimen of a man, and a strip of skin showed between his T-shirt and jeans.

She wanted to lick it.

She headed for him, full of determination.

Sawyer noticed her and uncurled from the pool table. "Hey, Kenzie. Are you—"

He stopped talking and watched her arm sweep the remaining balls, including the cue ball, into the pool table pockets.

"What are you doing?"

She didn't answer. Instead, she stalked toward him with one purpose.

"I wasn't done—"

She cut him off by grabbing his shirt and pulling him down, so she could kiss him.

Sawyer stood frozen for a second before throwing the pool cue aside, growling, and reaching for her.

After that, things went crazy.

As if Sawyer were afraid she would change her mind, he grabbed and attacked her like a caveman. He gripped her ponytail and tilted her head, so he could take her mouth at the angle he wanted.

It was silly because she had been scared that he might change his mind, too. She had been fighting him off for the last few days, and now that she had decided to have sex with him, she had been afraid he wouldn't want her anymore.

Sawyer yanked his shirt off so fast that she barely felt his mouth leave hers before it was back again. He unzipped her sweatshirt and pushed it off her shoulders before jerking her T-shirt over her head.

She wasn't wearing a bra, and when the cold air hit her breasts, her nipples puckered. Sawyer's frantic actions slowed as he dragged both hands down her body. After gently circling her nipples, he continued down her abdomen, and when he reached her pants, the caveman was back. He literally ripped the yoga pants right off of her. He wrenched the front down, and the seams gave away at the sides. Knowing how eager he was only fueled Kenzie's desire.

Now with her being completely naked, Sawyer picked her up and set her on the edge of the pool table. The cold of the wood shocked her bare ass, but only for a second because Sawyer flicked open his jeans, and his beautiful cock popped out. Long, thick, and ready.

Sawyer seized her hair again and wrapped it around his hand. She thought he was going to kiss her, but he didn't lean toward her. Instead, he pulled her head back to expose her throat. She had to put her hands down on the table behind her, so she wouldn't fall over. From the new angle, all she could view was his face and upper chest, and not being able to see what was going to happen next was freaking hot.

With his free hand, he boosted her butt just enough to bring her closer to him, pushed his way in between her thighs, and then—*holy fucking shit!*—Sawyer was inside her.

Just knowing that she was finally having sex with him turned her on so much that she thought she was going to come, and they'd barely even started.

She tried to bring a hand up to touch him.

"Arms down," Sawyer commanded as he pounded inside her.

She tried to move her eyes down.

"No. Just feel me," he said, giving her a couple of extra hard strokes before he resumed his previous rhythm.

Kenzie closed her eyes and simply felt. She would listen to him this time, but next time, she was going to touch him all over. And on the tail of those two thoughts, she came. And came. Her orgasm seemed to go on forever.

When her senses began to return to normal, she noticed that Sawyer had stopped moving.

She opened her eyes, and Sawyer tilted his head down until he looked into her eyes.

"Are you ready?"

"Ready for what?" she whispered, her voice hoarse.

"For me to come inside you and make this pussy mine."

She moaned and tightened around him.

"I'll take that as a yes."

He lifted her off the table, and at first, she was confused. Then, he brought one knee up and laid her down with him over her.

With a hand still in her hair, he kissed her again as his thrusts became more wild. He pulled back, and she was excited that she was going to get to watch this man come. She wanted to see him break apart as he came inside her. She was getting wet again from just thinking about it.

Right before he reached this climax, he tilted her head to the side and bit her shoulder.

She didn't get to see him orgasm as she shattered around him again so hard that she was pretty sure she also now had amnesia.

☾

Kenzie picked up her clothes from where they were scattered on the basement floor. She put on her shirt and sweatshirt, but when she got to the yoga pants, she held them up in the air. "You owe Anna new pants."

Sawyer pulled his T-shirt down over his head and turned around to look at her. "Who's Anna?"

"My brother's girlfriend," she said, letting her arm fall to her side.

Without the pants in between them, Sawyer's eyes dropped to the nude bottom half of her body. His eyes hooded, he stalked toward her. He yanked the article of clothing out of her hand and threw them to the side. He wrapped an arm around her, drawing her close. "I will buy her a dozen pants if I get to be inside you again."

Kenzie sucked in a breath. She was already primed to go, even after two orgasms.

But they needed to discuss some things first.

She put her hands on his chest to try to create some distance. "I would like that to happen again, too. But no more biting my neck and no sleeping together. Actual sleeping."

His brows drew together. "What?"

"You heard me."

Sawyer sighed. "Okay, I will go along with the first one, but what if I want to take you in the middle of the night?"

"Then, you can wait until morning."

He gave her a we'll-see-about-that look but didn't say no. "Whatever you say."

"Thank you. Now, we'd better go upstairs. I left some cookies in the oven, and I need to find some new clothes."

"You can just stay naked."

This time, she gave him a we'll-see-about-that look.

He shrugged. "What? A guy can dream, can't he?"

THIRTEEN

KENZIE SHOVED sawyer's arm off her waist, exited the bed, and headed for the bathroom to take a shower. After the water was warm, she climbed inside.

It wasn't long before thoughts started filling her head, whirlwind-style. She had hoped that if she showered first thing, before any coffee and before she fully woke up, she would remain in a semi-comatose state. Sometimes, showers were a time for her brain to go into overdrive, and today was one of those days.

It had been almost a week since Sawyer and she escaped from their kidnappers, and over the last few days, Sawyer and she had started sleeping together, in both the biblical and literal sense. Sawyer had stayed out of her room for all of four hours before he had woken her up the first night. He had fallen asleep after they'd done the deed, and after five minutes of trying to get him to wake up and leave, she had finally given up and gone back to sleep, too.

She couldn't deny that she liked sleeping next to Sawyer

each night. But she was getting way too used to it. There was no possibility it was going to last. They weren't going to live here in this house without any contact with the outside world for the rest of their lives. Reality would soon intrude. Kenzie's brother would come home eventually. Honestly though, she wanted it that way. Sawyer might think that they were mates and that he liked her romantically, but it was all pretend. Just because things were great between them now didn't mean it was real. Reality would be the two of them together after his memory returned, and they would go back to their regular lives.

Kenzie sighed and turned off the water. She grabbed her towel and stepped out of the bathtub. After she dried her body and hair, she used her towel to wipe the steam off the mirror.

Eyeing her body from head to the top of her thighs, Kenzie hoped that she wouldn't end up in the hospital anytime soon. She looked like an abuse victim, but the bite marks on her body were anything but mistreatment. When she'd told Sawyer that there was no biting her neck, she should have been less specific and said no biting at all. He had listened to her on this rule, but she had marks on her breasts, her pelvis, and—Sawyer's new favorite—her inner thighs.

She looked up and immediately saw the knowing smile on her face. She had to admit that her inner thighs were her new favorite, too. Sawyer would go down on her, using his mouth and hand, and right before she would come, he would bite her right next to her pussy. Every time, it would make her come so hard.

Despite Kenzie's numerous lovers and sexual adventures, Sawyer was the best she'd ever had. He knew exactly how to please her. Sometimes, he'd seem to know what she wanted before she did.

She frowned and shook her head at her reflection. Life definitely wasn't fair.

Kenzie went back into the bedroom and grabbed her now regular outfit of yoga pants, a T-shirt, and a sweatshirt. She was halfway dressed when she heard a deep hum. Wanting to be able to listen better, she paused in her movements. She knew that sound.

"Sawyer! Wake up!"

Sawyer, who had been sleeping on his stomach, jumped into a sitting position at the sound of her voice. "What? What?"

"My brother's home. I heard the garage door. Go put on some clothes."

Sawyer's eyes widened, and he stared at her.

"Go. What are you waiting for?"

Sawyer didn't respond, but he jumped off the bed and ran to the guest bedroom. Thankfully, the guest bed was still unmade.

Kenzie quickly threw on the rest of her clothes and flung the covers up on the bed. She wasn't trying to hide that she had slept there. She was just trying to hide the fact that she'd had sex and slept with Sawyer. Bastian didn't need to know about her private life.

Kenzie sprinted downstairs to the back door. As she waited for it to open, her mind raced with a ton of thoughts. *How am I going to explain to my brother what I'm doing here? How am I going to explain who Sawyer is? How am I going to explain why I don't have a car or our cell phones? And then the big question—could we be going home today?*

Kenzie heard two car doors slam in the garage and the sound of two voices. She groaned just as the door opened, and her brother's girlfriend stepped through.

"Oh," Anna said when she saw Kenzie. "What are you doing here?"

"Hello to you, too." Kenzie rolled her eyes.

Her brother had horrible taste in women. Anna was dressed in cream-colored slacks, an off-white sweater, a white trench coat, and taupe high heels. Her out-of-a-bottle blonde hair was pulled back in an updo with nary a hair out of place. Her appearance was as uptight as her attitude.

"Kenzie!" Bastian exclaimed when he saw her. He dropped the bags he'd been holding and gave her a big hug before letting go. "How are you?" His brow furrowed. "What are you doing here?"

"It's a long story. Maybe I can tell you the whole thing someday. First, I need to—"

"Holy crap," Anna said, interrupting Kenzie.

Kenzie looked over at Anna to see her mouth dropped wide open and her purse falling off her shoulder without her even noticing.

Kenzie turned to see what Anna was looking at.

Sawyer was coming down the stairs with a shirt half on and his jeans hanging low. Of course, he looked good, but Anna was probably staring at him because Kenzie had brought a guy to her brother's house, not because he was hot.

Kenzie looked back at her brother. "Bastian, this is Sawyer." When Sawyer reached her, putting an arm around her shoulders, she said, "Sawyer, this is my brother, Bastian." She looked over to see Anna's mouth snapped shut. "And this is Bastian's girlfriend, Anna."

Sawyer smiled and held out his hand. "Nice to meet you."

"You, too," her brother said with surprise.

Sawyer nodded a greeting to Anna since she didn't bother to hold out her hand.

"Kenzie has a boyfriend—and a handsome one at that," Anna said, more to herself than anyone else in the room.

"Anna," Bastian scolded.

Anna shook herself out of her daze. "I'm sorry," she said to Bastian. "It's just that Kenzie's never had a boyfriend, much less a good-looking one."

"I'm standing right here," Kenzie protested.

She looked out of the corner of her eye at Sawyer. He lost the welcoming smile that he'd previously been wearing.

Kenzie grabbed his hand and whispered, "It's okay. She's always like this."

"A bitch?" he whispered back.

Kenzie laughed out loud. "Yes."

"What's so funny?" Anna demanded.

"Never mind," Kenzie told her. She looked at her brother. "Bastian, I need to borrow your phone, and please tell me your computer is in one of those bags because I will probably need to borrow that, too."

Bastian reached into his coat pocket and withdrew his phone. It was like looking at a unicorn—rare and beautiful.

Bastian gave her a puzzling look. "Where is your phone?"

Kenzie snatched it out of his hand and gave him a weary smile. "That, my dear brother, is all part of the long story."

☾

Sawyer sat, watching as Kenzie paced back and forth in her brother's office. She was upset because all her attempts to contact someone had failed. He was trying to be supportive, but he didn't really care if they went home. He just wanted to be with her.

Kenzie used her fingers to start ticking off all the ideas she'd gone through. "First, I finally remembered Naya's number and called her phone. It was off, and now, it's been two hours since I left a voice mail. I emailed Naya. No reply. I called Vaughn's cell phone. Just like Naya's, it's off. And I don't know anyone else's number."

"Why can't your brother drive us again?"

She looked at him like he was an idiot. "And where would we go once we got there, Sawyer? My crappy apartment that has absolutely no protection? Oh, I know. We can go to Naya's parents' house because I'm sure the king and queen of the vampires would love to let a shifter and a human in the door. Even better, why don't we go back to Naya and Vaughn's house, the place where we got kidnapped from?"

Sawyer grabbed Kenzie's arms and pulled her between his legs. "I know you're frustrated, but making comments like that isn't going to do us any good. I'm sorry I don't remember anything, but you need to try to calm down if you want this to work."

Kenzie's face burst into a grin. "Sawyer, you're a genius."

"I am?"

"Work. Why didn't I think of that? Scoot." She nudged him with her hip. "I need the chair, so I can look up something on the computer."

Sawyer got up, and Kenzie sat down.

She started clicking away at the computer. "Yes," she said a few seconds later. She grabbed her brother's cell phone and punched in a set of numbers.

"Yes, what?" he asked.

She opened her mouth, but before anything came out, she held up her finger and moved the mouthpiece toward her lips.

"L and L Construction. This is Cindy. How may I help you?" a voice on the other end answered.

"Hello. Yes, I would like to speak to Vance Llewelyn."

"I'm sorry, but who am I speaking to?"

"Kenzie. Kenzie Swanson."

"Uh—"

"Look, I'm a friend of his son and daughter-in-law. Please, you have to put me in touch with him."

"Ma'am, I'm sorry, but Mr. Llewelyn isn't here, and I can't just give out his personal phone number to anyone."

"Well, can you give him my number and have him call me?"

"Well…"

At this point, the frustration was written all over Kenzie's face. "Can you hold, please? Just for a moment?"

"Yes, I suppose."

Kenzie pulled the phone away and covered the mouthpiece. "You need to talk to her, Sawyer."

"What? Why?"

"Because she'll know who you are."

"But I don't know her."

"That's okay. Just pretend like you do. All you need to do is get ahold of Vance, and then I will take over from there. Okay?"

Sawyer sighed. "Okay." He made a come-here gesture. "Give me the phone."

Kenzie blew out a breath of relief and handed him the phone. "Her name is Cindy."

"I heard."

Kenzie looked confused for a moment, and then she chuckled. "Oh, yeah."

Sawyer put the phone to his mouth. "Hi, Cindy. It's Sawyer."

"Oh. Hello, Sawyer."

"I need to get in touch with Vance. Can you please give me his phone number?"

"You don't have it?"

Shit, he mouthed. He had to think fast. "I lost my phone, and I don't have his number memorized."

"You?"

Now, he was getting frustrated with this chick. "Yes, me. Something came up. I really need to get ahold of him," he bit out.

"Okay, okay. Here is his phone number."

Sawyer grabbed the pen and paper on the desk and wrote down the number she rattled off.

"Thank you, Cindy." He pushed the End button on the phone. He turned the paper around to show Kenzie. "Happy now?"

She snatched it out of his hand. "Yes. Yes, I am."

FOURTEEN

THE LARGE SUV was silent as Kenzie tried to avoid looking across the seat at Sawyer.

It had happened. Her worst fear had come true. She had seen the change in Sawyer the minute Vance and three sentinels—Saxon, Tegan, and Camden—arrived. Not only had the look of confusion and then recognition crossed Sawyer's face, but when he'd said Vance's name before the alpha could speak, Kenzie had also known his memory had returned.

He hadn't looked at her since.

She'd known that it would happen. Sawyer was too strong of a person to remain amnesic forever. And while she had enjoyed the sweet, sexy side of him, she'd known that it wasn't completely real. So, why did she feel so despondent right now? She supposed that knowing the reality was different than the potential probability.

"Kenzie? Kenzie?"

"Huh?" She turned around and looked at Tegan in the third row. "I'm sorry. What?"

Tegan cocked her head. "Are you okay? You let out a pretty big sigh just now."

"I did?" Kenzie smiled at the white-blonde beauty. "I was just thinking, I guess."

Tegan smiled back. "That's understandable. You've been through a lot. I bet you're excited to go home."

"You have no idea. I hope my Crabby Abby is okay."

"Your cat? Yes, Naya made sure someone checked on her."

What a relief. The cat was a pain in Kenzie's ass, but it was still her cat.

"How is Naya? The babies?"

"Good. You'll see her when we get back to the Cities. She cried when we told her that we were bringing you home. I don't think she'll believe that you're okay until she can see you with her own eyes."

"I can't wait to see her either."

"So…how did you two pass the time without killing each other after your escape?"

Kenzie's gaze automatically met Sawyer's, who was practically shooting a death glare at her. She had to control the urge to roll her eyes at him. He acted as if she wanted the whole vehicle to know that they'd been fucking the last few days, only to have him dump her on her ass upon their return home.

God, he is so dense.

"We watched TV, played pool, cooked. It was really dull actually."

She looked at Sawyer, who started to relax once he realized that she wasn't going to say anything about them being intimate.

126

She directed her next statement toward him. "To tell you the truth, I've never been so bored in my entire life. It was a very, very blah time."

Sawyer narrowed his eyes and clenched his jaw.

Ha. Take that, you big jerk.

He, of course, knew that she was lying. After all, he'd been there when he made her come over and over, but she felt like the jab still stung him, and if it were possible, she'd pat herself on the back for a job well done.

Kenzie looked back at Tegan.

Tegan muttered, "Right…that's why you two smell like each other."

Sawyer turned his glare to Tegan, and Kenzie opened her mouth to say…*something*, but she didn't get the chance.

"When we get back, you two can tell us everything that happened," Vance said from the passenger seat in the front. "Then, we will fill you in on everything that you missed."

Sawyer and Kenzie knew a little of what had gone down after they had been kidnapped but not much. No one had wanted to say anything in front of Kenzie's brother, and after they had piled in the SUV, Vance had asked how long they had been at Bastian's, and that was about it. Neither she nor Sawyer had offered any more information.

Everyone fell back into silence, and not another word was spoken until they got to a house in the Cities that Kenzie had never seen. It was a beautiful big house on what appeared to be several acres of land surrounded by trees. The SUV pulled around to the back of the house to a big garage and another smaller house.

Everyone exited the vehicle, and Kenzie followed them all into the main house.

They entered the kitchen, and everyone headed for the next room. Kenzie stepped forward to follow, but she was stopped by a large hand wrapping around her bicep.

She looked back at Sawyer and scowled at him. "What?"

He pulled her close and spoke in a low voice, "You can't tell anyone that we"—he looked down at her mouth and licked his bottom lip—"were intimate. We'll explain that we had to pretend to be Vaughn and Naya and leave it at that. That should be enough of a clarification as to why we smell like one another."

She ripped her arm out of his grasp and scoffed. "As if I want them to know either." She rubbed her upper limb where she could still feel his touch, and she felt her birth control implant under her fingertips.

Two days ago, when Sawyer had discovered it, he had almost been upset.

She dropped her hand. Now, he was probably thanking his lucky stars that she wasn't going to end up pregnant from their time together.

"Look, I know you don't want them to know that you slept with a human, but did it ever occur to you that I don't want them to know I slept with you?"

Sawyer took a step back with a look of surprise on his face. "But—"

"But nothing, you conceited big oaf. Get your head out of your ass. You are not the great, wonderful catch that you think you are." She looked him up and down. "You really need to get over yourself because I can totally do better."

With that, she spun on her heel and followed the group into the other room.

☾

Phoenix's phone lit up from the nightstand next to where she lay. She grabbed the device off the table and checked the message. Sawyer was back. She needed to meet up with everyone to discuss what Sawyer had to say.

Urgency had her almost sitting up in shock, but at the last second, she remembered that Dante was sleeping on her hair, and she didn't want to wake him.

She was still at the vampires' compound, only leaving to hunt that rat-bastard Gerald. She'd continued to sleep in Dante's bed. She'd been doing it for so many days that she was actually getting used to sleeping during the day and hunting at night.

Dante and she never acknowledged that they slept in the same bed. They always went to sleep and woke up at different times. And he never touched her, not even by accident—except for her hair. Every evening, when she woke up, Dante would be sleeping on her hair.

It was the oddest thing because it wasn't like she fanned her long lengths out behind her on purpose. In fact, she had tried tucking it under her shoulders or putting it in a ponytail and even a bun, yet she always woke up the same way. Now, she didn't really care because he was always careful to keep his distance, and she was getting really good at moving her tresses out from under him without waking him up.

Phoenix gently nudged Dante from his back to his side as she clutched her hair in her other hand. As soon as he moved away, she tugged her long lengths out from under him. After she was free, she let go of him, and he rolled onto his back once more. She sat up to get out of bed, but she was momentarily distracted by the sight before her.

The covers had fallen down Dante when she moved him, and while he wore boxers to bed, they did nothing to disguise the large erection in his underwear.

"Holy shit," she whispered.

Phoenix didn't have a ton of experience with men, but she didn't live in a bubble. She wasn't a virgin, and with the Internet, it would have been pretty hard to never see a naked man. Plus, she was a shifter. Modesty and male cats did not go hand in hand.

Dante was freaking huge.

Without even thinking about it, she put her hands between her legs. While she'd had a couple of sexual encounters, the guys had been average and still always caused her pain. She couldn't imagine something as big as Dante's penis ever causing anything but agony.

Yet, at the same time, she was strangely curious about what sex with Dante would be like. He was always almost tender with her, even the time when he'd fed from her. He had tried to come off as intimidating, and she admitted that she had been for a moment, but in the end, he hadn't been rough or forceful with her. Because of this, even with his size, she couldn't imagine him purposely causing a woman pain. And she knew he had sex. He'd told her so himself, and he'd been pissed at her since she confronted him about needing to feed. She knew it wasn't something he'd made up because he was so angry at the time. So, how did he make it enjoyable for his partners?

She moved her eyes from his hard-on to over his abdomen and chest. He was muscular and smooth. His hairless torso was so different from all the naked shifters she'd seen, and he had a long scar that started on one shoulder and ended on his opposite hip. He was amazingly gorgeous, and his scar only enhanced his already apparent maleness.

She couldn't believe she felt this way, but she wanted to run her fingers over it. She slowly moved her hand above him, but right before she touched him, she stopped herself.

What am I thinking? She was crazy. Nothing good would come of this.

Dante would wake up the second her hand met his skin, and then...*what?* She would awkwardly walk away? She would actually attempt to be intimate with him?

She shook her head at herself. She had learned her lesson more than once already.

No matter how attractive she found Dante and how much of a gentleman she assumed he would be, any sexual contact they had would end the same as all her others. In disappointment. Hers and his. She would be uncomfortable and not enjoy it, and he would be frustrated that she couldn't get over her past and just relax. Or he would just use her body and not care if she had a good time or not.

She looked at Dante's face. Nah, he wouldn't be an asshole like that, but he would be disappointed. And, surprisingly, Phoenix found that she really didn't want to disappoint Dante. She didn't want him to be one more guy who thought she was a cold fish in bed.

She slipped out of bed and pulled the covers over him. As she moved to the closet to get dressed, she almost laughed out loud. It was like a fog had lifted, and she could think straight. Had she actually been thinking about having sex with Dante? She snickered. Maybe she really was crazy because she didn't think about sex ever. Whatever had just happened in bed a minute ago was a fluke. A sleep-induced irrational fluke.

There was no way she'd ever have sex again with anyone. Not even with Dante.

FIFTEEN

SAWYER LENNAR—REMEMBERING his last name made him feel good—watched Kenzie take her friend Naya into her arms after the female vampire had burst through the door, making a beeline for the human. The two consoled each other, but surprisingly, it was Naya who cried, and it was Kenzie who reassured her friend.

He tilted his head to the side in amazement. He had thought that the kidnapped victim would have been the more emotional of the two, but Kenzie was strong. After everything she'd been through, she still hadn't lost her spirit. He almost smiled with pride for her, but he stopped himself just in time.

Sawyer needed to get away from her because his body and mind was a mix of conflicting feelings and desires.

He was grateful that he had regained his memory. The difficult part was that he still remembered everything that had happened before his memory returned.

Everything.

He remembered the way she'd move when he was inside

her. The way she would come so hard all over his dick as he made her orgasm over and over. He had known she was experienced in the bedroom, and part of him had always thought of her as a little slutty, but after fucking her, he definitely saw the appeal. She knew what she liked, and she would take it. She wasn't shy, and she wouldn't force him to always take the lead.

Just the thought of her riding him to climax was enough to give him a hard-on from hell.

That was what made him immediately shut down his line of thinking. This was Kenzie he was thinking about. *Human* Kenzie. He needed to forget anything that had happened between them. He needed to forget how his stupid cat had thought she was his mate because he was never going to be mated to a human.

He needed to find a way to purge his mind of her. If only he could have swapped one memory for another. Unfortunately, amnesia didn't work that way.

Vaughn made his way over to Sawyer. Vaughn had missed the briefing where Sawyer and Kenzie had filled them in on their experience. Vaughn had only shown up when he brought his mate to see Kenzie. He had been speaking to Vance for the last few minutes, presumably to be told what he'd missed, and now, he was approaching Sawyer with his hand held out.

Sawyer put his hand in Vaughn's, and the other shifter pulled him close for a man hug and a pat on the back.

They pulled apart, but Vaughn didn't let go of Sawyer's hand. "I know you didn't do it on purpose, but you will never know how grateful I am to you and Kenzie for being kidnapped in our place. I can't imagine what would've happened to Naya and the twins if it had been us instead."

Sawyer opened his mouth. "Vaughn, you really—"

Vaughn yanked Sawyer forward a step. "This is where you say something like, 'You're welcome,' and nothing more." He raised his brow. "Understand?"

Sawyer couldn't help but grin. "You're welcome."

Vaughn released his hand and nodded. "That's better."

"So, I take it everything is good with the exception of Naya worrying about Kenzie?" Sawyer asked as Vaughn turned and stood next to him so that they could both see the females. "The pregnancy is going okay?"

Sawyer had been just as shocked as everyone when he found out that Vaughn had knocked up the beautiful vampire. However, after seeing how happy Vaughn was, Sawyer only wanted the best for the two of them and their future children.

Vaughn cracked a secret smile that previously wouldn't have bothered Sawyer, but after his time with Kenzie, he couldn't help but feel somewhat envious.

He shook off the foolish emotion.

"Yes, everything is good," Vaughn told Sawyer. "Did my dad tell you that we're having a boy and a girl?"

Sawyer shook his head.

"Naya's excited."

Sawyer gave Vaughn a questioning look.

Vaughn laughed, his blue eyes lighting up. "Okay, okay. I'm excited, too."

"As you should be. You deserve it, man."

"Thanks." Vaughn lost his smile and looked at Kenzie, who was going through her things that Naya had brought for her. "You know, you do, too. My dad says that Kenzie did very well out there. She's a tough chick, for a shifter or human."

Sawyer held up his hand to stop Vaughn from saying anything else. "I'm fine. I'm exactly where I want to be." Sawyer decided it would be best to just ignore the Kenzie comment.

Vaughn looked at Sawyer as if he was almost disappointed. It seemed like he was going to say something else, but the front door opened. Vaughn's younger sister, Payton, walked through the door, her hand held out behind her, obviously clasped in someone else's.

Sawyer was an only child but had known the Llewelyns since he was little. Vaughn was the closest thing he had to a brother, and he often thought of Payton as a little sister to him, too. The last time Sawyer had checked, the female shifter had still been single.

Sawyer quickly glanced at Vaughn to see if the sight alarmed him, but he appeared to be as relaxed as ever. Sawyer looked back at the door just in time to see whose hand Payton was holding.

It was a wolf.

"What the hell did I miss?" Sawyer exclaimed.

☾

Saxon watched as Phoenix walked from the Guardians' compound to his SUV. She had asked him to pick her up and bring her to the Llewelyns'. Saxon couldn't help feeling concerned for his friend. Normally, she was so independent, but ever since Dante had rescued her from Gerald, she wouldn't go anywhere by herself. No one had called her on it though. Oh, no, they were all smarter than that. She might not be her typical self, but she was still Phoenix.

Phoenix opened the door and slipped inside.

"Damn, girl. What did you do, bathe in the vampire?" Saxon hadn't seen her since their last rotation together a couple of nights ago on the hunt to find Gerald. Every time he saw her, she'd increasingly smell like Dante.

"Ha-ha. I'm not surprised since I've been staying there." She turned and grabbed her seat belt, muttering something else under her breath.

Saxon put the vehicle in drive and put his foot on the accelerator. "Can you please repeat what you just said? Because you don't smell like all the other vampires." He glanced at her for a moment before turning his eyes back to the road. "What gives?"

Phoenix sighed. "Okay, but this does not leave the car." She pointed a finger at him. "If you so much as even hint at what I'm about to tell you to someone else, you'll be singing soprano for the rest of your life."

He instinctively put his hand over his balls. "Jeez, Phoenix, I think you know me well enough to know that I won't tell anyone. I've kept your past a secret from anyone you don't want knowing, haven't I?"

"Yes, but this..." She paused. "It's different. You're probably going to laugh at me."

He smiled. "Well, now, you have to tell me."

She rolled her eyes. "I've kind of been sleeping in Dante's bed."

He immediately tensed. "What?"

"I've been sleeping in Dante's bed."

Saxon sharply turned the wheel to the right, making the tires screech, and they came to a forceful stop.

She grabbed the armrests. "What the hell, Saxon?"

He put the SUV in park before turning in his seat to face her, and she mirrored his actions.

"Why are you sleeping in Dante's bed? The vampires won't give you your own room? What has he done to you?" Saxon sniffed the air. "Do you smell so much like him because"—he swallowed—"he's forcing himself on you?"

He was going to rip the vampire to shreds. Saxon had thought Dante seemed like a good guy, and he had even warned the vampire a little about Phoenix's past to help him understand that she was special.

"Saxon, oh my God, you have it all wrong. No, Dante is not forcing himself on me. He hasn't done anything inappropriate to me or with me. Yes, the vampires gave me my own room, but…" She turned her eyes down toward her lap before looking back up at him. She chuckled. "You're going to think it's silly."

"Phoenix, I'm ready to drive back there and kick his ass. I don't care if he's been making you watch his daily puppet show. I just want to know that you're okay."

"Daily puppet show?" She laughed. "Can you imagine? That would be hilarious."

"Phoenix," he growled.

She rolled her eyes again. "I've been sleeping in Dante's bed because I feel safe when I'm with him." She shrugged her shoulders. "I tried sleeping in the room they gave me, but I tossed and turned."

He stared at her.

She raised her eyebrows. "You don't have to look so surprised."

He hadn't realized that his feelings were so obvious. "I'm sorry. I just didn't expect that to be your answer."

She turned to face forward once more. "I know. I don't know what's wrong with me. I don't know why he's the one who makes me feel safe. A vampire, out of everyone."

"Do you think you'll ever come back to the bunkhouse?"

She scoffed. "Of course," she said with conviction. But the next sentence was not spoken as strongly, "I'm sure that once Gerald is found, I'll feel better."

Saxon put his hand on hers. "Phoenix, it's okay to be a little vulnerable. And you know you can always sleep with me."

He wasn't hitting on her. He was telling the truth. It wouldn't be the first time he'd let her spend the night with him. His relationship with the female shifter was completely platonic. They were more like brother and sister than anything, but Phoenix still had the urge to be close to other shifters, so he'd let her sleep next to him.

"Yeah, and then everyone will think we're screwing. It's one thing to do it every once in a while on a night off, but if I stayed in your room every night, everyone would think we were doing it. No, thank you."

He put his hand on his chest. "Ouch. You wound me."

She gave him a you've-got-to-be-kidding-me look. "Please. You don't need my affections."

He smiled at her. "Yeah, you're right." He put his hand on hers again. "You're sure nothing bad has happened?"

"Yes, I'm sure." She shook him off. "Can we go now, please?"

He studied her for a moment. She seemed to be telling the truth, and he couldn't smell any lies, but something was off. It took him a couple of more seconds before he realized that she was embarrassed. He was so close to saying something to her because she never got embarrassed, but then he decided to keep his mouth shut. She'd been through enough.

Saxon turned forward and took off once again. "Just remember, you can talk to me about anything."

She smiled. "I know. Same here."

"I know."

"Now, tell me what you know so far about Sawyer."

SIXTEEN

KENZIE PUSHED OPEN her apartment door and stepped over the threshold, but that was where she stopped. She couldn't seem to go any further.

Almost all the shifters had been grateful for her assistance, but she couldn't help feeling like an outsider. All she had wanted to do was leave and go to her apartment. She'd missed it.

But now, being back home was…almost surreal.

"Vaughn, honey, can you stay outside in the hall?" Naya said from behind her.

There was a pause, and then Vaughn said, "Sure, baby."

Naya pushed Kenzie forward.

Right before the door closed, Vaughn said, "Good night, Kenzie. Glad you're back."

Kenzie was still too numb to respond.

Naya took Kenzie's purse off her shoulder and helped her remove her coat. All of Kenzie's things had still been at Naya and Vaughn's house where she had been painting the bathroom when she was abducted, except for her phone.

Her cell had been with the kidnappers, and the shifters apparently had been able to confiscate it from them. Right after Kenzie and Sawyer had escaped, the shifters had arrived at the house where Kenzie and Sawyer had been held. If she and Sawyer had waited a little longer, the shifters would have rescued them, and they would never have had to escape and take refuge at her brother's house.

Crabby Abby came around the corner and weaved her way through Kenzie's legs.

"I think Crabby Abby actually missed you," Naya said with amazement.

The *Crabby* in front of *Abby* was not a fun play on words. The cat liked no one.

Kenzie bent down to pet Crabby Abby, and the feline took off.

"Okay, maybe not," Naya said with a sigh. "Since I still have a key, Vaughn had some of the guys come here a couple of times to make sure she had enough food and water."

Kenzie turned to look at her friend. "Thanks."

Naya tilted her head to the side. "Kenzie, it was the least we could do." Naya put her hand on Kenzie's elbow and ushered her toward the couch. "Come and sit. Now, I heard your story from Vance, but I want to hear what really happened."

Kenzie sat. "What do you mean? We told everyone what really happened."

Naya, who was still standing, put her hands on her hips. "Mackenzie Rae Swanson, I am your best friend, and you had better not lie to me. I *know* something happened between Sawyer and you."

Kenzie sat back in her seat and raised her brow. "Did you just full-name me?"

Naya sat next to her. "Yes, yes, I did. I'm going to be a mother soon," she said, running her hand over her expanding belly. "I figure I have to practice my reprimanding." Naya turned in her seat and pointed a finger at Kenzie. "Plus, I know you're not telling me everything. Everyone else might buy that you two smell like one another because you had to pretend to be Vaughn and me, but I know you too well. There is more to the story."

Kenzie put her head back against the head of the couch and closed her eyes. "We had sex."

Naya gasped.

"Sawyer was confused with his amnesia. He thought that I was his mate. I tried to resist, but he was so…not Sawyer."

"Was it good?"

Kenzie snapped her head up, opening her eyes. "Really? Really, Naya? Out of all that, you want to know what Sawyer was like in bed."

Naya shrugged a shoulder.

"Vaughn has turned you into a sex fiend."

"Insults will get you nowhere."

Kenzie couldn't help but smile. "Okay, fine. He fucked like a god, all right? It was just as good as I had always imagined it would be."

Naya stared thoughtfully off into space. "Hmm…it must be a shifter thing. They must be born knowing how to please a woman."

Kenzie smacked Naya on the arm to get her attention. "You really are a sex fiend."

Naya smiled knowingly.

Kenzie just shook her head, but she did it with a smile. She had never thought she'd see Naya like this.

"So," Naya said, "what's with this mate stuff, and what do you mean by, 'not Sawyer'?"

◖

Kenzie was dragging her feet. The night before, after Naya had left, Kenzie had broken down and listened to her messages. She had been dreading it since she got her phone back because there had to be some on there from work. And she was right.

There were several heavily worded voice mails from her boss, Dave. First, he had sounded concerned, but after a few days, the worry had turned to anger until the last one that had told her she was fired. Now, she had to make an attempt to fight for her job back. The shifters had given her a letter from one of their physicians, saying that she had been in the hospital with pneumonia, but Kenzie had her doubts that it was going to work. Then, what would she do? She couldn't tell her boss the truth.

Well, Dave, you see, there are others out in the world who are not human. I was accidentally mistaken as the princess of the vampires and kidnapped. I finally made it home last night, and I came straight here this morning. Now, can I have my job back?

Kenzie snorted. Not only would she be betraying her friend, her boss would most likely laugh in her face. She would be better off with the letter saying that she had been too ill to come to work. Either way, waiting around wasn't going to change anything. She might as well get it over with.

She dressed in her best outfit as if it were another day at

the office and made sure her makeup was perfect. She didn't bother with breakfast because the knots in her stomach told her anything she might eat wouldn't stay down for long.

Kenzie took one last look in the mirror before grabbing her things and heading out the door. Her car was in its usual spot, thanks to Vance and his shifters who had returned it to her apartment from Naya and Vaughn's house where it had been left when she was abducted. She got in, rubbed her hands over the steering wheel, and then took off.

The quick drive to work was uneventful, except for her heart pounding in her chest.

Once inside the building, she made a beeline to her manager's office. She ducked her head as she walked. Many other hotel employees were roaming around, and she didn't want them stopping her and asking questions.

Kenzie was one of the head event and wedding planners at one of the oldest and most prestigious hotels in St. Paul, and she loved her work. Even the late-night weddings couldn't ruin her affection for what she did. She had been with the hotel since college—first, as an intern, and then as an associate before moving up to her current position.

As she knocked on Dave's door, she couldn't ignore the sinking feeling in her stomach that she was about to lose it all.

"Come in," her boss said from the other side of the thick wood.

Kenzie slowly pushed it open and stepped inside.

"Kenzie?" Dave said when he saw her, his ruby-red face showing complete surprise. "What are you doing here?"

"I work here," she answered, her voice full of hope.

Dave winced and opened his mouth to speak.

Kenzie held up her hand. "Wait. Please, before you say anything, I just want to let you know how sorry I am that you haven't heard from me for…" She paused. She didn't even know how long it had been since she worked last.

She started doing the math in her head, but it turned out that she didn't need to because Dave knew how long it had been.

"Almost three weeks," he said with his brow raised. "Because you haven't worked for almost that long. And you haven't answered your phone or replied to any of your emails either. Would you like to explain that?"

Kenzie quickly sat down in front of Dave's desk and pulled out her lame doctor's note. "I've been sick. I was in the hospital, and I wasn't able to get you word that I was there. I am very sorry. I never meant for this to happen."

Dave picked up her note and read it over for what seemed like an hour. "Pneumonia?"

Kenzie swallowed hard. She hated lying to her boss. "Yes."

Dave put the letter down on the desk and folded his hands. "Kenzie, while I am pleased to see that you are no longer ill, I find it hard to believe that you could not find one way to let us know you were sick, especially since you'd seemed perfectly fine the last day you were here."

Kenzie started to protest, and Dave held up his hand.

"It's your turn to wait. I don't want to hear any of your excuses." He shook his head. "Kenzie, I have always valued you as an employee and admired your work ethic, which was why it surprised me that you had done something like this. And because I like you, I would like to let this go, but I absolutely cannot. Your actions were too irresponsible. I can't, for the life of me, imagine that you didn't have anyone, whether it was family or friends, who could account for your whereabouts this whole time. It's almost like you disappeared off the face of the earth and then reappeared one day."

Kenzie winced. His words were so close to the truth.

"I'm sorry, Kenzie, but I have to let you go. In fact, we have already started interviewing people to replace you."

Her heart sank. She'd known it was a strong possibility, but a part of her had hoped this wouldn't happen.

"Kenzie?"

She made eye contact with her boss—with her former boss. "Hmm?"

"Is there anything else you need?"

She hadn't realized that she'd been staring off into space, and the man probably wanted her gone from his office.

"Um…" She licked her lips. "No." She stood from her seat. "I'll just be going."

Dave nodded. "I think that's for the best."

Kenzie slowly turned and walked out the door. She hung her head and covered her face the best she could as she left the building. If she'd thought that she didn't want anyone to see her face when she came in, the feeling was ten times worse now. She was completely embarrassed and ashamed. She didn't need anyone feeling sorry for her.

When she got to her car, she turned the heat up all the way because she was chilled to the bone. Maybe she was in shock from what had just happened. Probably not. She wasn't that lucky. Instead, she was going to have to drive home and stare at her empty apartment.

A sudden wave of loneliness crashed over her. Naya had a husband with children on the way, which was good. Kenzie was happy for her, but their relationship would never be the same. She'd just lost her wonderful, fulfilling career, and she was completely and utterly single. She had been fine with that before, but after her time with Sawyer and seeing Naya so happy, she couldn't help but feel all alone.

"Stop it," she told herself. "It's just because you lost your job. Naya is still your friend, and you don't need a stupid man to make you happy. Sawyer's an asshole anyway."

She was right. This was just a bump in her life road—a big bump but a bump nonetheless. She would go home, fire up her computer, and start looking for a new job. She would not let this bring her down.

SEVENTEEN

SAWYER CROUCHED low next to the abandoned house. He'd been home now for two weeks, and in the shifters' and vampires' quest to find Gerald, they had been making their way through the entire metro area, searching all the vacant homes. They had installed cameras in Gerald's home in case he went back. They had eyes on Brent, his son, twenty-four/seven. They had also hacked into every motel and hotel to receive updates on new customers checking in. The downside was that not every motel kept computerized records, but the shifters and vampires only had so much manpower.

With Gerald on the run for almost three weeks now, they were running out of options to find him. And they were starting to look a little pathetic. Sawyer didn't understand how one shifter could get away from them all.

Sawyer hadn't been the least bit shocked when he found out that Gerald had been behind Vaughn and Naya's kidnapping. Sawyer had never liked the guy. He was a sorry excuse for a shifter, and even though he was related to the boss, he didn't have a quarter of the alpha's integrity.

What had shocked Sawyer was the wolves' involvement. He hadn't been surprised that they were involved. He had already smelled them on the humans who abducted Kenzie and him. No, he had been surprised that the wolves would be involved with Gerald. Obviously, Sawyer had missed a lot during his kidnapping and amnesia. He had been filled in on everything that had happened—Payton's attempted capture, her rescue by Damien, Damien challenging his father, Dwyer losing and getting kicked out of Minnesota, and the pardon for the wolf-shifters to come back to the Twin Cities.

"Are you ready to go in?" Saxon asked from beside him.

"Ready when you are," Dante answered from the other side of Saxon.

Sawyer had been working with the vampires for the last two weeks, and he was finally getting used to it. He didn't have a problem with the vampires—they were better than humans—but it was still strange to be sharing so much information with them and trusting them to have their backs in situations like this. But he also understood how much they cared for their princess and that they weren't going to be left behind while the shifters did all the work in finding Gerald.

"I don't smell Gerald around here anywhere. Just humans," Sawyer told the other two.

"Yeah, me neither, but we still gotta check it out," Saxon replied.

Sawyer palmed the gun in his hand. It felt strange to use something other than his claws, but after Gerald had shot

Saxon and Zane, Vance had ordered them all to carry firearms.

Saxon, Dante, and Sawyer had glanced in all the windows, and after not seeing anything, they were getting ready to go in the front and back doors.

"I'll take the front," Dante told them. "Go around back, and I'll let you in."

Saxon nodded and headed toward the rear of the house while Sawyer followed him. It appeared that Saxon had no problem with taking orders from the vampire leader, but it seemed the two were friends. Sawyer didn't question it too much.

Just when Saxon stepped on the back porch, Sawyer heard a gunshot from inside the house, followed by Dante yelling, "Goddamn it."

Saxon kicked the back door open, so he and Sawyer could enter the residence. They looked for anything suspicious until they found Dante on top of a filthy human, holding the human's arms behind his back and tying something around his wrists.

"This fucker shot me in the leg. Can one of you find something to wrap around my thigh before I bleed all over the carpet? My jeans aren't going to soak up much more blood."

Saxon grabbed an old sheet lying in the corner. It was dirty, but so was everything else in the shithole.

"I don't get it. We didn't see anyone through the windows," Saxon said.

"Yeah, this asshole was hiding under a pile of who-knows-what. That's why we didn't see him," Sawyer replied.

"Ha-ha. I tricked you sons of bitches," the human said from underneath Dante.

"Shut up," Dante said before punching the guy in the jaw and knocking him out.

"We'll quickly check the other rooms, and then we'd better get out of here before the police show up. Someone had to hear that gunshot," Sawyer told the other two as he made his way down the hall.

Saxon and he cleared the other rooms and helped Dante up from the floor in the living room.

"I'm fine. I'm fine. I'll probably just need a couple of stitches. Can we swing by the vampire clinic on the way to our next location?" Dante limped out of the house.

"Dude," Saxon said, "I think you're done for the night."

Dante sighed. "Yeah, I suppose. Didn't hurt to try."

After they were all outside, Sawyer closed the door behind him. "Don't worry. We'll cover the rest of the homes on the list. We can do it with just the two of us."

The three of them hurried toward their vehicle down the street.

Thank God only one of us got hurt, was the last thought Sawyer had before his head exploded in pain, and it was lights out.

☾

Lexine was trying her damnedest to work with Phoenix, but it was hard. The more she was around the cat-shifter, the more Lexine disliked her. On a conscious level, she knew that it was petty jealousy. On an unconscious level, she didn't care because she should be the one in Dante's bed every night. It wasn't fair.

Lennox was driving while Lexine was sitting shotgun, so thankfully, she didn't have to look at the shifter's face. Although not seeing her didn't help much because the cab of the truck smelled like sunshine. Sunshine and Dante.

I think I'm going to puke.

Lexine knew they weren't having sex. One, because they never smelled like it, and two, because one of the other guys made a joke one night, and Dante had shut it down really fast. But it was almost worse that they weren't having sex. Lexine had never seen Dante in a relationship. She knew that he had girls who he would go out with, screw, and use for feeding, but none of them had ever come around the compound, and Dante had certainly never taken any of them on a date. Yes, this *thing* he had with Phoenix was much, much worse.

"Lexine!"

"Huh? What?" She hadn't even heard her brother talking to her.

"Did you hear anything I had to say? Did you even know I had a phone call?"

"No," she admitted embarrassingly. She could feel heat filling her cheeks. So much for being on alert when she was working.

She heard Phoenix huff from the backseat. Lexine turned and shot her a dirty look.

"Dante was shot and taken to the clinic," Phoenix informed her, annoyance or anger or both on her face.

Lexine looked at her brother to see if what she had said was true. "What?"

"It's true, sis."

"Oh, no. I hope he'll be okay," she said.

"He said to meet them there ASAP, so we will soon find out."

"He did?" A tiny flare of hope went through Lexine.

He could have told them to keep working, yet he had asked them to meet him there.

"Yes," Phoenix said, practically yelling. "Now, can we hurry the fuck up and get there already? If I knew where this clinic was, I would drive myself, but since I have to rely on you, I'd appreciate it if you'd stop driving like a grandma."

Lexine gasped. Phoenix didn't have to be such a bitch. Lexine looked over at her brother to see if he was as mad as she was, but the big dumb idiot was grinning.

"Lennox," Lexine scolded.

"What?" He shrugged. "It's funny."

Lexine rolled her eyes and counted the minutes until they arrived.

As soon as her brother stopped the vehicle, Lexine flew out of the passenger seat and into the building with Phoenix right on her heels.

"Take me to Dante," she demanded of the first person she saw.

The woman in scrubs put her hand on her hip and gave Lexine a look as Lennox joined them.

"Please," Phoenix added.

"That wasn't so hard now, was it?" The woman turned around and waved them back. "This way. Doc Montgomery is almost done cleaning him up."

Phoenix took a step forward.

Lexine put her arm out. "Where do you think you're going?"

"Lexine, let her go. Come on, it's not a big deal," Lennox said.

Lexine looked over her shoulder at her brother. "But it's the vampire clinic," she bit out.

The woman in scrubs turned around. "He said to bring the shifter, too. Now, will you three hurry up? I don't have all day."

Lexine looked at Phoenix, expecting to see a satisfied smirk on the cat's face, but she only appeared to be relieved.

Phoenix stepped forward again, and this time, Lexine didn't stop her.

They followed the woman to a room in the back. The door was closed, so the woman knocked first and waited for a response on the other side before entering.

She ushered the three of them into the room. Besides Dante, there was a woman in a lab coat with a stethoscope around her neck, who was clearly the doctor, and then another shifter, Saxon.

Lexine eyed Dante up and down to see how well he was doing. He was sitting up in the bed, shirtless, with the sheet pulled up to his waist. Lexine didn't notice a wound or bandage anywhere on his upper body.

"Hey, man. You gonna be okay?" Lennox asked Dante as they all crowded around the bed.

"Yeah, I was only shot in the leg. The doctor here assured me that I'm going to live."

Phoenix snorted. "'Only'?"

"Yes," the doctor said, "he was shot in the leg. I removed the bullet and cleaned the wound. He should be just fine in a week or so." She looked at Dante. "As long as you feed, that is."

"Thanks, Dr. Montgomery."

The doctor looked at everyone besides Dante. "Make sure he feeds, will you, please?"

Saxon pulled up his sleeve and stuck his arm out. "You can have my blood. Only the best for you, Dante."

Dante swatted Saxon's hand away. "Thanks, man, but no. Gross."

"That hurts, bro," Saxon said with mock sadness.

Heart pounding, Lexine took a step forward. It was now or never. There was a reason Dante had asked them to come. She knew he preferred women, like most adult vampires, unless he was on his deathbed. All she had to do was offer her blood, and he would be drinking from her. She would never wish a gunshot wound on him, but she couldn't help but be pleased by the turn of events. She took a deep breath and opened her mouth—

"Could everyone please leave the room, except for Phoenix? I need to *talk* to her," Dante said.

Black dots swam in Lexine's vision as she got light-headed. What was going on? This couldn't be happening.

He'd asked them to come because he wanted to feed from *her*? From a shifter? He would rather take the blood of a shifter than from another vampire? A vampire who was more than willing to share herself with him?

She had to get out of there.

Lexine spun around, marched to the door, and flung it open. She ran outside, not caring how cold it was. She couldn't be in there a second longer. She was a foolish lovesick woman, whose night had gone to absolute shit. Her only luck was that she hadn't said anything out loud because if Dante had turned her down in front of them—in front of Phoenix—Lexine didn't know what she would have done.

EIGHTEEN

SAWYER BLINKED OPEN HIS EYES. The room had minimal lighting, and he didn't recognize it.

He tried to sit up. "Oh, fuck." That made him dizzy, so he lay back down.

Suddenly, Kenzie was standing over him. "Shh…no need to rush getting up."

"What the hell happened?"

Kenzie snorted. "Apparently, the guy Dante tied up had a friend. Saxon thought he probably snuck out the window and then waited for you guys outside. This friend was pretty pissed about you tying up his pal, so he took a two-by-four to the back of your head. Your poor noggin. It keeps getting hit." All humor left her face, and worry flashed across her eyes. "Oh, no…you didn't lose your memory again, did you?"

He did a quick scan of everything and was pretty sure he was fine. He remembered being at the abandoned house and all the events leading up to when his head must have been bashed in. He was surprised his head didn't hurt more. It was just a dull ache at the moment. "No."

"Whew."

He looked around the room again. "Where am I? This is not the shifter infirmary."

Kenzie chuckled nervously. "No, they have you at the vampire clinic. Dante and you were both injured, and Saxon didn't have time to take you two to separate places. Since Dante's injury was worse, Saxon came here."

Sawyer nodded slightly. "That makes sense."

"You're not mad?"

"No. Why would I be?"

She looked at him like he was crazy. "Because you're Sawyer. You like to do everything by the book."

He knew she was right, but at the moment, he just didn't care. He shrugged. "Oh well."

"I'm a little worried, but I'm just going to go with it."

He picked up her hand from where it rested on his bed. "How did you get here? How did you know?"

She chuckled again. "Saxon called me."

He linked their fingers together. "That was nice of him."

Kenzie swallowed. "Uh...maybe I should go get someone."

Sawyer brought her hand to his lips and kissed it. "Why?"

"You're not yourself."

Sawyer drew her down until she was leaning over him. "I thought we had already established that."

"I don't think we should be doing this." Kenzie's breathing was shallow, and her face was flushed.

"Liar," he said. Then, he put his hands in her hair to pull her in for a kiss.

((

Phoenix watched everyone leave the room, and then she turned back to Dante with raised brows.

Dante sighed. "Look, I can't feed from any of the other Guardians. I need to keep some boundaries with them since I'm their leader, and I'm not calling anyone else to come and feed me because—"

Phoenix held up her hand. She didn't want him to say anything about the females he was intimate with. She would never admit it to anyone, but the green-eyed monster was starting to rear its ugly head. She didn't like it, but she couldn't deny that sinking feeling in her stomach as she pictured Dante feeding from some beautiful female vampire. "I'll do it."

He blew out a breath of relief. "Thank you."

She shrugged, pretending like feeding this male was no big deal when the first and only time it had happened was almost life-changing. "No problem."

Dante scooted over to the far side of the bed and patted the open spot he'd made for her. "Come and sit. I'd promise not to bite, but that'd be a lie."

Phoenix snickered and moved closer.

"Bad joke. Sorry. Just trying to lighten the mood."

Phoenix sat on the bed. "There's no need. I'm fine."

Dante lifted an eyebrow. "Phoenix, you might be able to cover your smell, but I can still read your body language. If you're unsure, you don't have to do this. I can wait."

At his words, she did notice how stiff she was, and she let her posture sag a little. One thing she did know was that she didn't want him to change his mind. She reassuringly put her hand on his arm. "Seriously, I'm fine. I want to do this."

"Okay. If you say so." He looked down at her hand. "Lift your sleeve, and give me your wrist."

An image of Dante with a beautiful female flashed through her mind again. Only this time, the female's head was thrown back in ecstasy.

Phoenix wanted to stab the fictional woman's eyes out.

Without saying a word, Phoenix removed her sweatshirt, leaving her in her V-neck T-shirt. Her messy knot of hair on the top of her head had been knocked loose by the removal of her sweatshirt, so she pulled her ponytail out and moved all her hair to the side and over her shoulder to leave the skin exposed for Dante. She looked him in the eyes. "I want you to take my neck."

Dante fidgeted in his seat. "Phoenix"—he swallowed —"you don't know what you're saying."

She raised her chin. "Yes, I do."

He closed his eyes and took a couple of deep breaths, and she was afraid he was going to say no.

He opened his eyes, and in a low voice, he said, "Come closer."

Without any hesitation, she moved closer to him.

Dante wrapped his arm around her waist and rubbed his nose over her neck. "You don't know the beast that you tempt, Red," he whispered.

She tilted her head away to give him more room.

He growled and struck.

Just like the first time, the sensation of his bite was something she'd never expected. She thought it would hurt, but his sharp fangs went smoothly through her skin, and when he started to pull on her neck with his lips, she moaned and grabbed the back of his head to hold him to her.

Dante shifted them until she was lying on her back, and he was in between her thighs.

"Dante, isn't this bad for your wound?"

His response was to grunt as he sucked harder. Then, he pushed his pelvis into hers.

He was hard.

Oh God. It felt good. *He* felt good.

His free hand moved up her leg, over her hip and waist, and up toward her breasts. She held her breath as he bypassed them and moved on to her shoulder where he grabbed her hair and wrapped it around his hand.

It made her remember the last time she'd fed him. He had pushed her up against the door, putting his hardness between her legs. He had cut his thumb with his fang and stuck it in her mouth.

His blood.

His blood had done something to her then, and she wanted it again. She pulled on the arm around her waist, and he complied.

She shifted her jaw enough that her sharp cat teeth emerged. She used her incisor to bite his thumb, and once she broke the skin, she shifted back and sucked.

She closed her eyes at the taste of his blood. Vampire blood was unlike anything she'd ever consumed. It was sweeter than her own and tasted like the cinnamon that he smelled like. Soon, she felt a tingling in her nipples and in her clit. She tilted her pelvis up toward Dante and rubbed.

She had to wonder if she was crazy. She had vowed to herself that she wouldn't have sex with anyone, and here she was, rubbing herself against a man. She might be the biggest dicktease there ever was.

Dante didn't seem to mind, and despite the single sheet covering him, he never attempted to move it or to remove her pants. Instead, he slightly pulled on her hair and ground his cock against her pussy. His blood, the friction of them moving together, and perhaps the simple fact that this was Dante were enough to give Phoenix the second orgasm of her life.

Fireworks went off behind her eyes, and her body tightened as she came. If this was what happened when people had sex, it was no surprise they enjoyed it so much. While she had never come close to climaxing during sex, she had come twice now by dry-humping Dante. She hoped he never found out because the whole situation was embarrassing. She was twenty-nine years old and had never had an orgasm until recently.

She was so lost in her head that she hadn't realized that Dante had removed his thumb and that he had stopped feeding from her neck. He was currently staring down at her face.

"Are you okay?" His voice was hoarse.

More than okay. "Yes."

"What are you thinking about?"

"Uh..."

His brown eyes sparkled. "I can practically see the wheels turning in that head of yours."

"Uh…" She couldn't tell him what she'd been thinking about.

"That's okay. I'm just glad you didn't run away this time."

"Uh…" She didn't know how to respond to that. She had run away the last time he fed from her. The intimacy of the moment and her unexpected orgasm had scared her. Another thing she was too embarrassed to admit.

Dante laughed.

She scowled at him. "What?"

"I was beginning to think 'uh' was your new favorite word."

She pushed at his shoulders. "Get off me."

He didn't move, so she pushed harder.

"Phoenix, stop. Please."

She complied.

"In all seriousness, thank you for feeding me."

She shrugged a shoulder. "No problem."

He looked at her like she was a liar—well, she was—but he didn't say anything. He just simply rolled off of her.

She sat up and noticed he was clutching the sheet in front of him. There was also a wet spot.

As she sat up, she quickly looked away to hide her satisfied smile. She'd been so in her own head and body that she wasn't sure if Dante had his own orgasm. Knowing she had pleased him helped with the jealous feelings of Dante being with other women.

Phoenix relaxed her expression and turned around to find Dante lying back on the bed with an arm over his face.

She reached for her sweatshirt and pulled it on. "Is everything okay?"

"Something is wrong with me."

She was confused. "Well, yes. I mean, you were shot."

"No, not that." He removed his arm and sat up. "Phoenix…"

She knew what he was going to say. Something about what had just happened between them and how it couldn't happen again. Never mind that he'd asked her. That was what was *wrong* with him.

All her previous satisfaction drained from her body. She didn't need to hear him make up excuses about why he couldn't feed from her again. She didn't need to hear about how she wasn't good enough because, despite his orgasms, they weren't having sex, and he needed sex.

"Sorry, Dante. I gotta go talk to Saxon."

He furrowed his brow. "Phoenix."

She turned around and marched to the door. "I'll talk to you later," she said over her shoulder as she pulled the door open and walked out.

She heard Dante yelling her name as she scrambled down the hall.

She hadn't been lying when she said she needed to talk to Saxon. She was going to tell him that she was moving back to the bunkhouse. Tonight.

NINETEEN

SOMETHING WASN'T right about this situation. Kenzie knew she should pull away, but the last two weeks had been hard with no job prospects so far even though she'd been working her butt off to find a new one, and she was beginning to feel incredibly lonely. Her. She thrived on being independent and single, but a few weeks with Sawyer, and it was like she'd lost that part of herself. Also, she was horny and obviously weak. Despite the fact that she should stop Sawyer from continuing to kiss her, she didn't.

He clutched the back of her head with one hand and put the other under her sweater. She thought he'd go straight for her tank top covered breasts, but he instead pulled the sweater up and over her head, pausing the kiss momentarily, before throwing her pullover in the corner.

Kenzie pulled away. "Wait. What if someone comes in?"

Sawyer jerked his head toward the door. "Lock it."

She didn't immediately get up, and Sawyer growled as he made a play for her camisole.

Apparently, he wasn't going to stop, unlocked door or

not, so Kenzie got up and flipped the lock. Just to be extra cautious, she also pulled the curtain closed in front of the door. She slowly pivoted and faced Sawyer.

He thrust his hips up in the air and said, "Take off your pants and get your sexy ass over here."

Kenzie bit her lip and pretended to be coy.

Sawyer laughed and groaned at the same time. "Woman, stop teasing me. I haven't been inside you for two weeks. I'm dying over here."

Again, she knew something was off because Sawyer wasn't like a light. He couldn't just flip a switch and suddenly want to be with her. But even if she might regret it tomorrow, walking over to the bed and climbing on top of him seemed very worth it now.

Kenzie kicked off her shoes and put one foot in front of her, gradually sauntering back over to Sawyer. As she made her way, she flicked her jeans open and gently pulled down the zipper. She stopped walking to turn around and show him her backside as she pushed her pants down over her butt. She was only wearing a thong, and she heard his intake of breath as he saw what little she wore underneath.

She tossed her jeans on top of her sweater but didn't turn back around yet. She crossed her arms to her sides and slowly drew her cami up and over her head. With her small boobs and her thick sweater, she'd forgone a bra when she got dressed that morning. Sawyer soon realized that because he moaned from his position on the bed. She flung her tank top on the growing pile of clothes and looked over her shoulder.

Sawyer was staring at her nearly bare ass, and the lust in his eyes only excited her more.

She pivoted on her heel, watching him, as his eyes followed her body up to her naked breasts and then up to her face.

"Come here," he practically whispered, his voice husky.

When she reached him, he grabbed for her, but she stepped aside.

She held up a finger, waving it back and forth, as she said, "Uh-uh, you need to wait your turn."

Sawyer dropped his hand and flopped back against the bed.

Kenzie pulled down the sheet covering Sawyer until it was mid-thigh. His cock popped out—big, proud, and hard. She wrapped her hand around him and squeezed.

Sawyer closed his eyes and groaned.

Kenzie pumped her fist a few times until she saw the clear fluid coming from the head of Sawyer's dick. "Tsk-tsk, someone's getting messy. We can't have that now, can we?"

Sawyer opened his eyes and watched as she climbed onto the bed and straddled him. She then leaned over him, making sure to put her chest right in his face, and grabbed a tissue from the table next to his bed with her free hand. She sat back against his legs and brought the cloth slowly up to his penis as if she were going to use it to wipe him off.

Out of the corner of her eye, she watched him try to decipher his emotions. He looked a little disappointed and confused about her actions, and that was exactly what she wanted.

Right before she touched him with the tissue, she said, "Oops…never mind. I don't think you're messy enough." She threw the cloth over her shoulder, bent over, and took

Sawyer into her mouth, sucking him in, until he hit the back of her throat.

"Holy fucking shit," Sawyer cursed from above her as he grabbed her hair.

Kenzie proceeded to give him the best blow job that she'd ever given. She knew by the sounds he made when he was getting close to coming, so she would back off. She wanted to keep him on edge for as long as possible. All the while, she could feel herself getting wetter and wetter. Giving Sawyer head was a real turn-on.

After teasing Sawyer a few times, Kenzie decided that she could no longer handle waiting to get off any longer, and she shoved her hand down her thong in search of her clit as she continued to suck Sawyer off to completion.

She was almost there when she heard Sawyer say something like, "I don't think so." He grabbed her hair and pulled her off his dick with one hand and yanked her arm out of her underwear with the other.

Kenzie blinked away her surprise and scowled. "What are you doing? I was about to come."

Sawyer pulled at her hips until she sat up on her knees. He slipped his fingers in her thong until they ripped off, hauled her body closer to his, and pushed her down right over his cock until he was balls deep inside her.

Kenzie moaned as Sawyer told her, "You're not coming unless I'm inside you."

He felt so good, filling her up, that she didn't bother protesting or telling him that he didn't get to boss her around.

She grabbed his neck and brought him to her lips. She kissed him as she began to ride him to the finish line. As they both neared their orgasms, Kenzie reluctantly broke their kiss to get more air into her lungs. Sawyer was so big and hard inside her that she could barely catch her breath. He felt so good.

Holding on to his neck still, she leaned back just a little, so his dick could hit her G-spot even better.

"Oh God, please don't stop," she begged him.

He thrust his hips up, over and over again.

He chuckled. "As if I'd ever want to."

The friction inside her built and built, and right before she went over the edge, Sawyer leaned toward her, sucked her nipple into his mouth, and bit down. Whatever she'd thought her orgasm was going to be was wrong because it ended up being ten times stronger and better. Her whole body shook as she spasmed around Sawyer. Her climax felt like it would go on forever, and she almost missed the fact that Sawyer was coming, too, but there was no mistaking his barbs filling her even fuller as he pumped his seed inside her.

Kenzie opened her eyes as Sawyer released her breast, leaving deep teeth marks in place. It would ache tomorrow, but she loved it. She loved the biting, the scratching, the barbs...everything. She looked up at Sawyer. If only she had been born a shifter.

She had never really wanted to be anything other than her human self until that moment. It wasn't as if she hated being human. She just felt that she would be an excellent shifter as well. The lifestyle didn't scare her, and then, of course, there was this man in front of her. She'd get to be with him. There would be no shifter-human conflicts.

Kenzie ran her fingers down the side of his cheek and over his neck.

Sawyer frowned and put his hand over hers. "What's wrong?"

She attempted a weak smile. "Nothing." She pulled her hand out from under his and rested her head on his chest. "I would just like to stay like this for a minute or two."

Sawyer wrapped his arms around her back in comfort. "Okay."

Kenzie listened to the beating of Sawyer's heart and started to relax. She wished she could stay there forever. She didn't want to go home, she didn't want to look for a job, and she didn't want to continue to drain her savings while she searched for work.

She was almost asleep when there was a knock at the door, and someone tried the handle. By that time, she'd felt Sawyer's barbs recede, and Kenzie knew it was time to get up and face reality. She grudgingly slipped from Sawyer's embrace, making sure to kiss him one last time, and got up to put her clothes on.

The knock at the door came again, louder this time. "Mr. Lennar?" the voice said from the other side.

Kenzie straightened her last item of clothing and looked at Sawyer. "You ready for me to open the door?"

He was covered again, this time to his chest, and he looked no worse than before, except for a little more tired. "Yep."

Kenzie went to the door, unlocked it, and swung it open. "Sorry," she told the lady in the white lab coat on the other side. Kenzie didn't offer any more of an explanation than that because she was only sorry to keep the vampire doctor waiting. She wasn't sorry for locking the door and fucking Sawyer.

Thankfully, the vampire was a professional and didn't let on that anything had happened in the hospital room that shouldn't have.

"Good evening, Mr. Lennar. I see that you're awake," the doctor said as she came in the room. "How are you feeling? I heard what happened to you a few weeks ago. Are you having any memory loss?"

Kenzie sat in the chair next to Sawyer's bed as he shook his head.

"No. At least, I don't think so. I remember everything up until what I assume was getting hit on the head. We were outside the house, I felt pain, and I blacked out."

The doctor nodded. "Good, good. I'm glad your memory loss didn't come back."

"Me, too."

Kenzie half-listened to the two of them discuss a few more things. Being that the doctor was a doctor for vampires, she gave him the best advice she could but told him to follow up with his shifter doctor to see what he or she recommended.

"Is there anything else?" the doctor asked.

Sawyer frowned. "Yes. I'm a little dizzy, but I don't have much pain. Isn't that odd?"

The doctor smiled. "Sorry. I forgot to tell you that I gave you a pretty strong painkiller. It's a narcotic, so you might not feel like yourself. I'm glad to see that you're pretty in control of yourself. I have some patients who get a little goofy on the meds. Some are affected more than others and in different ways."

Of course, Kenzie thought. *How could I have been so stupid?*

She must have made a noise because Sawyer and the doctor both looked at her.

"I'm sorry," the doctor said. "I forgot to ask if your mate had any questions."

Kenzie held up her hand and shook her head. "I'm not his mate," she said quickly. "And, no, I don't have any questions." She stood and grabbed her coat and purse. "In fact, I think it's time for me to go."

Sawyer frowned. "You don't have to leave."

Kenzie smiled sadly. "Yes. Yes, I do."

Sawyer didn't get it yet, but she did.

"Thanks, Doctor, for taking care of him."

The doctor looked confused but didn't say anything besides, "You're welcome."

Kenzie left the room and made sure to shut the door behind her. She leaned against the wall and held her coat up to her face. She really, really didn't want to start crying right there in the hall.

She calmed herself down enough to put on her coat and leave the building. On the way, she saw Saxon, but she didn't have time to stop. The calm before the storm was only going to last so long.

She hurried past him. "Thanks for calling me. I gotta go."

Saxon stood but didn't follow, and soon, she was out the door and headed to her car. She got inside, locked the door, turned on the ignition, and only then did she let the tears fall.

She was so stupid.

Of course, they had given Sawyer pain meds. Of course,

that was why he'd been acting different. Of course, that was why he'd wanted to have sex with her. She'd known he was off, but she hadn't realized how much she had hoped he'd had a change of heart until the doctor mentioned the pain meds.

Why do I keep doing this to myself? "Kenzie, he will *never* want to be with you. Ever. Stop hoping that he will change his mind." *And stop having sex with him.*

She would never be able to move on as long as she thought about and had feelings for Sawyer.

She wiped off her cheeks, blew her nose, took a deep breath, and made a decision.

This would be the last time she saw Sawyer. At least for quite a while. It was just too hard.

It would be awkward with Naya being mated to Vaughn and Vaughn being good friends with Sawyer, but Kenzie could do it. She *had* to do it. At this point, her heart was on the line, and she had bigger things to worry about in her life. She didn't need stupid man troubles when she didn't even have a job.

Kenzie put the car in drive and pulled forward out of the parking lot. She was determined to be strong, but she couldn't stop the longing look she gave as she took one last glance toward the hospital.

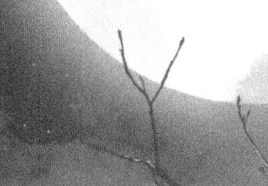

TWENTY

LEXINE STOPPED when she saw the sign for the bar. A drink was exactly what she needed right now.

Her phone buzzed in her pocket again. This was the fourth time, and it was getting on her nerves. But that was probably what—she pulled out her cell and looked at the screen—her brother was aiming for. She let the call go to voice mail and then pulled up her messages. She sent a quick text, telling him that she was fine and to leave her alone. Then, she put her phone on complete silence—no ringer and no vibrate.

Lexine pulled open the big wooden door and entered the bar, letting the warm air surround her. She'd left the hospital to take a walk and clear her head. At the time, the cold had felt good, but December in Minnesota was freezing, and one could handle it for only so long.

The bar was semi-full. Since it was close to the clinic, it was owned and frequented by vampires, but the occasional human would come in every once in a while. It would be nice to have vampire-only stuff, but that was pretty tough when humans outnumbered vampires. It was hard enough to hide a clinic, so there was no way they'd be able to hide a bar.

Lexine looked around for a vacant spot. She didn't feel like making any conversation tonight, so the farther away she was from everyone else, the better. She found a spot near the back, and the minute she took her seat, a server came over to see if she needed anything. It was perfect.

She ordered a shot of tequila and the largest beer they had on tap. She probably wasn't going to leave the bar sober tonight, but as long as she didn't think about Dante and Phoenix, she would be okay with that.

After about an hour or so, she knew she was on her way to getting drunk, but she had not succeeded in tuning out all thoughts of Dante. She just didn't get it. She didn't understand what he saw in that cat-shifter and why he wasn't interested in a vampire who would willingly and happily give herself to him.

Lexine knew she was pretty with her shoulder-length blonde hair and green eyes. Maybe it was because they worked together. Maybe she should quit. But she loved being a Guardian, and quitting wasn't a guarantee. No, she needed to do something to get him to notice her.

She wasn't sure if the group of females near her got louder or if she was suddenly unable to tune them out due to the alcohol, but Lexine could hear them bitching about the very thing that had brought her to the bar in the first place.

Lexine turned to them and said, "Men suck."

The three women, all vampires, stopped talking and looked at her.

"Excuse me?" the one with short brown hair said.

"I said, men suck. You're not the only ones with guy problems."

The one with long dark hair spoke up, "Would you like to join us?"

The short-haired one scowled at the speaker, but Lexine didn't care.

Lexine shrugged and said, "Why not?" She moved from her seat to their table.

The one with long dark hair introduced them, "I'm Michelle. This is Dani"—she pointed to the short-haired one—"and Analeigh."

Analeigh had long blonde hair and seemed to be the quiet one of the group.

"I'm Lexine."

"Hi, Lexine," Michelle said. "So, what is your guy problem?"

"Unrequited love."

Dani rolled her eyes, but Analeigh nodded in understanding.

"Unrequited love is a bitch," Michelle said. "Does this guy know how you feel?"

Lexine shook her head. "No. I was just thinking that I needed to do something to get his attention and make him see me as more than a coworker."

"What do you do for a living?" Dani asked.

Lexine took a drink of her beer. "I'm a Guardian."

The three women exchanged looks and sat up straighter in their seats.

Lexine waved her hand. "Look, if you're into something

illegal, I don't care, especially tonight. I just want to sit here and relax."

Michelle shook her head in protest. "No, it's just that we've never met a Guardian before. Sometime, you'll have to tell us all about your job."

Lexine opened her mouth to tell them that she couldn't share much when the door to the bar opened, and three guys walked in. They were loud as they seemed to be arguing about something. Lexine hoped they planned to sit far away from them, but to her surprise, they headed straight for the table where she was sitting with her new acquaintances.

"Guys. Guys," Michelle said, trying to get their attention.

The three males were still fighting when they reached the table.

Michelle had to practically yell at them to get them to stop, "Guys!"

The three stopped.

One of them turned and yelled, "What?"

Michelle shot him a look. "We have someone new with us tonight."

Now, all three males looked at Lexine as if they were just seeing her there for the first time.

"This is Lexine," Michelle continued. "She's a Guardian."

The way Michelle had pointed out what Lexine did for a job rubbed her the wrong way for some reason, but she couldn't pinpoint why. And she soon forgot about it as the men each reached out to shake her hand.

The short blond guy stuck out his palm first. "I'm Steve."

"Hi, Steve," Lexine said as she shook his hand.

She let go and watched as Steve pulled a chair up next to Analeigh. He kissed her on the cheek before throwing his arm over her shoulders. The two were obviously a couple.

Next was the tallest of the group with brown hair. "Hi, Lexine. I'm Mathis."

The two shook hands, and then Mathis sat down next to Dani. Thankfully, it was not too close, and Lexine felt relieved. She was beginning to think that the six of them were couples, and she'd have to make an excuse to leave. After everything tonight, she didn't want to be a third wheel —or, in this case, a seventh wheel.

Lexine finally looked at the last of the three guys and sucked in her breath. The vampire was hot with black hair that was about a month overdue for a haircut and deep brown eyes. In a way, he reminded her of Dante with his dark looks, yet the cool attitude he projected couldn't have made him more different.

Lexine held out her hand to him to shake, but the guy ignored it.

He did give her a nod and a quick, "Hey," before sitting down directly across from her.

Michelle pointed to the dark and handsome one with her thumb. "That is Lucas, and he's too cool for school."

Lucas snorted and gave Michelle the finger.

"So, what are you ladies talking about?" Mathis asked.

"Nothing much. Just making conversation. What took you so long?" Analeigh asked.

Steve shrugged. "Nothing. We just took our time." He

glanced at Lexine for a second before looking back at Michelle. "We can talk about it later."

Lexine wanted to ask questions, but she had just met them, so she kept her mouth shut. Instead, she asked how they had all met.

Several hours later, they were all laughing, and Lexine was beginning to feel like part of the group when they decided it was time to go home. Lexine was disappointed but took that as a good sign that she'd had a good time.

"So, Lexine, did you drive here? Or can we drive you home?" Michelle asked.

Lexine needed to check her phone and go back to the clinic. If Lennox had already gone home, she'd call him to come get her. "No, thanks. I already have a ride."

Michelle and a couple of the others looked disappointed but didn't push.

"Well, can I at least get your number, so you can hang out with us again?" Michelle queried.

"Of course."

Lexine exchanged numbers with Michelle, and they promised to meet up again soon. Lexine waved as they all piled into their two vehicles, and then she took off for the clinic on foot. When she got there, everyone was gone, except Dante was still in the hospital room. But she had no desire to go down and talk to him again.

Lexine pulled out her phone, expecting to see a bunch of messages from her brother. There were only two.

After her text to leave her alone, he'd responded with a, *Whatever.*

Two hours later, he'd told her he was going home, and if

she didn't come back, she could find her own way back to the compound.

She looked at her watch. That was over an hour ago. Maybe she should have taken her new friends up on a ride home, but it was too late now.

Lexine called her brother anyway.

"What?"

"Hey, Lennox. It's me. Can you come and get me?"

"Where are you?"

"The clinic."

"Where did you go?"

"A bar."

"Why? Why did you storm out of Dante's hospital room? You've been acting so weird lately."

She was not about to tell her brother about her crush on Dante. Lennox would think she was silly and would never understand. He never had a girl he couldn't get, and even if he did, he'd shrug it off as no big deal. He'd certainly never had a crush before.

"I…can't tell you."

"Can't or won't?"

"Come on, Lennox. Will you come and pick me up or not?"

"Not."

"What?"

"You heard me. Not. Until you can talk to me and not be so secretive, Lexine, you can find another way home."

"Lennox."

"Later, Lexine."

"Lennox? Lennox!"

It didn't matter how many times she said her brother's name. He was already gone.

Lexine stared at the phone in disbelief. She never thought her brother wouldn't come and pick her up. *Now, what am I going to do?*

"Hey, Lexine."

She spun around at the sound of her name to see who had spoken it. It was Saxon. He was with Sawyer and her favorite cat-shifter, Phoenix.

Oh, great.

"What are you still doing here?" Phoenix asked. "I thought everyone went home a while ago."

Lexine ignored the cat-shifter's question about why she had been left behind. "They did."

"Do you need a lift home?" Saxon asked. "We had to wait around for them to discharge Sawyer."

Lexine thought about her options. She could call a cab or get a ride from these guys. It wasn't going to kill her. "Sure. Why not? I suppose Phoenix is going to the compound anyway."

Phoenix shook her head. "Nope. I'm going back to the bunkhouse tonight."

Really? This was very interesting news. *What happened to make Phoenix go home?* Lexine had to fight to control her grin. "In that case, I would love a ride home."

"Come along then," Saxon said. "We'd better get Sawyer out of here before he falls over."

"Fuck you."

"There's the Sawyer I know and love. Pain meds wearing off?"

"Fuck you."

Saxon just laughed and guided the injured cat out the door. Phoenix followed behind them with Lexine on her heels, beaming. No matter what else happened that night, she had already heard the best news, and getting ditched by her brother and hitching a ride home from three cat-shifters wasn't going to ruin her mood for the world.

TWENTY-ONE

KENZIE WALKED down the stairs in her father's house to the living room where her dad was sitting on his favorite old recliner. Next to him was her mother's empty one. After Kenzie's mom had passed away from breast cancer, Bruce Swanson hadn't done anything to change the house where Kenzie had grown up.

"Dad, what do you say we go do something tonight?"

Her father grunted and kept his eyes on the TV.

"We could go to a movie or go bowling?"

Her dad sighed and looked at her. "Look, Kenzie, I just want to stay home and watch TV. I appreciate you coming to visit for Christmas, but I had a long day at the factory, and I don't want to go anywhere."

"Right." She didn't know why she'd expected anything else from him.

Her father hadn't wanted to do anything when she was growing up, and it had only gotten worse since her mother's death.

Kenzie was starting to regret coming back to Iowa to

visit for the holidays. "Well, I can't sit here another night. I'm going out."

Her father grunted again. He had already turned back to his show. He didn't even bother to ask her where she was going, and he probably didn't care.

Grabbing her coat and purse, Kenzie headed for her car and then to who-knew-where. The bad thing about growing up in a small town was that all her friends from high school had moved away. While some of them might be in town to visit family, like she was, she didn't even have anyone's number. And truth be told, she really didn't feel like making small talk. She wasn't married, she didn't have kids, and now, she was out of a job and soon-to-be homeless. None of those things were worth talking about with former classmates.

Kenzie drove down the road, unsure of where she wanted to end up. As with other tiny communities, finding something to do was limited. That was why, after she had graduated, she'd moved to a large metropolitan area. She'd hated living in a small town. Unfortunately, if she didn't find a job soon, it looked like she might be moving back here to live with her dad. It was a depressing thought and the reason she decided to go to the local bar and grill. At least they had good appetizers.

She was seated in a nice booth and ordered a drink and nachos. That would give her something to do for a while. Kenzie checked her phone while she waited, but she didn't have any messages, emails, or notifications. Of course she didn't. Just another thing to add to her loser status.

"Kenzie? Kenzie Swanson?"

She snapped her head up at the mention of her name to

see one of her old classmates, a former high school boyfriend, standing there. "Jake Bancroft. How are you?"

He hadn't changed much. He still had the same light-brown hair and deep blue eyes along with the same lanky build, but he had filled out a little more since high school. He looked more like a man instead of a teenager.

Jake eyed the seat across from her and then skimmed the room.

"I'm here alone. Dad's at home. Would you like to sit?"

Jake hesitated.

"Unless you're busy."

He smiled down at her. "No, not busy at all." He slid into the booth. "So, how are you? It seems like I haven't seen you in forever."

This was what she had wanted to avoid, so she simply said, "Good. How are you?"

"Good. Busy."

The waitress came over to see if Jake wanted anything, and he ordered a beer.

"I have nachos coming, if you want to share," she told him.

He nodded. "Sounds good."

The waitress left, and Kenzie asked him, "So, are you still working in Omaha?" She might not have seen Jake for a long time, but it was a small town, and people kept up on others.

Jake laughed. "I wish. I came back home about a year ago to run the hotel."

"What? I'm shocked."

Jake had wanted out of their small town just as much as she had. His family owned the only hotel in town, and that was where Kenzie had first gotten her interest in hotel management. But Jake had two brothers, one of whom Kenzie had been sure would have taken over the business.

"You and me both. But Dad got sick, and it became too much for Brandon to handle, so I moved back to help."

Kenzie leaned forward a little. "So...do you hate it?"

Jake laughed again. "Actually, it's not that bad." He jerked his chin toward her. "What about you? You still in St. Paul?"

Kenzie swallowed. "Yes. For now."

"And you work for a hotel there?"

"I went into the field, thanks to you and your parents, and I'm glad I did. I like it." She hadn't really answered his question, but she hadn't totally avoided it either.

"That's good. That's good. My mom will be so proud when I tell her."

"I think she already knows."

Jake looked confused. "How?"

"Well, she is my friend on Facebook, so she's probably seen my place of employment."

"Figures. She did always like you."

"Yes, we always got along. But she doesn't post much. I didn't realize anything was wrong with your dad."

Jake sighed. "He had a massive heart attack, and the doctors told him to take it easy."

"Oh, I bet he didn't like that."

Jake chuckled. "Not in the least. But when they explained to him that he could work hard for about another year or take it easy for another ten, he decided on the latter, especially now that Brandon has a kid. My dad didn't want to miss out on that."

The waitress interrupted them, bringing their drinks and food.

After a few bites, Kenzie asked, "What about you?"

"What about me?"

"Kids? Wife?"

"Not me. I came close once, but it didn't work out. You?"

Of course, she immediately thought of Sawyer. And she'd been doing so well at trying to forget him over the past week, ever since she'd had sex with him again.

She cleared her throat. "No, I'm not married or dating anyone."

"You don't seem so sure about that."

"Oh, I am. Trust me. I am definitely not in a relationship."

"Well, that's too bad."

Thinking about how complicated it would be to be in a relationship with Sawyer, she said, "Nah, it's probably for the best."

They continued talking, and before she knew it, they had been sitting there for three hours.

"Oh my gosh," Kenzie said when she looked at her watch.

Jake looked down at his. "Oh, wow. Time sure flies, huh?"

"I'll say."

"I'd better get going. Tomorrow is Christmas Eve," she said, grabbing her coat. Not that she and her father had anything planned.

"Big plans?"

Kenzie laughed, embarrassed. "Uh…actually, no. It's

just my dad and me. Bastian went to his girlfriend's parents' house for Christmas."

Jake pushed his own jacket up over his shoulders. "Listen, my family is having dinner tomorrow night. Why don't you and your dad come?"

Kenzie didn't know what to say. It was a sweet proposal.

Jake mistook her silence for a no. "You know what? It was a silly idea. Never mind."

Kenzie reached out and touched his hand. "No, I would love to. I was just thinking about how I was going to convince my dad to come."

Jake grinned at her. "Great. My mom will be excited to see you, ya know. Actually, the whole family will be."

Kenzie smiled back. "I look forward to seeing them, too. And if I can't get my father to leave his chair, then I'll just come by myself."

"Sounds like a plan."

They both stood and made their way for the door.

Once outside, Kenzie asked, "What time should I be there?"

"How does five sound? We're having hors d'oeuvres and drinks first."

"Is your mom making tortilla roll-ups and her famous cheeseball?"

"You know it."

Kenzie clapped her hands. "Yay. I can't wait."

Jake leaned over and kissed Kenzie on the cheek. "See you tomorrow then."

"Tomorrow."

Kenzie turned around and walked toward her car with a smile on her face. For the first time in the last few weeks, she had something to look forward to. Even if it wasn't her family, family and friends were just what she needed this week.

As she unlocked her vehicle and got inside, Kenzie also realized that, besides the one mention of dating, she hadn't thought of Sawyer once. Maybe she really could forget about him and move on. The thought made her smile harder.

TWENTY-TWO

"WOULD YOU SHUT UP?" Sawyer practically yelled at Zane.

The two of them were sitting in the living room of the bunkhouse, watching a movie. Well, Sawyer was *trying* to watch the movie. Zane wouldn't stop talking, and now, Sawyer had missed half of it already.

"Damn, son, you are fucking crabby," Zane said.

Sawyer wasn't in the mood for Zane's sense of humor. "I didn't ask for your opinion."

Zane hit pause. "Yeah, well, you're going to get it."

Now, Zane stops the movie?

After all his yakking, he'd hit pause when Sawyer didn't want him to because he knew what Zane was going to say, and Sawyer didn't want to hear it.

He narrowed his eyes at the fellow cat. "Hit play."

"No," Zane said as he shook his head. "Since you got back, you've been walking around here more surly than usual. And let me tell you, you're not exactly happy to begin with."

"Are you done?"

"*No*. You need a wake-up call. Do you know how lucky you are? You have a wonderful female who, for some strange unknown reason, likes you. *You*. She likes your grumpy ass and all. And you just"—Zane flung his hand out like he was tossing a Frisbee—"throw her away like she doesn't mean anything to you."

Sawyer sat forward in his seat. "I am not discussing this with you. It's none of your damn business."

Zane swung his legs off the couch. "Maybe, maybe not, but I'm your friend, and I just don't understand why you're willingly making yourself miserable. I would give anything to be in your position. Especially now."

Sawyer rolled his eyes. Zane needed to get over that stupid female wolf-shifter. She wasn't coming back, and he barely knew her.

"Don't roll your fucking eyes at me. You know I'm right. That girl would be with you in a heartbeat," Zane scoffed. "And don't tell me you haven't fucked her. I could sme—"

Sawyer jumped up from his seat and pointed his finger. "I told you to shut your goddamn mouth, Zane. I am not now, or ever, talking to you about this. Unless you want me to rip your fucking head off, you should keep quiet right now."

Zane opened his mouth, and Sawyer lunged for him, only to be stopped by Phoenix, who had come into the room from who-knows-where.

"It's not worth it," she told Sawyer.

"He doesn't know when to mind his own business," Sawyer said to Phoenix but kept his eyes on Zane.

"Sawyer," Phoenix said. "Sawyer."

He looked at the female.

"Yes, Zane can be a dick sometimes."

"Hey!"

"But this is nothing new. Why don't you and I go downstairs and work out? You could pretend the punching bag is Zane's face."

"I'd rather just punch Zane."

"I know. But it's not worth it."

Sawyer sighed.

"Let's go downstairs," Phoenix said again.

"Okay." Sawyer took a step back, not realizing that Phoenix had been holding him away from Zane the whole time. Sawyer ran his hands through his hair. "Yeah. Let's go downstairs."

Sawyer turned and made his way for the basement when he heard Phoenix say, "Don't you dare follow us. I'm not stopping him next time."

Zane said something else, but by that time, Sawyer was thankfully far enough away that he didn't have to hear what else the loudmouth might have said.

Soon after he'd made it to the basement, Phoenix followed. The two worked out for about half an hour before Sawyer began to feel the tension that Zane had caused leave him. He was having a hard enough time forgetting Kenzie without Zane opening his big mouth.

Sawyer put the barbell back after he'd finished bench-pressing his last set of reps, and he closed his eyes. He pictured Kenzie above him, riding him in the hospital room. He was getting hard from just thinking about it. He'd been drugged up, and his inhibitions had been lowered, but he could still remember everything.

He really needed to stop fucking up with her. First, his memory loss, and then the pain meds in the hospital. She was going to think that he wanted a relationship with her, and he was finding it harder to stay away.

In a moment of weakness, he'd almost gone to her apartment to apologize for what had happened at the hospital. Thankfully, Naya had mentioned something about Kenzie going home for Christmas, and Sawyer had saved face. He needed to stay as far away from the human female as possible. While his brain had told him she was bad news, his dick couldn't give a flying fuck. And if he were really truly honest with himself, a slight part of his cold heart didn't care either.

The time at her brother's had shown him what it could be like if he accepted her as his mate. They had been happy in their own little world with his memory of what had happened to his family gone. And a part of him wanted that happiness back.

Suddenly, the image of Kenzie was gone, and all Sawyer could picture were his parents the last time he'd seen them. His hard-on disappeared, and it was replaced with an ache in his chest.

No matter how much Sawyer wanted Kenzie, it wouldn't matter. What mattered was what he owed to his parents and that little boy who would never see them again. He might have strong feelings for a human, but he wouldn't break the promise he'd made to his dead parents. Someday, he would find a female cat-shifter who would make him happy enough. He didn't need Kenzie, and he definitely didn't need the guilt that would come with her.

Suddenly, Sawyer felt a hand on his arm. He'd been so

lost in his head that he forgot where he was, and the outside touch caused him to sit up quickly and hit his head on the barbell. "Ow."

Phoenix winced and took a step back. "Sorry. You weren't moving or anything, and I called your name, but you didn't hear me. I wanted to make sure you were okay."

Sawyer rubbed his head. "Yeah, I'm fine. Just thinking, is all."

Phoenix bit her lip, like she wanted to say something but was holding herself back.

"What?"

"I know Zane is an ass sometimes, and he really needs to learn some tact, but he is partly right."

Sawyer raised an eyebrow. "Oh, really?"

He couldn't believe Phoenix, of all shifters, was going to give him advice on his love life, or lack thereof. She was wound tighter than he was, and at least he'd fuck a few select females every once in a while. For all he'd known, Phoenix was asexual. She hadn't shown interest in either males or females, and when she had gone into her heat, she had locked herself away until she was over it. It wasn't until recently that Sawyer had seen another side of Phoenix.

"Yes, really. You deserve to be happy, Sawyer. You can't let the past dictate your future so much."

Sawyer burst out laughing.

Phoenix scowled. "What's so funny?"

"You giving me advice on my love life."

Phoenix crossed her arms over her chest. "What about it?"

Sawyer stood and put his hands on Phoenix's shoulders. "Phoenix, you're a great cat-shifter, and I would trust you to have my back any day, but you don't know shit about relationships."

She knocked his hands away. "Oh, and you do?"

"No, I don't. But at least I know that I don't know shit about relationships."

"Whatever. That's not the point. I might be single, but I do live in this world. I see what others are like, and I know that if you would let Kenzie in, she could make you happy."

At the mention of Kenzie's name, Sawyer stopped laughing. "I'm not talking about this with you either."

"Why? I'm trying to help you here. Zane's just upset because that Isabelle chick left him, and he's taking his frustration out on you."

Sawyer gritted his teeth. "Look, I appreciate you wanting to help, but I'm fine, okay?" He took a step around Phoenix. It was time that his workout was over.

"I don't believe you."

Jeez, what is with people today?

Normally, he never talked about this stuff with Zane or Phoenix. She was getting almost as bad as Zane.

Sawyer swung around. "Okay. You want to talk about relationships?" He shrugged. "Let's do that then." He took a step toward her. "But maybe we should start with you."

Phoenix wrinkled her brow. "Me?"

"Don't play dumb. Yeah, you. Maybe we should talk about why you let a certain vampire feed from you or why you choose to stay with him."

"You're right. This isn't a conversation we should be having. I apologize for overstepping."

Sawyer rocked back on his heels. "So, the shoe is on the other foot now, and someone doesn't like it."

"Don't be a jerk."

"Jerk? I just want you to be happy, Phoenix. Vaughn mated a vampire. No one will judge you if you do, too."

Phoenix flared her nostrils. "That's not going to happen."

"Why? Because of your past? I don't know what happened, but you should just let it go. That's what you told me to do. Maybe you should take your own advice."

Phoenix lost some of her anger and actually looked vulnerable. "You son of a bitch. You have no idea what you're talking about."

He leaned forward. "And neither do you."

She straightened her shoulders. "You're right. Forget I said anything." Walking right past him, she took toward the stairs. "You can rot in hell for all I care. I hope you live a long and lonely life, and your dick falls off. You're an asshole."

He had accomplished his mission, and he felt relieved—until he saw Phoenix wiping her face as she rounded the corner and went upstairs. A sliver of guilt settled in.

But she should learn to mind her own business.

Sawyer flopped down onto the nearest seat as Saxon came down the stairs.

"Dude, what the hell happened? Phoenix ran past me into the bathroom."

Sawyer shook his head in frustration. "We got into a fight. She was trying to talk to me about relationships. She told me that I needed to forget the past and move on. I told her that she needed to do the same."

Saxon looked down at Sawyer with disappointment. "That was really not cool. You owe her an apology."

"Why? Pot, kettle."

"Sawyer," Saxon started before he sat down and told him something that rocked his core.

"Shit," Sawyer said. "You're right. I do owe her an apology." He really was an asshole.

Saxon slapped him on the shoulder and went upstairs as Sawyer got on the treadmill and flipped it to the fastest setting. He needed to compose himself before he went and apologized to Phoenix.

TWENTY-THREE

KENZIE PICKED up her glass of wine and relaxed in her chair. Christmas Eve dinner was going great. Even her father seemed to be having a good time. There was nothing extravagant about their meal, but Jake's parents' house felt homey, and with the whole family around, it really felt like a holiday.

Kenzie and Jake had dated for two years in high school, so his mom and dad had almost become like second parents to Kenzie. Her breakup with Jake had been mutual, and there had been no hard feelings, which had helped her keep a good relationship with the Bancrofts.

"So, Kenzie, we know you've been in the Minneapolis-St. Paul area for years, but have you ever thought about moving home?" Sandy, Jake's mom, asked.

If this question had been presented to Kenzie only a couple of months ago, she would have said a loud, *Hell no*, but today, with her current jobless situation and no hope for a future one, she had to give the honest answer of, "Yes, actually, I have." At least living with her father would be rent-free.

Sandy shared a look with Jake's dad, Tom, and then glanced over to Jake and Brandon.

Kenzie set down her wine glass and sat up in her seat. "What's going on?"

"Well," Sandy said, "we were wondering if you would like to come back and work for the hotel."

"What?" Kenzie asked, surprised.

"We need someone to run the banquet room and ballroom. We probably don't get anywhere near as much business as you're used to, but we keep pretty steady with weddings, birthdays, and anniversaries."

"What happened to Celine?" For as long as Kenzie could remember, Celine had worked at the hotel.

"She retired. We've been trying to do without her, but we're falling behind," Tom said. "We've placed advertisements for the position, but the few applicants we've gotten have either not been good enough or have ended up going somewhere else."

"Wow. This is really unexpected," Kenzie said. She was tempted to say yes right away. Her future looked so bleak, but at the same time, she wasn't excited to move back home to Iowa.

She would be leaving her whole life behind, including Naya. And even if she didn't want to think about him, Sawyer flashed across her mind, too. It was silly, but if she moved away, there would never, ever be a future for them. She mentally shook her head at herself. There was never going to be a future with him, and it was foolish to even consider it.

Putting Naya and Sawyer aside, she was a little worried that if she said yes, right after returning to Iowa, she would get a phone call from one of the various places she had applied to in the Cities. She didn't want to turn around and tell the Bancrofts that she couldn't stay after accepting the position.

"Why don't you think about it?" Jake said.

Kenzie laughed nervously. She'd been thinking so hard that a couple of minutes passed without her giving an answer. "I will definitely consider it. I have a lot to think about before I make any decisions."

"That's understandable, dear," Sandy said. "On that note, how about we have some dessert?"

Tom rubbed his hands together. "Sounds great."

Later, after the dishes were cleaned and put away, Kenzie joined Jake on the all-season porch.

"How are you feeling?" he asked her.

She turned her head and smiled at him. "Great. I needed this."

"This?" he questioned.

"Some downtime with family even if it's not my family. Things have been...stressful lately."

Jake looked concerned. "Do you want to talk about it?"

Kenzie gave him a half smile. "I'm afraid to sound like a big whiny baby."

Jake chuckled. "How about I promise not to judge you? Too much."

Kenzie laughed. "Thanks a lot."

"No, seriously, I'm here if you want to unload."

She shook her head, embarrassed. "Just the usual. Girl's best friend gets married and is going to have babies while girl couldn't be any more single, which makes her feel lonely sometimes. But girl does like one boy who wants nothing to do with her. Girl has trouble at work, and there doesn't seem to be an end in sight. Cue fake violin music because people are out there with real troubles."

"Just because there are worse things that could happen doesn't mean you don't have a right to feel the way you do."

"Thanks. That's very nice of you to say."

"Well, we all have problems."

"What about you?"

"Me?"

"What problems do you have?"

"Let's see. Besides the hotel stuff, my ex-girlfriend came back for Christmas, and all she can do is complain. Pretty soon, she's going to start crying, and then I'm going to be forced to comfort her. Before we know it, she'll be crying in my arms, which will lead to pity sex, and then I'll have to let her down the next morning by telling her that we can never have a future together."

Kenzie playfully shoved him. "Shut up," she said with a laugh.

"Kidding. I'm kidding," he said, rubbing his arm.

"Oh, that didn't hurt."

He laughed and dropped his arm. "You're right. It didn't. Things are actually okay right now," he added, answering her question.

"I'm glad one of us is good."

"Say, what are you doing next week?"

"Next week?"

"Yeah, New Year's. I'm actually coming up to the Cities to visit some friends. I'm sure you already have plans, but if you don't, you're more than welcome to come and hang out with us."

Kenzie sighed. She'd almost forgotten that Naya was having a New Year's party. Vampires loved New Year's. It was a holiday always celebrated at night, so they tended to live it up. Kenzie wanted to go and celebrate with her best friend, but she was afraid that Sawyer would be there.

"I'm supposed to go to a party. My best friend's actually. It'll be her last before she gives birth, so I feel like I really should go."

"You don't want to go?" Jake asked.

"Part of me does, but part of me doesn't. It might be a little awkward."

"Ah, the guy you like will be there."

"Probably."

Sawyer would be there, and then there was the fact that she would most likely be the only human. Besides Sawyer, everyone was nice to her, but she still felt like an outsider.

"I'll still go because I love Naya. Hopefully, the night will be good."

"Well, the invitation still stands."

"Thanks. I appreciate it. You never know what'll happen."

☾

On the ride home, Kenzie asked her dad, "What do you think about the Bancrofts' offer?"

"What do you mean?"

Kenzie sighed. Until now, she hadn't realized that a piece of her had hoped that her father would say he wanted her to take the job. "What do you think about me taking the job at the hotel and moving back here?"

She glanced away from the road to see her father shrug.

"I think it'd be fine. You should do what you want to do."

"Do you not want me to move back?"

"I didn't say that." Her father's voice was starting to get tight.

"Yeah, well, you didn't say you wanted me to either."

Her dad huffed out a deep breath and threw his hands up. "Kenzie, I don't know what you want from me. I'm trying to be supportive and let you make your own decisions."

Kenzie counted to ten before she said something she would later regret—like how sometimes she wished that her father had gotten cancer and that her mother was the one who was still alive. Her mom would have been so excited for her to move back, and she would not have been shy about letting Kenzie know that. On some level, Kenzie understood her father was trying not to pressure her, but it would be really nice to know that she was wanted and loved. Lately, it'd seemed like no one wanted her.

"Forget I asked," she told her dad. "I wouldn't be able to live on my own at first, and I'm guessing you wouldn't want me around all the time."

Her father turned in his seat. "When did I ever say that?" He scoffed. "Women," he muttered under his breath. "Listen, you are more than welcome to come and live with me, if you decide to move back," he said, this time louder so that she could hear. "I never said you couldn't move in."

Kenzie didn't say anything right away. It wasn't exactly

the warm welcome she had hoped for, but at least she knew she wasn't going to have to be homeless. She raised her chin in mock confidence. "Thank you. I appreciate the offer."

Her dad shook his head and muttered, "Women," again under his breath.

TWENTY-FOUR

PHOENIX GLANCED AROUND THE PARTY, knowing she should have stayed home that night. Naya was being a wonderful hostess, and Vaughn had tried to engage her, but it was stupid of her to come. She couldn't deny that she'd wanted to catch a glimpse of Dante. There was no way she would ever seek him out, but if she were to accidentally run into him at a party that they had both been invited to, that would be an entirely different situation.

The only problem was that he wasn't there. Vaughn and Naya's party had started over two hours ago, and she had been waiting almost the whole time to see him. She'd attempted to socialize when she first arrived, but she wasn't feeling it. That was when she'd had to admit that she'd only come to see Dante.

It was crazy of her to even want to see him. But she couldn't deny that she'd missed him. Another thing that made her stupid. She had been just fine before she met Dante, but now, he'd made her want something that she couldn't have.

She pushed herself off the wall where she'd been lean-ing, drank the last bit of her beer, slammed the empty bottle on the counter, and headed for the door. It was time for her to leave.

The first step of rehab was admitting that she had a problem.

Phoenix stopped in her tracks. And her problem was the sexy, dark six-three vampire who had just walked through the door.

She cursed under her breath. First, she'd wanted him there, and he hadn't been. Then, when she'd decided it would be better not to see him, he'd shown up. She must have been a horrible person in her past life because she really hadn't done anything in this life to deserve this.

She had to get out of there.

Someone stopped Dante to talk, and Phoenix took that as her chance to escape. She turned around and sprinted as fast as she could through the crowd, heading for the back door. The only problem was that her shoes and coat were by the front door. Thankfully, she had her car keys in her pocket, but in just her socks and bare arms, it would be a cold jaunt around to the front of the house where her vehicle was parked. Hopefully, the snow wasn't too high to walk through.

Stupid Minnesota winter.

She slipped out the back door that led to the garage. She flipped the switch on the wall, turning on two dim bulbs in the three stalls. Off to the side, on the ground, she was ever so grateful to spot a pair of Vaughn's work boots lying there. They'd be too big on her, but she didn't care because they'd also be warm. She slipped them on and then went out the door leading to the backyard.

"Holy shit." She had thought the garage was cold, but outside was freezing. She'd need to haul ass if she didn't want to get hypothermia.

She reached behind her to close the door, not wanting to leave it open for just anyone to walk out, when a hand wrapped around her wrist and pulled her back inside.

Phoenix raised her opposite hand, ready to strike the person in the nose. As she swung around, her arm was knocked to the side, and she was hauled up against her attacker as he slammed the door behind her.

Cinnamon.

She sensed cinnamon.

She stopped fighting. "Dante?"

"What are you doing out here in barely any clothes?" His brown eyes were filled with a mix of concern and frustration.

She tried to shake him off. "You make it sound like I'm almost naked."

"You might as well be with what you're wearing out here."

At the mention of the cold, she realized how warm Dante was. He was warm, and he smelled delicious. He must have showered before he'd shown up at the party because she sniffed soap on top of his scent. She wanted to nestle into him.

She attempted to shake him off again, and this time, he let her. She took a step back to create even more distance between them. She was not going to let herself lean on him.

"I wasn't planning on being out in the cold for long. I was going to my car."

"Is there a reason you didn't go out the front door where your coat and shoes are, along with everyone else's?"

"Uh…" She did not have a good reason for why she hadn't just left via the front door. "Because."

"Because? Is *because* also the reason you're wearing men's boots that are several sizes too big for you?"

She might as well keep going with her flimsy non-excuse. "Yep."

"Phoenix, why can't you just admit that you were trying to get away from me?"

Her mouth fell open. *He knows? But how?*

"I saw you the moment I walked in the door. I always know where you are when we're close. And I know you were panicking, and since you were going in the opposite direction of me, you were probably trying to get away from me."

She didn't know what to make of his words. She was secretly pleased yet a little creeped out. "How do you know where I am and how I'm feeling?"

He shook his head. "That's not important right now. Why are you avoiding me? Did I do something?" He took a step forward and lowered his voice. "Did I hurt you when I fed from you?"

She took a step back. "What? No, you didn't hurt me."

He'd only given her the second orgasm of her life. Hurt was far from the list of what she had felt that night.

A look of relief swept across his face.

"Why did you think you hurt me?"

"Because you left my hospital room in the middle of our conversation. Because you didn't come back to the compound. Because you haven't answered any of my phone calls or texts."

She hadn't responded out of self-preservation. He'd only tried to call and message her a few times right after that night. She hadn't heard from him since. Maybe if he hadn't quit trying, she wouldn't have gotten curious and shown up at the party, looking for him.

"You didn't try *that* hard," she said under her breath.

"What?"

"Nothing. Look, I just thought it would be better if I didn't stay at the compound anymore. I was sleeping in your bed, and you fed from me twice." That made Dante the person she'd been the most intimate with in her whole life. "I thought it'd be best to put some distance between us."

He looked a little confused, and she didn't understand why because she felt her reasons made perfect sense.

"But that was just sleeping and feeding, a form of nourishment. It's not that big of a deal."

His words were almost like a slap in the face. He didn't see what had transpired between them as anything important while he had been making her feel and experience things she'd never felt before. And those two reasons were why she needed to get out of there.

"You're right. I'm just being silly," she managed to say.

What is wrong with me? This was what she wanted. She wanted there to be distance between them. She didn't want him to want her in a romantic way. If he didn't want her, then he would never pursue a relationship, and she would never let him down.

So, why was she so sad and disappointed once again?

"Look, Phoenix, I thought we were friends, and I just wanted to make sure you were okay."

She sidestepped him. "Yes. Friends. Sorry I didn't answer your messages. I'm fine though." She took off Vaughn's shoes at the door and put them back where she'd found them. "I'm just going to grab my things and get going."

She turned the knob as Dante said, "Phoenix."

"Yes?" she said but didn't turn around.

"I'm sorry."

Sorry? "Whatever for? You have nothing to be sorry for." Because the blame was all on her.

She pushed the door open and stepped inside. Despite the crowd of people, she'd never felt so alone in her entire life.

TWENTY-FIVE

SAWYER WAS BEING SNUBBED by two women. It was a first for him.

Phoenix had been avoiding him since their argument. Although, to be honest, tonight, she had seemed preoccupied, and he hadn't even tried to approach her. He still owed her an apology, but so far, she hadn't let him get one in, and tonight was not the night to try again.

Then, there was Kenzie. Sawyer might as well not even exist. She hadn't gone out of her way to avoid him, but whenever they were around each other, she'd act like he was pretty much a stranger. He hated to admit that it bothered him. He wanted to pull her aside and remind her that he'd been inside her and that he knew her body better than she did. He was definitely no stranger.

"Don't you think you should take it easy?"

Sawyer turned and looked at Vaughn. Sawyer hadn't heard him approach. He wasn't sure if it was because of the music and loud voices or because he'd been lost in his own head.

"Everyone is always telling me that I don't relax enough, and now that I've had a few drinks, you're telling me I've had too many," Sawyer told Vaughn.

"We want you to let loose, not get rip-roaring drunk. You have no tolerance, and no matter how much you drink, it's not going to make her come over and talk to you."

"My tolerance is just fine. Thank you very much. And who are you talking about?"

Vaughn gave him a don't-be-stupid look. "You've been watching Kenzie all night. I'll give you credit because you've been trying not to, but you can't keep your eyes off of her."

"Shut up."

"I'm just saying, dude."

Sawyer looked over to the person they were talking about. Kenzie was standing with a group of women, but she didn't seem to be paying much attention to them because she was looking at her phone, something she'd been doing all night.

What is so important?

A smile broke over her face, and she began typing furiously in reply. Now, he really wanted to know whom she was talking to.

Is it a—

Vaughn hit Sawyer on the arm.

"What?"

"Quit staring. Or go talk to her."

"No."

Vaughn rolled his eyes. "You're pathetic, you know that?"

"I don't believe I asked for your opinion."

"I guess you didn't need to, seeing as how I'm your

friend and all." Vaughn leaned closer to Sawyer's ear as his voice got more serious. "You either need to go talk to her or let her go."

Sawyer leaned back, so he could look Vaughn in the eyes. "Let her go? She's not mine to begin with."

"Oh, yeah? Then, why don't you tell everyone here that because we all think you've marked her?"

It wasn't what everyone thought, and Vaughn knew it. Sawyer had bitten Kenzie to protect her. It had nothing to do with wanting her for himself. Sawyer opened his mouth to tell Vaughn just that, but Vaughn didn't even give him a chance to speak.

Vaughn held up his hand. "Don't even give me that same bullshit line you always do. You can try to lie to yourself, but you can't lie to me. I've known you for too long."

"You don't know what you're talking about. And why has everyone been so interested in my life lately?"

"Because we're your friends, and we want to see you happy."

Sawyer gritted his teeth. "I am happy," he spit out.

Vaughn snorted. "Yeah, you certainly sound like you are."

Vaughn had a point.

"Well, I would be if everyone would just leave me alone and stop asking questions."

"Regardless, I still don't believe you."

"You should."

Vaughn looked around the room. For a second, Sawyer was worried that he was looking for Kenzie, planning to bring her over to their conversation, but his eyes kept searching until they landed on a female cat in the corner of the room. Sawyer didn't recognize her. She was medium height with long blonde hair and a generous chest. She was very attractive, but that didn't matter to him.

Vaughn pointed to the female. "See her?"

"Yes."

"That's Sienna, and she's single."

"Okay. What is your point?"

"And for some strange reason, she was asking about you."

"Ha-ha. You're hilarious."

"Listen, if you really don't care about Kenzie and are serious about not having any claim over her, I want you to go talk to Sienna."

"You're crazy. No."

"Then, I'm going to go over to Kenzie and tell her—"

Sawyer slammed his bottle down. "Fine. I'll go talk to her." Anything to get Vaughn to leave him alone.

He'd just make sure that he didn't get too close to Sienna. If they didn't touch, then no one would think he was interested in her sexually.

Sawyer started walking backward toward Sienna and held up his arms. "Happy now?"

Vaughn shook his head and chuckled without humor. "Fuck no. But it'll do for now." He brought his beer up to his lips before he took a long drink. After he was done, he said, "Now, I'm going to go find my mate, so I can look at her and remember why I'm glad that I'm not you."

Sawyer gave Vaughn the finger.

Vaughn laughed, spun around, and walked toward his mate.

Sawyer swung around and headed toward Sienna.

It turned out that she was a nice girl, but she didn't do anything for Sawyer. He didn't know why because she was pretty and seemed to be easygoing—unlike someone else he knew.

Unfortunately, that wasn't the only thing he compared between them. Even talking to an attractive she-cat, who apparently was interested in him, couldn't make him forget about Kenzie. There was a possibility that he had a problem.

Not wanting to give up yet, he tried to imagine what it would be like to be mated to Sienna. He pictured her pregnant as she happily cooked him supper every night and did everything he'd asked of her. Sure, he would be content with that, but at the end of the day, it just seemed…boring.

Soon, Sienna's face turned into Kenzie's, and he imagined her full with his child. But, unlike his image of Sienna, Kenzie was not cooking him dinner. Instead, he pictured eating every fast-food craving she'd demand that he bring home. Life with Kenzie would not be easy.

"Sawyer? Sawyer." Sienna shook his arm.

Sawyer looked down at her with a bit of embarrassment. He'd been daydreaming as she was talking to him. "I'm sorry. What were you saying?"

Sienna gave him a sad smile. "You know what? Never mind. Your human went upstairs."

"Huh?"

"I know you're interested in that human female. You've been watching her almost the whole time we've been talking. I thought you were looking for her just now. She went upstairs first to do something, but she then said something about leaving after that."

Kenzie is leaving?

"It's not even after midnight yet," he said to himself more than to Sienna. He didn't know why, but he was suddenly filled with panic. He couldn't just let her leave. Something wasn't right.

TWENTY-SIX

KENZIE STARED at her pathetic self in the bathroom mirror—correction, her jealous, petty, pathetic self.

Up until now, the night had been going okay. She was enjoying Naya's New Year's party well enough, and she'd been texting with Jake most of the night. She'd forgotten how fun he had been back in high school. It was silly that they hadn't stayed friends just because they had broken up. Tonight, he'd been insisting that she ditch the party and hang out with him and his friends. She'd been telling him no because she felt like she should stay at her own best friend's party, but now, she was done.

Kenzie hadn't talked to Sawyer all night, and that had gone well. Before coming tonight, she had decided that the best way to handle the party would be to just pretend like nothing had ever happened between them. Sawyer was never going to change, and being mad at him for basically being the person that he was would only make her bitter and angry.

She just needed to accept that they were never going to be…anything. Not even friends. Her relationship—or rather, non-relationship—was like gas prices. She could wish and wish that things were different, but there wasn't anything she could do about it, so she might as well accept it.

And Kenzie was tired. She was so tired of fighting with Sawyer. She didn't have the energy anymore. With every-thing that was going on in her life, she had bigger things to worry about, like where her next paycheck was going to come from.

Arguing with Sawyer as some sort of weird foreplay wasn't worth the effort anymore. That was why she hadn't talked to him all night. She just didn't want to fight. If he had spoken to her, she would've politely talked back, but she had refused to initiate any conversation with him.

And everything had been fine until Sawyer had started talking to a very beautiful woman, and it'd continued for quite some time. Kenzie really hated to admit it, but she was jealous. And hurt. *Stupid emotions.* If only there was a way to shut them off.

But she couldn't control the way she felt, so she'd decided to take Jake up on his offer and get out of there.

Kenzie used the bathroom facilities and washed her hands. One nice thing about having one's best friend host the party was that she could use the private bathroom in their room. No waiting to get in. No one pounding on the door, telling her that she was taking too long. She could use this time to compose herself before she walked back downstairs.

Kenzie smoothed her purple dress down over her hips.

She loved this dress. It always made her feel pretty, even on bad days, but tonight, it wasn't working. She sighed. She really was tired of life. Maybe she was even a little depressed. She'd had a roller coaster of a time over the last few months. Once she found a new job, maybe she should see someone for counseling.

Her phone vibrated on the bathroom counter, and she picked it up.

Jake: So, are you really coming? I was just giving you crap about ditching your party. You don't have to come if you're having a good time there.

Kenzie: So, first you want me to come, but when I say I am, you change your mind?

Jake: What? No! That's not it at all.

Kenzie: Relax, cowboy. I was only teasing you. Jeez, you can dish out the crap, but you can't take it, huh?

Jake: I guess I deserve that.

Kenzie looked up from her phone and noticed the smile she wore in the mirror. It wasn't a crazy-in-love smile—she already knew that she would never be romantically or sexually attracted to her ex again—but it was a carefree smile. And she knew that she needed some worry-free time before she figured out the next step in her life.

It was good to know that she had someone who could provide that for her. Maybe that was what was nice about hanging out with Jake. She didn't like him in that way, and he definitely didn't give off any of those vibes to her either, so hanging out with him would be easy.

Kenzie: I'll be there as soon as possible. Naya lives kind of far away, so it might take me an hour or so.

Jake: Take your time. And please don't drive if you've been drinking.

Kenzie: Just one drink two hours ago. I'm good.

Jake: See you in an hour then.

Kenzie took one last look in the mirror just to make sure everything was in place, and then she turned off the light as she opened the bathroom door. Naya and Vaughn's bedroom was dark, and the hallway just had some faint light coming from the first floor. Kenzie knew where all the furniture was, so she didn't wait for her eyes to adjust to the darkness before she walked out of the bathroom.

Unfortunately, she didn't get very far.

"Oof," was the sound she made as she ran into a hard body. Assuming it was Vaughn coming to use his own bathroom, she said, "Oh, sorry. Naya told me it would be okay to use your bathroom."

Arms came up and gripped her biceps. "Why are you leaving?"

Kenzie tried to take a step back. "Sawyer?"

He growled. "Who else did you think it would be?"

"I thought you were Vaughn, seeing as how this is his room and all."

"Does Naya know you are secretly meeting her mate in their dark bedroom?"

This was what she had been avoiding all night.

She brought her arms up and knocked them down over Sawyer's arms to get him to let go. "I'm not doing anything with Vaughn, and you know it. Does being an asshole come really easily to you, or do you have to work hard at it?"

Sawyer sighed. "Apparently, it's been coming pretty easily to me lately."

"Just lately?"

Her eyes were starting to adjust to the darkness, and she saw Sawyer scowl.

"Yes, just lately."

She needed to stop this fight right now. "Well, good luck with that. I hope you have a good night."

She tried to step around him, but he moved into her path.

"Why are you leaving?"

"I think it's best that you and I avoid each other as much as possible, don't you?"

"That doesn't mean you have to leave the party."

"Oh." She had assumed he was asking why she was leaving the room. "How did you know I was leaving the party?"

He waved his hand in front of him. "That doesn't matter. Look, I don't want you to leave on account of me."

Why's he being nice all of a sudden? "Uh...I'm not." At least, she wasn't leaving *all* because of him.

She stepped around him again from the other side, and this time, she succeeded in getting past him.

She heard him mutter under his breath, but she couldn't make out the words. However, the next thing out of his mouth made her stop.

"Are you going to meet up with a male?"

Kenzie slowly pivoted around. "Excuse me?" she asked ever so carefully.

He'd made it very clear that they would never be together. He'd just been flirting with some girl downstairs, and he'd had the nerve to ask if she was meeting up with a guy.

"You're unbelievable," she said, her voice full of disbelief.

He scrubbed his hand down over his face. "I think I have a right to know."

Kenzie could feel her anger rising. She took a deep breath because it was taking everything in her not to go off on him. She was barely able to maintain an even voice as she said, "No, you don't. You have made it clear over and over again that you don't have or want that right. Not that it is *any* of your business, but yes, I am going to meet up with a guy."

She saw Sawyer tense up, and she told herself to tell him that it was an innocent friendship, but she didn't. She was petty and immature because she liked seeing him jealous. If he was going to push her away, then she didn't owe him any kind of reassurance that she wasn't dating anyone.

"Who is he?" Sawyer's voice was getting harder.

"My old high school boyfriend, if you must know." She crossed her arms over her chest in satisfaction while the small mature part of her mind screamed, *Shut up, Kenzie. Don't do this. Don't goad him. It will only end badly.*

Sawyer cracked his neck. "High school boyfriend. Did he take your virginity?"

Kenzie felt her eyes widen. That was a ballsy question for him to ask. Why she didn't turn and walk away, she didn't know. "Again, none of your business, but yes. We did date for a long time and actually talked about marriage."

"Are you fucking him now?"

That's it.

She was done. The virginity question hadn't done it, but his last question had. She was out of there.

But not before she had the last word. "*Yes*," she hissed. "He fucks me so good."

The growling sound that came out of Sawyer was almost frightening.

Get out. Get out. Get out, get out, get out, get out! she yelled at herself.

TWENTY-SEVEN

KENZIE SPUN on her heel and sprinted for the door, but she didn't get anywhere. Sawyer snatched her around the waist and slammed his body against hers as she dropped her phone on the carpet. With his free hand, he grabbed her hair and pulled her head back so far that it almost hurt.

He ran his nose up along her shoulder and over her neck until he got to her ear. "Fucking liar. You don't smell like anyone but me."

Okay, this was perhaps a good thing. He was really angry, and now that he knew she wasn't sleeping with anyone, maybe he'd calm down.

Trying to defuse the situation, she said in a joking voice, "Okay, you got me. I lied." She wiggled in his arms. "You can let me go."

"Were you lying about the whole thing? About meeting up with your ex?"

She didn't know what to say. The situation was intense, and she wanted to say she had lied about everything, but

Sawyer would smell her lie. She was too emotional to even attempt to hide her scent from him.

"No, I wasn't lying about that part."

Sawyer's arm tightened around her.

"But it's not what you think. He's just a friend now."

"Was he really your first fuck?"

"Damn, you have a dirty mouth. Yes, he was the first guy I had sex with, but that was way back in high school."

Sawyer nipped her shoulder, and she couldn't help but moan as she grew wet.

"Doesn't matter. He still knows what it's like to be inside you."

Since Sawyer was holding her practically off the ground, it was very easy for him to move her up against the wall.

She started to panic. She didn't have the strength to tell him no because she knew deep down that if she told Sawyer to stop, he would, but the stupid, sick part of her wanted him. She needed to try to convince him that he didn't want to do this.

"Sawyer, we were kids. We barely knew what we were doing back then." She swallowed her pride and said, "It's not like when I was with you."

He grunted. "I know that, but I think you need reminding."

He sucked on her neck, and she squirmed in his grip as the area between her legs started to throb.

"No, no reminding needed," she tried to joke as he set her down, flipped her dress up, ripped her underwear away, and pushed two fingers inside her. Her last syllable turned into a long loud moan as she squeezed herself around him.

Sawyer chuckled. "You are on fucking fire and dripping

wet. I think you might be right. You don't need reminding…"

She held her breath, now worried that he would walk away and leave her like this.

"But I'm going to anyway."

She barely sighed with relief before Sawyer pushed his pants off his hips and shoved himself inside her. He let go of her hair and loosely wrapped his hand around the front of her neck as he began to pump into her over and over.

She was a perverted individual because he felt so good that she never wanted him to stop. She wanted Sawyer to keep going until she was sore and raw.

Apparently, she had spoken that request out loud because Sawyer replied, "No problem, mate. You'll still be feeling me between your legs next week."

Thankfully, she was too far gone to even care that he'd heard her, and she barely even noticed his use of the pet name he'd given her while he was without his memory.

She felt her climax approaching and knew that Sawyer wasn't far behind her. He tilted her chin to the side and bit down as they both came. A small part of her knew that she should try to get him to release his teeth from her neck, but it felt so good that she started to wonder if her orgasm would ever stop.

She barely caught her breath before Sawyer started moving inside her again. She knew he had come. She'd felt it in his body and in between her legs, but he had already recovered and was on to round two. Her next release didn't last as long, but it was just as strong. Thinking this would be the end, she was shocked to find out that Sawyer wasn't finished with her.

When all was said and done, Sawyer had come in her four times, gotten her off five, and left four deep bite marks —two on each side of her neck. She was definitely going to be sore tomorrow, and there was no way she'd be able to meet Jake and his friends like this.

Shit. Jake.

Kenzie's orgasmic euphoria faded quickly, and she shook Sawyer off. He'd already let go of her neck and waist, but he was leaning against her and was still inside her. As she pushed on his chest, he stood up and stepped away. He slipped from between her legs, and she immediately felt his wetness there.

She was a stupid, stupid fool.

Sawyer had marked her good. His bite marks were on her neck. His scent was all over her skin. And his seed was between her legs. He had to know that she wouldn't be meeting anyone tonight, no matter how innocent that relationship was.

Kenzie needed help. She couldn't believe that she'd kept doing this to herself. You would think she would have learned. But no, she'd kept putting herself in these situations with Sawyer, and she had no one to blame but herself.

Tired and defeated, Kenzie limped back toward the bathroom to clean herself up, so she could go home.

"Kenzie," Sawyer practically whispered behind her.

She didn't know if he regretted what they had done or if he could read her body language, but she didn't have the strength, either mental or physical, to turn around and confront him. All she wanted to do was go home, crawl into bed, pull the covers over her face, and pretend like she'd never met Sawyer Lennar.

"Just go," she practically begged, her back to him.

"Kenzie."

"Please."

"Can I at least get you anything?"

She needed her keys, purse, and coat before she could go home. With the last of her pride gone, she told him where her stuff was and asked him to get it. "Will you please just leave my stuff on the bed and tell Naya that I had to go?"

Sawyer sighed but didn't protest. "Yes."

Kenzie went into the bathroom after Sawyer had left the room, but she didn't turn on the light. She couldn't look at herself right now. She quickly cleaned up, and when she heard Sawyer in the hall, she closed the bathroom door until she heard him leave again. He had stood there for several seconds, and for a second or two, she was worried that he would never go.

She quickly grabbed her stuff, including her phone from the floor, and even though it wasn't easy, she managed to sneak out of the house without seeing Naya. One good thing about winter was that she could hide in her big, bulky coat and pull her hat down low over her ears.

Kenzie drove home on autopilot. Once in her apartment, she took off her dress and underwear and threw them both in the garbage. Her underwear had barely been hanging off her waist anyway, and she never wanted to see her purple dress again. It would only make her think of Sawyer, and she wanted to forget about him.

She threw her bra on the floor and slipped into bed, naked. Just as she was starting to feel sorry for herself, she heard her phone vibrate against the kitchen counter as it rang. Worried that it might be Naya, Kenzie slipped from her bed and picked it up.

It hadn't been Naya, although she had sent Kenzie a text, but Jake.

She closed her eyes. She'd forgotten about him again.

Her phone vibrated once more, this time shorter. Jake had texted her. She walked back to bed as she read his message.

Jake: Hey, Kenzie. I tried to call. Just worried about you. It's been almost two hours, and I haven't heard anything. I wanted to make sure you didn't get into an accident.

Kenzie: I'm sorry, Jake. I ran into some troubles with a friend. I won't be able to make it tonight.

Jake: I understand. I hope everything's okay.

Everything was far from okay, but that didn't mean she had to wallow in self-pity. She'd gotten herself into this mess, and it was up to her to get herself out.

Kenzie: Everything will be fine. Thanks for caring.

Jake: No problem.

Kenzie: Will you do me one favor first?

Jake: Sure. What is it?

Kenzie paused before replying, but she knew it was time to make a change.

Kenzie: Tell your parents I accept their job offer.

With that, Kenzie shut off her phone, set it on her nightstand, and rolled over to go to sleep. She might have made a mistake tonight, but with everything in her, she would make sure that it was the last one.

TWENTY-EIGHT

KENZIE PUT the last of her summer clothes in the box and taped it up. Looking around the room, she felt pretty pleased with herself. She'd been busy packing all week, and her efforts really showed. It probably helped that she hadn't had anything else to do, like work, so packing had become her temporary job.

She grabbed her phone and looked at the clock. She had just enough time to take a shower and meet Naya for dinner. They were going to one of their favorite restaurants. Naya thought it was just a girls' night out. What she didn't know was that Kenzie was going to break the news about her new job in Iowa. She'd been putting it off since she told Jake that she accepted the job at his family's hotel. But she couldn't leave Naya in the dark forever.

Kenzie showered, dressed, put on makeup, and headed to the restaurant. Naya was already there, sitting at their table, when the hostess brought Kenzie over.

Naya smiled when she saw Kenzie. "Hey, how was work? Did you have a lot of traffic?"

Normally, Naya would have come to Kenzie's apartment before they went to dinner, but Kenzie had wanted to explain her plans to Naya rather than having Naya figure it out from her half-empty living room and the boxes stacked against the wall. Kenzie had lied and told Naya she would meet her on her way home from work.

Rather than furthering the lie, Kenzie only answered the second question, "Traffic was fine. How was it for you?"

"Good. I made it here earlier than I'd thought I would."

The server came over with their menus and asked if they wanted anything to drink. Naya ordered water due to her current state. Kenzie ordered wine. A little liquid courage couldn't hurt.

Not wanting to be interrupted by anyone, Kenzie made small talk until after they ordered their food. After the server left with their orders, Kenzie started to get a little nervous about telling Naya she was moving. The good thing about best friends was that they could read each other well. The bad thing about those friends was that they could read each other well.

Naya sat back in her chair. "All right, Kenzie, spit it out. I know you have something to say."

Naya had said the words with a smile on her face, probably thinking that whatever Kenzie had to say wouldn't be that bad. But the second Kenzie said, "I'm moving back to Iowa," all happiness left Naya's face.

Naya jumped forward in her seat as much as she could with her rounded belly. "What?"

Kenzie fidgeted in her seat. "I'm moving back to Iowa."

"When?"

"Saturday."

"Saturday! That's only a few days away. I thought you were going to say next month, not Saturday. Why so soon? What is going on? Why the rush? What about your job?"

This was the part that she really didn't want to tell Naya about because she knew Naya would feel guilty and responsible even though it wasn't Naya's fault that Kenzie had been kidnapped.

"Well, I actually haven't been working since I came home from my...ordeal."

Naya shook her head. "I don't understand."

Kenzie sighed. "They fired me, Naya. And I haven't been able to find another job since I came back."

"Why?"

"Naya, I was gone from work for, like, three weeks. There was no way they were going to let that slide."

"But I thought you had a note saying that you were sick and in the hospital. I thought Vaughn's family did that for you."

Naya seemed to be getting very upset, thinking that the Llewelyns hadn't taken care of things, so Kenzie put her hand on her friend's.

"Naya, they did give me a letter from the doctor saying that I was in the hospital with pneumonia, but my boss didn't think it was enough." Kenzie removed her hand. "And he was right. If I were really sick, I would have called in way before missing three weeks of work. Or I would have had someone else call work for me. I'm surprised Dave didn't come out and call me a bald-faced liar. But even if he had, there was no way I could tell him what had really happened."

"But I don't understand why you can't stay here and find a new job."

Kenzie shrugged. "I've been looking since it happened. No one wants to hire me. There are tons of hotels in the area, but when it comes down to it, it's a small community, and I've been blacklisted. No matter what my reputation was before I was kidnapped, all they know now is that I didn't come to work for three weeks without telling anyone beforehand. I applied to probably thirty hotels, and I didn't get one phone call. Not a single one. And I only have so much money in savings."

Naya looked like she was going to start crying as their server brought their food over.

"Is there anything else I can bring you?"

"No, thank you," Kenzie said with a smile in hopes that he would leave them alone. Their food looked delicious, but Kenzie didn't know how much she'd be able to eat with the ball of nerves still knotted in her stomach.

After the server walked away, Naya asked, "What are you going to do in Iowa?"

"Well, first, I'm going to move in with my dad for a while. It's rent-free. And you've heard me talk about my old boyfriend from back home, Jake, right?"

Naya nodded.

"Jake and his parents offered me a job at their hotel. So, not only will I have a place to live, but I'll also have a job."

"But you hate your hometown. You love the Cities. I'm here."

Kenzie laughed. "I know. And I am going to miss you like you wouldn't believe, but right now, beggars can't be choosers. And I am way beyond begging at this point."

"I don't want you to go."

"I know, honey. I don't want to go either."

The two of them picked at their food in silence. Kenzie could see that Naya was processing all the information Kenzie had given her.

Suddenly, Naya said, "I know."

"What?"

"My family has connections. Vaughn's family has connections. They can find you a new place to work."

Kenzie smiled sadly at her friend. "That is really sweet, but I don't want their handouts."

Naya scowled. "Kenzie, it would not be a handout. It would be what you are owed for what you went through. You're lucky that the only thing you lost was your job. You could have lost your life."

Naya's voice was starting to rise, so Kenzie quickly said, "You're right. I understand where you are coming from."

"But that's not it, is it?"

Kenzie cringed. She really didn't want to tell Naya this part, but it seemed like there was no avoiding it. "No," Kenzie said, shaking her head. "I can't stay here with Sawyer around. It's gotten to the point where we are almost toxic to each other."

Naya set down her fork. "Kenzie, what else are you not telling me? Why are you keeping all this stuff bottled up inside?"

Kenzie shrugged again. "I don't know. Because you're pregnant. Because you're married to Sawyer's good, if not best, friend. I don't want to put you in the middle of anything."

Naya rolled her eyes and let her arms fall to the table.

"Kenzie, I have known you way longer than Vaughn or Sawyer. And, of course, I love my mate, but my loyalty is to him and you, not to Sawyer. Now, tell me what is going on."

Kenzie slowly pulled back the collar of her sweater to reveal the sides of her neck.

Naya put her hand up to her mouth and gasped. "Oh my God."

Kenzie released her sweater and held up a hand. "They look a lot worse than they are."

"Kenzie," Naya said, dumbfounded, "you have two huge bruises on your neck and shoulder. And those are not fresh bruises. They're several days old. Are they from the party?"

Kenzie nodded.

"So, they are almost a week old, and they look that bad still. What in the hell happened?"

"Sawyer happened."

Naya's eyes blazed with anger, and she pushed her chair back as if she was going to get up, walk out of the restaurant, and find the man who had done that to her friend.

"Naya, will you let me tell you what happened before you go and kill someone?"

"Fine," Naya said, pulling her chair back up to the table. "I'll let you finish. But I still reserve the right to commit murder after this is said and done."

Kenzie laughed. "Shh…someone might hear you."

Naya did not think the situation was funny like Kenzie did. "So? I really don't care right now. Spill it."

"Sawyer found out that I was going to meet Jake after your party. At first, Sawyer made me so mad that I lied and told him that Jake and I were having sex. Then, I told him the truth—that our relationship was platonic—but Sawyer couldn't get past the fact that I was still meeting up with my ex and that he was the first guy I'd had sex with."

Naya sucked in a breath, and her eyes widened.

Kenzie leaned closer. "He went fucking ballistic. I've never seen him like that. He kind of seemed to lose control. My bruises are from him biting me during sex. At the time, it felt good. I pretty much can't have an orgasm anymore without Sawyer biting me, but this time, he bit me really hard. I didn't notice until the next day. And not just that…"

Naya leaned closer, eager to hear the rest of Kenzie's story.

"My fricking crotch hurt for, like, three days. I actually put an icepack between my legs quite a few times over the first couple of days. I have never been fucked so hard in my life."

Kenzie leaned back, and Naya did the same.

"The thing is, Naya, it would be kind of hot to tell you this story, knowing that someone wanted me this badly. And as caveman as it is, it's still a little hot to think someone would be that jealous over me. But the sad fact of the matter is that Sawyer doesn't want me." Kenzie paused and thought about her last sentence. "No, that's not right. Sawyer wants me. He just doesn't want to want me, and that's another reason I have to leave."

Naya opened her mouth.

Kenzie cut her off, "At least for a while. If I could make it so that Sawyer and I would never see each other again, that would make things easier. But that is not possible with you and Vaughn being mated. Sawyer is never going to get over the fact that I am human, and he's never going to move past his dislike of humans. And unless I'm gone, he is never going to stop wanting me."

Kenzie looked down at her hands. "And I'm never going to get over him. Because, despite the fact that he can be a world-class asshole, I unfortunately saw that other side of him when he lost his memory and didn't remember that he hated me. I saw how good things could be if he would just let himself love me the way I could love him." She sniffled, trying not to cry. "Hell, the way I probably foolishly already do love him." She looked up at Naya. "Why am I so stupid?"

Unlike Kenzie, Naya wasn't attempting to hold back her tears. "Oh, Kenzie, that is so sad."

Kenzie shook her head. "No, Naya. Unfortunately, that's life."

TWENTY-NINE

SAWYER AND VAUGHN were sitting in the living room of the bunkhouse, playing video games. Since Naya had gone out to dinner, Vaughn had come over to hang out. Since both of them had the night off from patrol, they decided to play some games.

From his spot on the couch, Sawyer heard Vaughn's phone ringing again. "You'd better answer that, man. Your phone has rung three times. What if something is wrong?"

Vaughn paused the game. "Oh, shit. You're right."

From the chair across from them, Tegan made a sound of disgust. "Men. You are so lucky that Naya loves you."

Vaughn scowled at Tegan as he answered his phone, "Hey, baby."

"Where are you?" Naya said from the other end. No hello from her. She was all business.

"I'm at the bunkhouse."

"Is Sawyer with you?"

Vaughn turned to look at Sawyer.

Sawyer shrugged. He had no idea what Vaughn's mate wanted with him.

"Yes," Vaughn answered.

"Good. Don't go anywhere. I'll be there in half an hour."

"Okay, baby."

"Okay. By the way, don't *baby* me. I know you were too busy playing video games to answer the phone."

The next sound was the beep Vaughn's phone made when the call ended. Vaughn pulled the phone away from his ear and looked at it as if just making sure Naya had really hung up.

Tegan laughed. "Oh my God, I love your mate."

Vaughn narrowed his eyes at her but didn't say anything. Instead, he turned to Sawyer. "What in the hell does my mate want with you?"

"How should I know? I hardly ever talk to her."

Vaughn grabbed a handful of chips. "Yeah, and it'd better stay that way."

Sawyer rolled his eyes. "Dude, I don't want your woman."

"I know. But I'm still going to make sure you know that she's mine."

The man had a point.

"That's fair."

Vaughn unpaused the game, and the two of them continued playing.

About half an hour later, they heard the sound of a vehicle pulling up, followed by a car door slamming shut.

Tegan went to the window to see who it was. She gave a long whistle and said, "Holy shit, that is one pissed off pregnant female headed straight for us." She looked over her shoulder at Vaughn. "What did you do?"

"Nothing. She's here to see Sawyer, remember?"

Tegan looked at Sawyer. "Well then, what did *you* do?"

Sawyer shrugged. "Nothing."

Tegan shook her white-blonde head and turned back to the window. "Nothing, my ass. That's what all men say when they've done something."

"I'm serious." And Sawyer was. He had no idea what he could have done to make Naya so mad at him. Like he'd told Vaughn, he rarely even talked to her.

Tegan quickly scrambled away from the window and sat back in her chair. She put her feet up on the armrest, trying to make it look like she had been sitting there the whole time, as the door swung open, and Naya came barreling into the room.

Pissed off pregnant female didn't even begin to cover it. If Naya had been a cartoon, she would have had smoke coming out of her nose as she charged toward them.

As she approached the couch, she walked right toward Sawyer. He instinctively scooted back as far as he could get.

"You are a fucking asshole!"

"Naya!" Vaughn exclaimed from beside him while Tegan said, "Holy crap, I just heard the vampire princess say *fuck*."

Sawyer, still having no idea what was going on, put his hands up in surrender. "Naya, I'm sorry, but I don't understand."

"You! You are the reason my very best friend is moving away. All because you're too damn stubborn and selfish."

Vaughn stood and pulled Naya back a few steps from Sawyer.

Sawyer put his hands down and leaned forward. "Wait. What now?"

"Kenzie. Kenzie is moving back to Iowa."

Sawyer swallowed, and a horrible panicked feeling came over him. "She's moving?"

"Yes. Because of us"—she gestured to herself, Vaughn, and Sawyer—"she lost her job at the hotel and hasn't been able to find work. Her boss didn't buy her sick story, and she couldn't tell him the real reason. Now, no hotel in the area will hire her."

"She's moving away for a job because we got her fired?" Vaughn asked.

"Yes," she told her mate. Then, she put her hands on her hips and glared down at Sawyer. "But even if she could find a job, she'd probably still be moving because of you and your pigheaded, stubborn, selfish, biased, speciesist self."

Sawyer jumped up from the couch, and Vaughn used Naya's shoulders to pull her farther away.

She pulled away from him and stepped forward, putting her finger in Sawyer's face. "I do not understand what is wrong with you. You have a beautiful, vibrant female who would do nothing but love and cherish you if you would give her half a chance."

Sawyer sighed uncomfortably. "Naya, it's not that easy."

She shook her head in disbelief. "Yes, it is. Kenzie is giving up her whole life here—her job, her friends, her apartment, everything—to move back to a place she hates, to live with her father who didn't even know she was missing over Thanksgiving, to a job that won't be half as good as the one she had. And do you know why?" She poked Sawyer in the chest with her next words. "Because she's keeping our secret. She can't tell anyone about us, and she is willing to give up everything she loves…for us. Do you know what that is?"

Sawyer just shook his head.

"It's the opposite of selfish," Naya said, her voice wavering. Her anger was turning to sadness, and she looked to be on the verge of crying.

"Naya, baby," Vaughn said, trying to touch her again.

"No." She shook him off. "He needs to hear this." She turned to Sawyer. "You are so blind to anything else but your hate that you can't even see when others are suffering, too. You are so caught up in your own feelings and jealousy that you can't see that you are breaking Kenzie. You don't want her, but you can't let her go either. I saw what you did to her the night of my party. She has bruises, Sawyer. Bruises. Still. All because you are too selfish to think of anyone but yourself."

Sawyer recoiled. He'd known that he was rough with Kenzie that night, and he had regretted it ever since, but he'd had no idea that he hurt her that much.

"But the worst part is not the marks you left on her body. It's what is going on inside of her. You might hate humans, but she is still an individual. She has wants, needs, and desires just like you. And she has feelings. Feelings that you have stomped on over and over again like they mean nothing. I know you went through something when you were younger, but that doesn't give you the right to treat someone the way you've treated Kenzie. Kenzie didn't even know you back then, and she has nothing to do with your past. You have to stop punishing her for what someone else did."

With those parting words, Naya spun around and headed for the door.

Sawyer was stunned by the princess's words, and he had to sit back down before his legs gave out. She'd had some really good points.

Sawyer looked up to see that Vaughn had followed her to the door and was saying good-bye.

Tegan was sitting quietly, staring at Sawyer with a look of shock on her face. "I can't believe that just happened," she muttered.

Neither could Sawyer.

Naya left, and Vaughn walked back into the room.

Nobody said anything at first, but then Vaughn broke the silence. "So, Naya is going back to be with Kenzie for the night. Kenzie is moving on Saturday, and Naya wants to spend as much time with her as possible."

Sawyer, who had been staring off into space, snapped his neck up to meet Vaughn's eyes. "What?"

Vaughn almost looked sorry for Sawyer. "Yeah. She's moving on Saturday. Apparently, she already has almost all of her apartment packed up. We have to get what little is left of Naya's things out of the second bedroom before then."

"Saturday?" Sawyer said.

"Yes. She's not messing around or making idle threats. She's really moving."

Sawyer was stunned. This was a lot of information to process.

"Sawyer?"

Sawyer looked at Vaughn again.

"I'm not going to tell you what to do or offer you advice on what you should do, but I think you should know that she's getting a job with her old boyfriend from high school. All I'm going to say is that this might be your last chance."

THIRTY

PHOENIX WALKED into her bedroom and gently tossed her stuff on her bed. Tegan was sleeping, and Phoenix didn't want to wake her.

Despite the long night of being on patrol and the late hour, she wasn't tired. It was another night of patrol that had come up empty. She was beginning to think that they were never going to find Gerald, and at this point, she kept expecting their alpha to call off the search. As much as it pained her, there would be a point at which they'd have to give up. He could be in Hawaii by now, for all they knew, and they could be just wasting their time looking for him.

Phoenix stripped off her warm winter clothes and put on shorts and a tank top. Maybe a light workout would help her burn off some energy, so she could fall asleep. After dressing silently in the dark, she walked quietly through the bunkhouse to the basement. Thankfully, everyone else had gone to bed, and she didn't have to face anyone on her way downstairs.

Expecting the workout room to be empty, Phoenix was

surprised to see Sawyer down there. She almost turned around because she hadn't talked to him since their last conversation in that room, but he looked troubled. And she wasn't really mad at him anymore.

She knew that some of the things Sawyer had said were because of his own insecurities that he was trying to pass on to her. But she'd still been avoiding him because she didn't feel like having a make-up conversation with him. She knew Saxon had told Sawyer about her past, and it made her feel awkward. She was hoping that they both could just forget about what had happened, but every time she saw Sawyer, she could tell he wanted to apologize.

Now, she knew she would be a bad friend if she didn't at least ask Sawyer if he was okay.

She slowly walked into the room and advanced toward him. He was sitting on the workout bench, staring at the floor, and he didn't even look up as she approached.

"Sawyer," she said as she put her hand on his shoulder.

Sawyer jumped at the touch.

"Sorry. I didn't mean to scare you."

He shrugged in response and looked down again.

Phoenix sat beside him. "Are you doing okay?"

"I have no idea."

What does that mean? "Do you want to talk about it?"

"No."

Okay then. At least I tried.

Phoenix started to stand, but before she was fully upright, Sawyer spoke again, "Kenzie is moving to Iowa."

Phoenix dropped back into the seat and blew out a deep breath. "No wonder you don't know if you're okay."

"Yeah."

"But this is kind of what you wanted, right? Once she moves, a lot of your problems will leave with her."

Sawyer sighed. "I know. It's just…"

"You'll miss her," Phoenix offered.

Sawyer gave Phoenix a side glance and winced. "Yes."

Shocked that Sawyer would even admit to that, Phoenix was momentarily speechless. Then, she asked, "So, what are you going to do?"

Sawyer sat up straight and rubbed his hands over his face. "I have no idea. The worst part is that she's moving back to go to work for her ex-boyfriend. She'll see the bastard every day at work. And that pisses me off. And it pisses me off that I'm pissed off. My life would be so much simpler if I had never met her."

"Yes, it would be easier, but you did meet her. And whether you want to or not, you feel something for her." Phoenix knew she was treading into dangerous waters, but unlike their last conversation, Sawyer seemed to be open to advice. "Can I ask you a question?"

"Why not?"

"Why don't you want to be with her? Why don't you claim her as your mate? She would obviously accept you."

"Because, Phoenix, I just can't get over the fact that she is human. Plus, she's totally not my type. I like quiet, demure girls, and Kenzie is anything but that."

Phoenix couldn't believe how blind Sawyer was. "First of all, no, you do not like quiet, demure girls."

Sawyer turned and scowled at her.

"You *want* to like those girls because you think finding someone like that will make your life easy and simple, but you are not actually attracted to them."

"What?" he asked in disbelief.

"Oh, you want an example? How about that girl you met on New Year's? I had already left for the night, but I heard all about it. She was sweet and nice and just the type you claim to want, yet here you are, still single. You didn't even give the girl one date."

Sawyer scoffed. "Okay, I'll give you that one, but she's only one example."

"If you think she's the only one, you're fooling yourself."

"Maybe," he admitted.

"Secondly—going back to your reasons for not mating with Kenzie—it's not that you can't get over the fact that she is human. It's the fact that you don't *want* to get over the fact that she is human."

"Whatever."

"I'm serious, Sawyer. Have you ever tried to move past what happened to you when you were younger?"

"Well…"

"That's what I thought. Can you keep something between the two of us?"

Sawyer looked confused. "Yes."

Phoenix swallowed. She couldn't believe she was about to tell Sawyer her biggest and most embarrassing secret. "Please don't laugh, but the one thing that no one knows about me is that I really want to be a mom."

Sawyer's eyes rounded.

Phoenix laughed. "I know, right? Me. But I've always wanted to be a mother. If I could, I would have a dozen kids. Ever since I was little, the only thing I saw about myself as a grown-up was the fact that I would be a mom. It's the only thing that I've ever truly wanted in life."

"Phoenix," Sawyer said.

She could hear the sadness in his voice. "Please don't feel sorry for me."

"I would never."

Phoenix playfully elbowed him in the arm. "Yes, you would."

"And get my ass kicked? No, thank you."

She nudged him, but then she turned the conversation serious again. "The thing is, Sawyer, I have tried to get over my past. I have tried to not let it shape me. I have done everything I can think of to move on with my life. Do you know why?"

Sawyer shook his head. "No."

"Because I want to be happy. I want to find a mate and have a bunch of kids." She turned to look Sawyer straight in the eyes. "But you…you hold on to your past. You hold on to all the hurt and anger. I don't think you want to move on."

"But why? Why wouldn't I want to move on?"

"That's easy. Because you blame yourself for what happened. You are punishing yourself, Sawyer, for some-thing that wasn't your fault. I know you feel like you played a role in what happened to your parents, and maybe you did. But, Sawyer, you are not to blame for what happened. All you were really guilty of is being young and in love and trusting the wrong person. You did not make them do what they did. You did not ask them to do what they did." She put her hand on his. "You are not responsible for other people's actions."

Sawyer sucked in a deep breath and let it out.

Since he hadn't stopped her so far, she kept going. "I

also wonder if you're having trouble trusting yourself and your heart. I'm guessing that's why you want a quiet girl because you think something like that won't happen again. But I have news for you. Sometimes, those quiet girls are even worse. You just don't know it because they're quiet."

Sawyer smiled.

"But, listen, you can't doubt the feelings that you have now because of what happened years ago. Kenzie is not that girl from your past, and it's not fair for you to treat her as such. Also, it's not fair for you to hold all humans accountable for the actions of three. Right now, we shifters are still a secret, but what if we aren't forever? What if one shifter does something that makes all humans scared of us? That wouldn't be right, would it?"

Sawyer shook his head. "No."

"Exactly. So, not only is it not fair to Kenzie, but it's not fair to you. You are denying your own happiness, Sawyer." She squeezed his hand and let go. "I'll leave you with that. Ultimately, you have to decide what you want and what is best for you, but please do so with your eyes wide open."

Sawyer nodded and cleared his throat. "I will."

Phoenix stood up and headed for the stairs.

"Aren't you going to work out?" Sawyer asked.

She turned and smiled. "Nah, I think I'm good. Suddenly, I'm pretty tired." She twisted back around.

"Phoenix?"

She spun back to Sawyer once again.

"I'm sorry."

She smiled at him. "Don't worry. I know."

THIRTY-ONE

KENZIE STACKED her last box and looked around her apartment, trying to suppress her feeling of melancholy. It was a very sad day for her because tomorrow was moving day. She was going to have to say good-bye to her life of the last ten years.

She took another walk through before going to bed. Naya's room was completely empty—she and Vaughn had come to pick up everything a few days ago—and it seemed this made Kenzie the saddest. Despite her hands being tied and knowing she was moving because she had a job, she knew that she and Naya would never be the same, and it was possible that, after time, they would lose touch altogether. Naya was the only thing Kenzie had left, and sooner or later, she would be gone, too.

Quit feeling sorry for yourself. Life happens. Shit happens. That's just the way it goes sometimes.

With a sigh, Kenzie closed the door to Naya's room and wandered to her own room. All that Kenzie had left was her bed and a vacant nightstand. It looked so empty and lonely. Kind of like her.

She really needed to get a grip on her poor-me routine. She knew things could be worse. Once the movers got there in the morning and she was actually driving down to Iowa, things would feel better.

Kenzie set her phone alarm to go off at four thirty in the morning. The movers were set to be at her place at six, and she wanted to be showered and ready before they got there. It was only eight in the evening, but she knew she would have a big day ahead of her, so she wanted to go to bed early. Plus, she could feel the beginning of a migraine coming on, so she had taken her prescription half an hour ago, and she would pretty much be a zombie on the medication. She'd been told that she had done and said things on it that she couldn't even remember. It was for the best for her to just go to bed now. And even though she was going to bed early, she was going to be exhausted tomorrow morning for the first few hours. Her medicine worked wonders on her headaches, but it would stay in her system for what seemed like forever.

She changed into her pajamas and slipped into bed. She stared at the crack in her ceiling that had been there since she moved in. She fell asleep while staring at the jagged line, thinking about how much that crack resembled her life and how appropriate it was to be the last thing she saw before closing her eyes.

☾

Sawyer knocked on Kenzie's door and waited for her to answer.

He'd had a lot to think about during the last few days. With Naya yelling at him and Phoenix opening up and sharing a part of herself, Sawyer knew that he needed to take a step back and look at his life from a different perspective.

It was hard to let go of some of his hate toward humans and his biased views, but he'd realized that Phoenix was right and that he was punishing himself. He understood that he still needed work and that he couldn't just expect everything that he had felt and thought for so long to change in a split second, which was why he had taken the biggest step he'd ever taken by seeing a professional. He'd only had one meeting so far, but for him, it was a huge effort to change his life for the better.

His second step was coming to Kenzie's home to apologize to her. He had some other things to say, and knowing that she was leaving, he couldn't put it off any longer.

After Sawyer realized that Kenzie wasn't going to answer, he looked down at his watch. Eight thirty. Not that late, and Naya had confirmed that Kenzie would be home all night, packing up her things for tomorrow, and he had seen her car in the parking lot.

Why isn't she answering?

He sighed because he really wanted to do things right, which meant being a gentleman by knocking on her door and waiting for her to answer and invite him in. He rapped his knuckles on the wood again, a little louder this time. He waited another minute or so before he turned around and reluctantly walked away. He supposed he would just have to call her even though he wanted to talk to her in person.

He got to the end of the hallway before he stopped, turned around, and marched back to her door. *Screw being a gentleman.* He couldn't do this over the phone. He'd broken in before. What was one more time? Besides, what if something had happened to her, and he had just walked away? He snorted at his lame justification for entering her home illegally, but lame didn't stop him from proceeding. He promised himself that he would sit quietly and wait for her to come home, if she were out, and that he would sit in full view of the door so as not to scare her like the last time he'd broken in.

Sawyer jimmied the lock and slipped in. The apartment was dark, except for the kitchen appliance clock and the streetlights illuminating the room through the open curtains. Boxes were everywhere, and it made the fact that Kenzie was moving all the more real. Any hesitancy he had before about entering her apartment without permission completely disappeared. He needed to see her before she left.

Sawyer put his nose in the air and sniffed. He smelled the distinct scent of lemon, but it wasn't from household cleaner. It was Kenzie. Funny how he'd never admitted to himself what she smelled like before, but now, there was no mistaking the aroma.

With her fragrance so strong, Sawyer knew she had to be there, so he was confused as to why all the lights were off in the apartment. He quietly walked to her bedroom and pushed the partially closed door open all the way. Lights from the parking lot penetrated the room, and he was surprised to see Kenzie's outline in her bed. Knowing the early hour of the night, he was worried at first until he saw the rise and fall of her chest under the covers.

He was unsure of what to do next. Last time he'd come into her room while she was sleeping, he'd scared her. He didn't want to do that again.

Kenzie's cat, who had been sleeping on the end of her bed, suddenly perked up and started meowing when she saw him. He stepped into the room and swept the cat up before she woke Kenzie, who stirred in her bed. The stupid cat had a hard-on for him. She'd stopped meowing and started purring as soon as he picked her up. He was trying to do things the right way, but everything was getting fucked up.

He gave the cat a few more rubs and a pep talk about being quiet before he set her down. Then, he approached Kenzie and lightly put his hand on her leg to gently shake her. He figured it would be less scary if he was at her feet rather than looming over her. But she didn't move.

He stepped forward and rocked her hip next. She still didn't wake up.

Reluctantly, he sat down next to her on the bed, hoping that would be less frightening when she awoke. He brushed her hair out of her face and whispered her name.

THIRTY-TWO

"KENZIE. KENZIE."

She heard her name from far away and realized that her dream was changing, which was a relief. She'd been dreaming that she was standing on the edge of a cliff with Naya and Sawyer standing at the bottom, looking at her with confused eyes. She had wanted to go down there, but she'd known that the fall would kill her.

But now, her dream was transforming into something better. She felt fingers brushing her face as her name was being whispered in the dark. She opened her eyes to see Sawyer crouching over her with a look of concern on his face. At first, she didn't understand because Sawyer didn't worry for her. Then, she understood, and it made sense that she would dream of this before leaving her home.

She reached up and touched his jaw. "You're back."

He furrowed his brow. "I'm back?"

She ran her fingers over his lips and face, taking advantage of her dream. "Yes. Amnesia Sawyer, you're back."

"What makes you think that I'm not regular old Sawyer?"

He's so silly. But, of course, Amnesia Sawyer wouldn't understand how Memory Sawyer was. "Because I can see that you care, and there is no disgust in your eyes."

He closed his eyes, as if he were in pain. When he opened them again, he looked sad. "That's really how I look at you? Like you disgust me?"

She shrugged. "Yes."

She didn't understand why he was talking to her about this. It wasn't important right now. She had no idea how long she'd been sleeping or when her alarm would wake her, and she didn't want to waste time talking about Memory Sawyer. In all the weeks she'd been home from their ordeal, she had never once dreamed of Amnesia Sawyer, and she feared that this would be the one and only time that it would happen. Even though it wasn't real, she wanted to enjoy the moment while it lasted. She didn't want to talk about how Memory Sawyer—the real Sawyer—hated her.

He closed his eyes again. "I really am an asshole," he said, seemingly to himself. When he opened his eyes and looked at her, he said, "I'm so sorry, Kenzie."

She just smiled and continued to touch him. His apology was nice, but she didn't understand where it was coming from. Memory Sawyer would never apologize, and Amnesia Sawyer didn't remember anything he had done, so it seemed she was dealing with a new Sawyer. But that was okay because Dream Sawyer didn't stop her from touching him.

He clutched the hand that she had been using to touch his face and hair. "I'm serious. I am so sorry for the way I have treated you."

Again, she didn't know why he was wasting time telling her this stuff. She wanted him to take off his clothes and make love to her. She wanted the *last time* she was intimate with Sawyer to be making love, not the jealous, hate-fueled fucking that he'd given her on New Year's.

Not knowing what to say to get Dream Sawyer to stop talking about how he'd treated her and move on to other things, she simply said, "Okay."

"No, Kenzie. I need you to understand that I was in the wrong. I need you to accept my apology."

If that's what it takes. She smiled at him. "Apology accepted."

His shoulders slumped with relief. She hadn't realized how tense he'd been. Well, she was about to make him even less stressed.

She reached for the bottom of his T-shirt and tried to pull it up.

He put his hands on hers, stopping her movements. "What are you doing?"

She thought that was obvious. "Taking off your clothes."

"Why?"

She was beginning to think Dream Sawyer was stupid. "So, you can make love to me."

He yanked her hands off his shirt. "Kenzie, I didn't come here for that. I've messed things up with you before with sex." He shook his head. "No, we aren't having sex until we talk more. I haven't even said the things I've come to say."

Kenzie blew out a breath of frustration. "This dream is not going the way I want it to."

"What dream? Kenzie, this is real."

She reached up and cupped his face. "Aren't you sweet?" Even though things weren't going the way she wanted them to, she knew that the real Sawyer would never come to her house and tell her that he was sorry for being an ass. No, this was definitely a dream.

He leaned down and touched his nose to hers. "And you are frustrating, woman." His tone was a mix of teasing and irritation.

"You wouldn't have me any other way," she teased back.

He lost all humor and said, "You're right. I wouldn't. I want you just the way you are."

The words were spoken so seriously that she felt the beginning of tears in her eyes. But she didn't want to cry. She didn't want to wake up and be tormented with this Dream Sawyer. That would just be too painful. Sex, no matter how intimate it was, was something she could live with and replay in her mind. This sweet, accepting Sawyer was just her mind being cruel to her.

Why do I continue to want what I can't have?

Knowing that she needed to stop things from progressing to where her heart would break all over again, she pulled his head down and kissed him.

He growled into her mouth and began running his hands all over her. Before he could change his mind, she grabbed for his shirt and ripped it over his head while he did the same with hers. Immediately bringing their lips back together, they continued to kiss as she pushed off her pajama bottoms and reached for the button of his jeans.

After they were both naked, Sawyer sat up, pulled back the covers, and…just stopped.

"What's…wrong?" she asked through her heavy breathing.

Sawyer stood, threw the comforter back over her, and put his hands up in the air. "I told you that I didn't come here to have sex with you."

Kenzie took in his glorious body. Had he always been this sexy, or was her imagination building him up in her mind? She paused at his groin and tilted her head. Now, that part of him she was sure she was exaggerating, but that was beside the point right now.

She looked back to his eyes. "That huge erection you're sporting says otherwise, big guy."

Sawyer instantly swung his arms down to cover himself.

Kenzie clicked her tongue in disappointment.

"He's not in charge. I am."

She flipped back the covers on her bed and opened her legs in response.

Sawyer groaned, as if he were in pain. "I'm serious, Kenzie. I am not having sex with you."

She opened her mouth, but he seemed to know what she was going to say before she said it. Of course, he was part of her imagination, so it made sense that he could anticipate her next words.

"I'm not fucking you or making love to you either."

She closed her legs, frustrated. "You're no fun."

He sat at the end of the bed with his side facing her and ran his hand through his hair. "I've heard that before."

They seemed to be at an impasse. He wasn't going to have sex with her, and she was suddenly afraid her dream would end. She had to think of something quick before he disappeared. She wasn't ready to say good-bye.

"Kenzie."

She looked up at Sawyer, not realizing that she'd been staring into space.

"I'm sorry. I'm not trying to hurt your feelings. This happens to be something I feel very strongly about. I don't want you to hate me tomorrow. Besides, you're obviously tired."

"That's ridiculous," she said with a yawn. "I wouldn't hate you tomorrow. I could never hate you. I might not like you and some of your actions sometimes, but I could never hate you. I love you." She yawned again. "But I am tired for some reason." How she could be tired when she was already sleeping, she didn't understand. "Will you at least lie with me?"

Sawyer slowly stood and stared at her, as if in shock.

"What?"

"I can't believe you said that," he whispered.

"Said what?" She was confused. "Asking you to lie with me?"

He smiled and shook his head. "No. Never mind though." He jerked his chin up. "Move your sexy butt over. I would love to lie with you."

She moved to the other side of the bed to give him room.

Sawyer paused before lying next to her, his smile a full-fledged grin. "Do you promise not to try anything, or do I have to put my clothes back on?"

"I promise." She held up three fingers. "Scout's honor."

"You were never a Boy Scout."

"No, but I was a Girl Scout, so that counts for something, right?"

"Sure," he said as he lay down. He put his arm around her, pulling her close.

She rested her head on his chest and breathed in his earthly scent. "I could fall asleep like this for the rest of my life."

He squeezed her arm. "Maybe you'll get to."

She smiled sadly. She knew that wasn't going to happen, but she wasn't going to argue with Dream Sawyer. He didn't seem to understand that all this wasn't real, but then again, he wasn't real, so in the end, it all made sense.

She started to drift, and she realized her dream was fading. She hoped her next one would be even better, but instead, she fell into a dreamless deep sleep.

THIRTY-THREE

KENZIE GRADUALLY AWOKE, buried underneath the covers. Still tired, she didn't want to get up yet, especially knowing the big day that she had ahead of her. She'd rather just go back to sleep.

She tried to do just that since her alarm hadn't gone off yet, but instead of sleeping, her thoughts turned to the two dreams she'd had last night. The first with her standing on a cliff had just been weird, as a lot of dreams were, and she briefly wondered what it meant, but she decided not to waste time trying to figure it out.

Her second dream had been something else. She moved her hands along her sides and legs just to confirm that she still had her pajamas on, which she did, and she found herself a little disappointed. It had seemed so real that she'd half-expected to find herself naked.

But, of course, Sawyer would never come to her in the middle of the night and apologize to her. It was better to not think about that right now. Still lying in bed, she felt like it had actually happened, and that made her a little sadder.

She could think about it on her five-hour car ride today when her reality would be truly in front of her as she made her way down the highway.

Kenzie rolled onto her back, still leaving the covers over her. She was surprised with how rested she felt. Yes, she wanted to go back to sleep, but she'd thought that she'd be way groggier from her meds. It was almost as if she had slept later than she had planned.

Feeling a little worried, Kenzie stuck her hand out from underneath the covers and searched around for her phone. She hit her hand on the nightstand, which was weird because she knew exactly where that thing was, but it suddenly seemed to be taller than it normally was.

She found her phone and pulled it under her shelter with her. She hit the power button, and when she saw the time, she about had a heart attack. *7:28 a.m.!* She'd overslept by several hours, and she hadn't heard the movers knock on her door. Cursing herself and the movers for not calling, going by the lack of missed calls on her display, she threw back the covers, ready to give someone a tongue-lashing, when she noticed her surroundings.

"What in the hell?"

Kenzie had no idea where she was. This was not her room, and this was not her stuff.

"Oh God." *What happened while I was sleeping?*

She knew that she'd had conversations and done a few things, like go to the bathroom and pull food out of the fridge, when she was on her migraine medication, but she had never woken up in someone else's bedroom.

She looked down at herself to confirm that she was still in her pajamas. She hoped she hadn't gone out in public like this. She obviously hadn't changed into regular clothes. Had she found some guy and gone home with him, and that was why she had dreamed about Sawyer?

She dropped down onto the bed as her legs gave out underneath her. She didn't know what to do, and despite the fact that she and Sawyer would never be, it made her sick to think that she had found some guy and gone home with him. That was ironic because, before Sawyer, that had kind of been her thing.

She put her head in her hands as her mind began to race. She had no idea what to do. She needed to get out of there. She needed to call the moving company. She needed to get back to her apartment. She needed to go back in time and stop whatever had happened. She needed to use her brain and think.

She looked down at her phone. *Naya!* She would call Naya. Maybe she could have Vaughn come pick her up—after Kenzie figured out where she was. She pulled up the map on her phone and used the GPS to find out her location. She was in Eden Prairie. That was all the way on the Minneapolis side. She was never taking her medicine again, migraine or no migraine.

Now that she had her location, she could call Naya, and then after that, she could find out whose house she was in. And, just in case he was an ax murderer, she could warn him that someone was coming for her.

"Hello?" Naya answered the phone.

"Thank God you answered."

Naya's voice immediately went on alert. "What's going on? Was he a jerk to you again? He promised that he would be nice if I helped him. I should have known—"

Kenzie cut her friend off, "What are you talking about? You know what? Never mind. I need your help. I have no idea where I am, except that I'm somewhere in Eden Prairie. I'm freaking out because I must have done something crazy last night. If I give you my coordinates, do you think Vaughn could pick me up?"

The other side of the line was silent.

"Naya?" Kenzie said, panicked.

"So…you have no idea where you are?" Naya asked calmly.

"Yes!" Why wasn't her best friend more worried about her? "For all I know, I could be with a rapist or murderer. I'm lucky that I didn't wake up tied up with duct tape on my mouth."

"He might be a jerk, but I don't think he's that bad," Naya said under her breath.

"What are you talking about? And why aren't you more worried about me?"

"Kenzie, have you even left the room yet?"

"No. Did you not hear me? I don't want to die."

Naya started laughing, and Kenzie thought about hanging up on her. Unfortunately, she didn't know whom else to call. She momentarily thought of Sawyer, but she really didn't want to call him to rescue her.

"Kenzie, listen. You're not going to die. Just leave the bedroom, and I promise, everything will be okay. At least, it'd better be. I don't care how pregnant I am. Someone can still get his ass kicked."

Kenzie was about to protest Naya's suggestion when the bedroom door was pushed open a crack, and a cat walked into the room and jumped on the bed. But it wasn't just any cat. It was Crabby Abby. Kenzie would recognize her anywhere.

What in the hell?

"Kenzie? Kenzie!" Naya called from a distance.

Kenzie looked down at her hand, not realizing that she had let the phone fall away from her ear. She slowly brought her cell back up. "Naya, what is going on?"

"That is for the two of you to discuss. Just go talk to him. Then, call me later. I want to hear everything."

"Who is *him*?" Kenzie asked, but it was too late.

Naya had already hung up.

Kenzie slowly rose from the bed, clutching her phone in front of her. It obviously wasn't going to save her if she opened the bedroom door and there really was a murderer on the other side, but it was all that she had.

Crabby Abby jumped off the bed, meowed, and walked back toward the door. When Kenzie didn't move fast enough for her, Crabby Abby came back to Kenzie, meowed, and walked toward the door again.

"I'm coming, okay?" she told her cat. "Give me a minute. My life might be shit right now, but I still want to live."

Crabby Abby sat down, lifted her leg, and started licking her butthole.

"Yeah, same to you, cat. I knew I should've gotten a guard dog."

Crabby Abby paid no mind to Kenzie and rose to walk to the door, this time disappearing around the corner of it.

Kenzie crept closer and slowly opened the door, hoping it was well oiled and wouldn't creak.

The first thing that she saw was her boxes against the

wall in the hallway. She knew they were her boxes because they had her handwriting on the sides of them.

The whole situation was just getting weirder.

Maybe she was still dreaming. That had to be the only explanation.

Kenzie pinched herself. *Ouch*. Okay, so maybe she wasn't dreaming.

She heard a voice coming from down the hall, and Kenzie followed the sound as she vowed to God that if she was killed, she would haunt Naya for the rest of her life. When she got to the end of the hall, it opened up into a living room with a kitchen beyond that. Kenzie was more than stunned to see Sawyer standing there on the phone with his back to her.

Sawyer moved the phone away from his mouth as he put his nose in the air and inhaled. He instantly swung around, and she guessed that he must have smelled her.

He put the mouthpiece back up to his lips. "She's here. Listen, let me call you back." He pushed a button on his phone and threw it on the couch.

Kenzie stared at him, completely confused. "What in the hell is going on?"

THIRTY-FOUR

SAWYER STARED AT KENZIE, not knowing where to start explaining.

"Where the hell am I?"

That was an easy question. "My parents' house. My house." *Our house now.* "I inherited it after my parents passed away." He gestured toward the couch. "Will you please sit? I'll try to explain everything."

Kenzie eyed him like he had three heads as she slowly lowered herself onto the couch and set her phone on the coffee table, but at least she wasn't arguing with him.

Sawyer sat down next to her, making sure to give her some space so that she wouldn't feel claustrophobic. Despite her messy hair and the indents on her face from her pillow, he still thought she looked beautiful.

He couldn't believe how freeing it was to think that. Before, he would have stopped himself from coming close to admiring her, but now, he felt like he had been liberated.

Kenzie waved her hand in front of his face. "Dude, why

are you grinning like an idiot? You're kind of freaking me out."

"Sorry," he said, but he didn't stop himself from smiling at her. He could watch her all day.

"Sawyer?"

"What?"

"Are you going to tell me what's going on? Or are you going to sit there, like a lump on a log, staring at me?"

"Sorry," he said again. He cleared his throat. "I guess I don't know where to start."

She raised her brow. "Well, you could start with why I am here and not on my way to Iowa right now."

Sawyer winced. "That's kind of a long story." *How can I say this? How should I explain this?* "Okay, I guess I'll start with Naya coming to see me." He looked down at his hands in shame. "She yelled at me for the way that I'd treated you the night of the New Year's Eve party." He peeked up at Kenzie for a second. "And Naya was right. I behaved horribly. I was jealous and mad, and all I could think about was your ex-boyfriend touching you." *Touching what's mine.* "Instead of being an adult and talking to you, I reacted on instinct and jealousy. The instinct part you can blame on my cat half, but the jealousy part is all me being a stubborn idiot."

Sawyer looked up at Kenzie, who was staring at him with her mouth halfway open.

"What?" *Do I have food on my face or something?*

"I-I-I," she stammered. "I'm in shock. I can't believe you just admitted that to me." Her eyes widened. "Hell, I can't believe you admitted it to yourself."

"After Naya yelled at me, I had a long talk with Phoenix, and she made some very valid points. Our conversation made me realize some things about myself that I'd been blind to, and I decided that I needed to make a change, or I'd end up living a long and lonely life."

"Wow. Can I ask what you realized?"

Sawyer smiled. "Of course. I don't want there to be any secrets between us."

"I am so confused," Kenzie said as she rubbed her head.

"Let me go back to the beginning. I grew up in this house with my parents, and when I was about ten, I think, we had new neighbors move in next door. My parents and the couple next door had a lot in common, including an only child of the same age, and they hit it off almost immediately. They became good friends, and the only thing that the neighbors didn't know was that my parents were shifters."

"Your neighbors were humans and friends with your parents?" Kenzie asked in disbelief.

"Yes."

"But you hate humans."

Sawyer cringed. "Hated," he corrected. "And I'm getting to why I felt that way."

"Felt?"

"Yes. Now, the neighbors had a daughter named Megan, who was the same age as me. I didn't care for her at first because I was a ten-year-old boy, and as far as I was concerned, she had cooties. But after a few years, that changed. Not only did we become friends, but—"

Kenzie closed her eyes. "You became boyfriend and girlfriend."

"Yes. And like any young romance, I thought I was in love. I thought we would be together forever, but I knew that it could never last if she didn't know the truth about me. Megan was very kind and caring. I had no doubts that she would accept me as a shifter. I figured it would come as a shock, of course, but after she processed it, I figured we would live happily ever after, as they say."

"But that didn't happen."

Sawyer shook his head. "No. When I told her, she didn't freak out or anything, but she told me that she needed space and time to think. I was disappointed but not surprised, and I agreed to leave her alone for a while." He clenched his hands. His story was getting hard to tell. "I hadn't heard from her for about two weeks. It was the weekend, and I went camping with a friend and his family. Apparently, that weekend was the same weekend that Megan decided to tell her parents the truth about my family. I don't know what made Megan's parents react the way they did, but apparently, in a fit of rage, they confronted my parents. I don't know the details, but I know the neighbors brought a gun and shot my parents."

Kenzie gasped.

"When I came home from camping, I found them in the backyard, dead. They had died the night before, so it was obvious that they were gone when I approached. I will never forget how they looked, lying there."

"Oh my God, Sawyer." Kenzie moved closer to him and grabbed his hands. "I'm so sorry. That's awful."

He squeezed her hands to let her know that he appreciated her being there. "The police investigated, and it was discovered that it was the neighbors. They didn't even deny it when the cops came looking for them. Thankfully, humans don't know or believe in shifters, so the neighbors came off as crazy, and the jury didn't buy their defense. Both of them are currently locked up in prison. I was fifteen years old."

"And Megan?"

"She committed suicide after her parents were arrested. I never spoke to her after I revealed my secret. I don't know why she told her parents. I don't know why her parents reacted the way they did. All I know is that if I hadn't told Megan, then my parents would be alive."

"Oh, Sawyer."

"I blamed myself all these years, and of course, I blamed humans for what had happened. Only recently, I understand that I was punishing myself for what had happened to my family. But I couldn't admit that I was punishing myself, so I put all my self-hate into hating humans. Toward you. It's going to be a long journey, but the first step is admitting these things out loud. I've even started therapy."

"Wow, Sawyer. It's no wonder you hate humans."

"But it's not right. It's no better than saying all cat-shifters are bad because of what Gerald has done. Not all cat-shifters are villains, and not all humans are like Megan or her parents. I realize, especially now, that it was wrong of me to lump you all into one category."

"I appreciate the fact that you recognize I would never hurt you like that."

"I'm sorry it took me so long to understand that. I've been horrible to you. I have treated you like no man should ever treat a woman."

"So, you brought me here to apologize? Am I getting that right?"

"Yes," he said, relieved that she understood his motive behind bringing her to his house.

She pulled her hands from his. "What I don't get is why you didn't just come to my apartment to talk to me."

"I tried. You were out of it. You kept telling me that you were dreaming."

The color drained from Kenzie's face.

"What's wrong?"

"I am an idiot. Of course last night wasn't a dream." She put her head in her hands. "I can't believe the things I said to you, thinking you were just a part of my imagination."

Sawyer knew he shouldn't laugh, but she was so cute. "Kenzie, it's okay. I know you thought you were dreaming. I barely remember what you said." Now, he was lying to make her feel better because there was no way in hell he'd ever forget her saying she loved him.

"I'm still embarrassed. And I don't embarrass easily."

"Then, we'll just pretend like it never happened. How about that?"

She peeked at him before sitting up and dropping her arms. "Yeah, right. Sure. But I guess I'll have to take what I can get. I'm still a little confused. Why did you bring me here? Why is my stuff here? I saw my boxes sitting in the hall."

"Since I wasn't able to speak to you last night, and your movers came so early this morning, I just had them bring your things to my place. I figured you had to be out of your apartment today, and I wanted to talk to you about something else before you decided to move down to Iowa."

"What is that?"

"Naya also told me that you had lost your job because you couldn't account for your whereabouts during our kidnapping."

Kenzie groaned. "She wasn't supposed to say anything. I didn't want anyone to feel guilty."

"Don't be ridiculous. We put you in that situation. If it weren't for us, you'd still have your job."

She shrugged. "I've found a new one."

"In Iowa," Sawyer pointed out. "Naya made it very clear that you do not want to move back there."

She shrugged again. "That's life."

"But, Kenzie, Naya made it seem like you hate it there."

She threw her hands up in the air, obviously getting frustrated. "Well, hotshot, what do you want me to do about it? I tried everything that I could think of to get a job in the Cities. Nobody wants me. Nobody. I couldn't even get an interview." She stood up. "Now that I have admitted my failure to you, I would like to go and figure out how I'm going to get my stuff down to Iowa because I have a job to start in another couple of days."

Sawyer jumped up and grabbed her wrist. "No, you don't understand. We found you a job at a great hotel."

She shook her arm, knocking his grip loose. "I don't want anyone's handout. I don't have much left of my pride, but I do have some, and I don't want anyone's pity."

"Kenzie, it's not a handout or pity. This is what is owed to you. You earned this," he practically begged her to understand. "You can't move to Iowa."

She lost some of her anger. "It is what it is, Sawyer. And I shouldn't be mad. Tell…whoever…got me this job, thank you. I appreciate it, but I can't stay here." Her eyes grew sad. "It's too hard. Maybe even more so now."

"I don't understand."

"That's okay. You don't need to."

She picked up her phone and started walking back toward the hall.

Even though he knew that she wasn't leaving right that second, a sense of panic came over him, and he blurted out the first thing that came to him, "You can't go. I love you."

She stopped walking, keeping her back to him.

"And I know you love me, too. You said it last night."

She slowly pivoted around on her foot. "You told me that you didn't remember anything and that we'd forget it ever happened."

He shrugged a little regretfully. "I lied."

THIRTY-FIVE

KENZIE STARED AT SAWYER, speechless.

"Did you hear what I said? I love you, and I don't want you to move to Iowa."

Kenzie had been given a lot of information today, and she didn't even know what to make of Sawyer's current news. "I think I need to sit down."

He stepped over to her and guided her down to the closest recliner. "What's wrong?" he asked as he knelt between her legs.

"You're asking me what's wrong? I should be asking you that." *Hmm…*

Kenzie put her hands up to Sawyer's forehead and face.

"What are you doing?"

"Checking to see if you have a fever." She pulled her arms back, so she could look at him better. "Oh my God, you're dying."

He rolled his eyes. "I'm not dying."

She leaned forward and said in a low voice, as if it were a secret, "Are you sure?"

He burst out laughing. "Yes."

She moved back, insulted that he would think his death was funny. "Well, I think it's a legitimate question. Up until now, you've hated me."

Sawyer grabbed her hips and pulled her closer to him. He looked and smelled so good that she had a hard time not touching him.

"Have you not heard anything I've said in the last hour?"

"Obviously, I have," she said. "But I thought that was all a part of your therapy, all a part of the healing process."

He gave her a funny look. "I've only gone once. That would have been one heavy-duty therapy session."

"And how was I supposed to know that?"

He nodded once. "Good point. You couldn't have known."

"I don't know what to think of all this."

Sawyer pulled her closer and ran his nose and mouth along her neck. Just like that, she was wet.

"What does your heart tell you?"

Kenzie closed her eyes, taking in the feel of his touch. "Mmm," was all she managed to say as she brought her hand up to grab his hair.

Sawyer nipped her neck and continued to rub her there. "That's it? Just 'mmm'?"

"Well…" She paused and licked her lips. "It's saying…"

Sawyer sucked on the spot where her neck met her shoulder, and her pussy throbbed.

"Oh God, I don't know what it's saying. I can't concentrate."

He ran his nose back up her neck until he reached her

ear. "Is it saying yes? Is it telling you that it wants me to mark you?"

His words, while sexy, actually gave her the willpower to open her eyes, put her hands on his chest, and push slightly away.

His eyes were filled with concern. "What's wrong?" he asked.

For some reason, she'd thought he'd be mad that she had stopped him, so seeing him worry made it easier for her to talk to him. She put her forehead on his. "I don't know what to think. I feel like I'm in the middle of a tornado, and I don't know where I'm going to be set down or what shape I will be in when it happens. I don't want to be hurt again."

Sawyer moved his forehead from hers, kissed her brow, and cupped her face. "Oh, Kenzie, I really did a number on you, didn't I?"

She felt guilty saying yes, so she shrugged.

"How about if I tell you how I feel and what I think about the situation?"

"Okay."

"The moment I met you, I felt an attraction like I have never had with any female, shifter or human, before. I tried to fight this pull I felt toward you, but even though I denied it until now, my cat knew that you belonged to me."

Kenzie was about to protest the belonging-to-him part— while she liked where this was going, she belonged to no man—but Sawyer cut her off with a quick kiss.

"Let me finish. Then, you can list all your grievances when I'm done, okay?"

She couldn't help but smile. "Okay. Continue, please."

Sawyer theatrically cleared his throat. "As I was saying,

my cat knew you belonged to me, and that rat bastard has no clue as to what gender equality or the feminist movement is, so you might just have to live with him the way he is."

Kenzie bit the inside of her cheek, so she wouldn't laugh, but she couldn't stop the grin from spreading across her face. She had never seen this side of Sawyer.

"As I was saying, you got under my skin anyway. And instead of embracing what we could have, I tried to fight any attraction to you or feelings for you, which only led me to do some foolish, jealous things."

"Like what?" she asked.

He gave her a look. "As if you don't already know. But I will indulge you and tell you anyway."

"Okay," she whispered eagerly.

"There was the time you threatened to fuck Saxon, so I pulled you into the restroom of the nightclub and made you come before marking you." His brow furrowed as he seemed to be distracted by another thought. "By the way, please don't ever threaten to fuck my friends again."

She held up three fingers with one hand and crossed her heart with the other.

"Good. Now, do you remember that night I broke into your apartment to try to find Vaughn?"

She nodded.

"Man, did I want you that night. And you were wearing those pajamas without a bra. It took everything in me not to bend you over the couch."

"You could see that I wasn't wearing a bra?" she asked, surprised.

"Of course. I have cat vision after all. I had to hide behind the damn counter, so you wouldn't see my erection.

And then, when you opened your hall door in the same pajamas, the thought of anyone seeing you like that practically drove me crazy."

"I had no idea."

"I know. I hid it all behind anger. Anger was my friend, and it was an easy way to push you away." He rubbed his hand down her arms. "Then, there was the kidnapping, but we don't want that to be a part of our romantic past, do we?"

"Not really."

"But after we got away, I lost my memory. When I gained it back, it was really hard to stay away from you and deny myself. I saw what it could be like if I didn't let my past affect me so much, but apparently, I wasn't ready to let go of all that bitterness yet."

"That was the hardest for me. Knowing what it would be like to truly be your mate, if you liked me."

"I'm so sorry, Kenzie."

"I know."

"Anyway, so after we got home and my memory returned, I had to go and get myself injured. I'm sorry that I took advantage of you when I was on narcotics."

She winced. "When you say it like that, I should be the one to apologize. You were drugged up, and I should have known that something was wrong by the way you were acting. Maybe a part of me did, but I missed being with you so much that I was willing to risk it."

"So, we're both sorry. We'll leave it at that then." He sighed. "That brings us to the night of the party. I know I already apologized, but I want you to know that the thought of your ex touching you made me crazy. I know it's not an excuse, but all I could picture was the way you look when you come, but instead of me giving you that look of pleasure, it would be someone else. My cat was definitely in charge that night, but if I hadn't still been fighting my feelings for you, I never would have treated you like that. Just thinking about it makes me sick to my stomach."

Kenzie reached up and ran her fingers over his jaw. "I don't know if it helps, but I never did anything with my ex, and I wasn't planning to either. He's more like a brother to me now, and I actually think he's dating someone. Truth be told, if you hadn't been so mad that night and hadn't done what you did for the wrong reason, it would have been the hottest sex I'd ever had."

Sawyer smiled at her words. "Thanks for that."

She shrugged a shoulder. "I don't want you to be completely miserable."

"Thanks," he said with a chuckle. "Anyway, then I found out you were moving. I guess a part of me thought you would always be around. I realized that I had been taking you for granted, and if I didn't step up, man up, I would lose the greatest thing that had ever happened to me."

She sucked in a breath at his words.

"So, here I am, without anger or jealousy, telling you that I love you, Kenzie Swanson. I know we have a lot to work on, but I want you to stay here with me. I want you to live here in this house with me, I want you to wear my mark, and I want you to yank that stupid birth control out of your arm, so I can give you lots of babies."

She loved everything that he was saying, and her heart was about to burst, but she had to point out one thing to him. "They'd be half-shifter and half-human babies."

"No, they will be half Kenzie and half Sawyer, just the way they are meant to be. I love you. The rest doesn't matter."

Kenzie grabbed him and kissed him as she moved off the couch and onto his lap.

Sawyer broke their kiss and asked, "Does that mean you'll stay?"

She nodded her head and grinned. "Yes, I'll stay. I'll take the job at the hotel—after I check it out—and I'll stay here with you. But do you really think we should go from fighting to moving in together?"

He kissed her nose. "The way I see it, we've already wasted seven months."

She raised a brow.

"Okay, I've wasted seven months, and I don't think we should waste any more time. Besides, you already gave up your apartment, and your stuff is all here. I think it was meant to be."

She considered his words. "You're probably right." She held up a finger. "But I think you should wait to mark me. I mean, I know you've already done it plenty of times, but I think you should wait this time since it'll be official."

He scowled at her. "Fuck that. I'm marking you the second you let me inside your body."

She loved when he talked dirty to her. "Then, I guess I'd better not let you have your filthy way with me."

Sawyer growled in protest and went for her neck again as his hand moved between her legs.

She was so easy when it came to this man. "Okay, you can have your filthy way with me."

He brought his head up and grinned knowingly at her. "Damn straight I can."

"You're lucky I love you."

Sawyer beamed from ear to ear. "You have no idea how lucky."

（

Sawyer rocked back on his heels on the bed as he took in his naked mate. Her chest was rapidly rising and falling from the orgasm he'd just given her from going down on her. As she regained her breath, Sawyer stripped off his clothes and placed himself over her, in between her legs.

Kenzie reached up and ran her hands over his chest. "I will never get sick of touching you, and I love the fact that I don't have to hold back any longer."

"I love it, too."

She dragged her hand down his torso until she reached his cock. She squeezed him tight, and he bucked in her hand.

"God, that feels good."

She smiled coyly at him and squeezed again.

He removed her fist from around him and kissed her palm. Then, he spread her legs wide and placed himself at her entrance. "Are you ready, Kenzie? There's no going back after this because I will never let you go."

She bit her lip and nodded. "I'm ready. Make me yours, Sawyer."

He slowly pushed inside her and closed his eyes. She had the sweetest fucking pussy. He would never tire of this feeling, and he was one lucky asshole for having the privilege of being there.

He began to thrust inside her with hard, deep strokes, and she clutched at his back as he brought her closer to another orgasm. When he knew that she was close, he put his mouth in position and bit down as he slowed his movements. He wanted her to feel his bite more than what he was doing to her between her legs.

She dug her fingernails into his back and hip, and a slow moan escaped her lips.

He let go of her neck and drew back enough so that he could admire his work for just a second. Then, he picked up his speed again as he whispered in her ear, "Come for me, mate."

THIRTY-SIX

DANTE STRETCHED his neck back and forth while he leaned against his SUV and waited for the gas tank to fill. Tonight was his night off, so he was relaxed and not really paying attention to what was going on around him. Yet something caught his attention. He glanced up and was shocked at what he saw.

Gerald Llewelyn was exiting the gas station and making his way toward an old beat-up Ford.

All this time that they had spent searching for the bastard, and here Dante had found Gerald when he wasn't even trying.

Dante quickly stopped the pump on the gas even though his tank wasn't full, screwed on the gas cap, and hit *No* for a receipt. He jumped in his SUV just in time to follow Gerald out of the parking lot.

He stayed far enough away so that Gerald wouldn't notice that he had a tail, and soon, they came up on an apartment building. Gerald pulled into the parking lot, and Dante parked on the street as he cursed.

There was no way he'd be able to follow Gerald inside without being discovered. Gerald would smell Dante in a second, and going by the age and look of the building, the hallways were probably long and narrow with no place to hide if Gerald suspected that he was being watched.

It would just make finding Gerald that much harder but not impossible.

A second later, a light turned on in an apartment.

Bingo.

Unless someone else had just come home, Dante had found out where Gerald was staying.

Dante picked up his phone and flipped it open. He scrolled down to Vance's number and paused. He knew that he should be calling the cat-shifter alpha. Gerald was a cat-shifter and Vance's cousin, and Vance deserved to know what Dante had found. Instead, Dante scrolled back up to the Ps. He didn't know why he was about to do what he was going to do because, as a leader, Dante felt it was his responsibility to follow the rules and do the right thing.

However, without another moment of hesitation, he hit Send.

☾

Phoenix ignored the vibrating in her pocket for the second time. Saxon and she were busy clearing their last abandoned house, and she didn't have time to answer the phone. Not that it mattered anyway because the house was empty. After weeks of this, Phoenix was really starting to feel like the whole thing was pointless. They were never going to find Gerald.

She met Saxon back in the living room. "Nothing, right?" she asked.

"Nothing."

"Let's go then. The sooner we get through our list, the sooner we can get home."

A few weeks ago, if they had gotten through their list of uninhabited and foreclosed homes early, she would have asked for more. Now, she just wanted to be done, so she could go home and sleep.

They walked toward their vehicle when her phone went off again. Irritated, Phoenix pulled out her cell and looked at the number. It was Dante. She hadn't seen or heard from him since New Year's Eve, and she was very close to not answering. But if he had called three times in the last five minutes, then it must be something important.

"Who is it?" Saxon asked.

It was on the tip of her tongue to tell him that it was Dante. After all, the two of them were friends, but for some reason, she didn't. "Uh...it's Tegan. Why don't you go warm up the SUV while I see what she needs?"

"Sure."

After Saxon was out of hearing distance, she hit Accept on her phone. "Hello?"

"Phoenix, this is Dante."

As if she didn't know. Not only had his number come up on her display, there was also no way she would ever mistake his voice for someone else's. "What do you need?"

"I need you to come to the address I'm about to text to you."

"What? Why?" He was crazy if he just thought she

would drop everything and show up to some random address somewhere. "I'm working."

"Phoenix," he stressed her name. "I found Gerald."

Instantly, her heart began to race, and her palms began to sweat. "Are you sure?" *Please don't let it be a mistake.*

"Without a doubt. Now, get your ass over here."

Phoenix hit End and jogged over to the SUV.

As she climbed inside, Saxon asked, "What did Tegan want?"

"Oh, you know, girl stuff."

Saxon looked at her like she had two heads. "Girl stuff? You?"

Phoenix knew she wasn't what someone would call feminine, but she was still insulted. "Yes, girl stuff. In case you didn't know, I am a girl."

Saxon put the car in drive. "Yeah, I know you're a girl. I just wasn't sure you knew."

Phoenix held up her middle finger and glared at him. "Fuck you."

Saxon simply laughed and pulled away from the curb.

She had been wondering how she was going to ditch Saxon without telling him what was going on, but now that she was irritated with her friend, she didn't care if he questioned her about where she was going.

She pulled up the address Dante had sent her on her GPS and looked for the nearest cross street. "I need you to drop me off somewhere."

"Where?"

She told him the corner that she needed to go to.

"Phoenix, that isn't the best neighborhood. Why do you need to go there?"

She wanted to tell him that it was none of his business, but she didn't want him to question her more. "I'll explain later, but I can't say right now."

"Phoenix," Saxon said in a parenting tone.

"Saxon, I'm not going to argue with you on this. Either take me or don't. I'll just grab my car when we get home."

He sighed. "I'll take you. But if something happens, I will kick your ass, girl or no girl."

She rolled her eyes. "Fine."

They drove the rest of the way in silence, and when Saxon pulled up to her destination, she practically jumped out of the vehicle before he'd even stopped. Right before she closed the door, Saxon grabbed her arm.

"What?" she asked.

"I know you don't want to tell me what's going on, but please be careful."

Despite his worry that she was doing something that she shouldn't, it was also nice to know that he cared. "I will."

He let go of her arm, and she slammed the door. She waited for Saxon to pull away before she took off running down the street. With the snow and ice on the sidewalk, it took her longer than she would have liked, but eventually, she made it.

As she approached the address Dante had texted her, a car door opened, and Dante got out of his SUV. He looked amazing, as always, and part of her wanted to run into his arms, to thank him for calling her with his find instead of calling her alpha, but she didn't.

She stopped before touching him. "So, he's in there, huh?" She nodded toward the apartment building.

"Yep, basement level."

Dante's dark brown eyes studied her, and she had to control the urge to fidget.

"No wonder we never found Gerald. We've been concentrating on motels and abandoned houses."

Dante ran down the plan to apprehend Gerald, and she agreed with his strategy.

"So, you ready to bring this asshole in?" he asked.

"Yes." More than anyone could ever know.

Dante checked his weapons and nodded at her. "Let's go then."

Just before he took off for the building, Phoenix put her hand on his arm.

He looked over his shoulder at her. "What's wrong?"

"Nothing. I just wanted to say thank you."

Dante turned around. "Phoenix," he started, his voice tender.

She didn't want to hear any tender words or sentimental thoughts, so she cut him off, "I just wanted to say thank you. Now, let's go." She marched past Dante, determined to find Gerald.

She heard Dante sigh, but he followed on her heels.

No other words were spoken as they silently made their way into the building and up to the door of Gerald's apartment. Not that it mattered how loud they were. Someone close by was having a party and had the music cranked up to full blast.

As they neared the apartment, Phoenix could smell the fucker's scent outside the door, and it made her sick. She tried not to picture him leaning over her in the motel room where he'd tied her up, but it was hard.

She looked over at Dante's chiseled features and

breathed in his cinnamon scent. She hated the thought of needing anyone, but just knowing that he was there grounded her and gave her the ability to concentrate on what needed to be done.

They each positioned themselves on one side of Gerald's door, and they nodded to each other to signal they were ready. Dante knocked lightly, and they both moved out of the direct view of the peephole. Gerald would be able to see someone, but he would have no idea it was them. Then, they could push their way in and knock him out. Phoenix would kick him in the balls a couple of times while he was unconscious, and then they would bring him in. Easy and efficient. Of course, Dante hadn't included the crotch-kicking part, but she figured an extra step in their plan wouldn't hurt anyone.

Unfortunately, things didn't always work out as one had intended.

She didn't know if it was adrenaline or what, but everything happened so fast. Gerald pulled the door ajar, and Dante kicked it open. Phoenix followed right behind him and kicked the door closed before anyone walked by.

She didn't know how it'd happened, but within seconds, Gerald had pulled out a gun and fired twice.

Dante's body jolted from the force of the gunshots, and Phoenix screamed. Dante fell to the floor, clutching his chest, and without a second thought, she shifted into her cat and went for Gerald's throat. A faint thought crossed her mind that she was supposed to be bringing Gerald in alive, but all she could think about was Dante bleeding on the ground.

What if he dies? The thought was more than Phoenix

could bear, and she bit down with all her strength until she felt the life leaving Gerald's body.

She let go and stepped back as he slumped to the floor. Instead of feeling satisfied, she wanted him to come to life again, so she could kill him all over.

The sound of Dante coughing pulled her from her vengeful thoughts.

Phoenix quickly shifted back to human, practically tripping over her clothes. They were ripped from her shifting, and she pushed them off her body. She barely felt the cold air as she fell over Dante.

"Dante." She scanned his body, trying to find his bullet wounds, but he was completely covered in blood, and she had no idea where to put pressure. With no other options, she laid herself over him, hoping that it would help.

"Phoenix," Dante said as he tried to reach up and touch her. His arm fell back to his side.

"Shh…Dante. Don't try to talk," she told him as she used her leg to pull her pants over to her. She reached in the pocket and pulled out her cell. It hadn't been that long since Saxon dropped her off, so hopefully, he could come back and help her save Dante.

"You got Saxon."

"Saxon, I need your help."

"You weren't careful, were you?"

"No."

"Shit."

Phoenix gave Saxon her location and the apartment number, and then she hung up.

"Dante, help is on the way." She looked down around

them at all the blood that was on the floor. "Please, don't die, Dante."

Dante coughed, and blood came out of his mouth, giving Phoenix an idea. She just had to keep him alive long enough to get him to the vampire clinic. She put her wrist up to Dante's mouth and shook him.

"Dante, you have to feed from me, okay?"

Dante moaned but didn't bite down.

"Dante."

She shook him again, but he didn't move. She took her wrist away and shifted her other hand enough for her claws to come out. She cut herself deep enough to make herself bleed and put her arm back to Dante's mouth. After a few drops hit his tongue, he finally bit down and started sucking.

Relieved that her plan was working, she relaxed on Dante's chest and let him feed.

After a minute or two, Phoenix began to feel sleepy. She knew her adrenaline was wearing off, but she had never felt so exhausted. Just as her eyes began to close and her consciousness faded, the door opened, and someone walked in.

Her last thought was that she hoped they were safe.

THIRTY-SEVEN

TWO DAYS LATER

SAXON FLIPPED through the channels on the TV, feeling bored. There was nothing on worth watching, but he had promised Dante that he wouldn't leave the hospital room. It was the last thing Dante had said right before he closed his eyes.

From the bed beside him, Phoenix stirred and opened her eyes.

Saxon turned the volume down. "Sleeping Beauty awakens," he said as he smiled down at her.

"What happened?" Phoenix barely managed to say. Her voice was hoarse and low.

Saxon grabbed the glass of water sitting on the stand next to her bed. "Here, drink some of this." He held the straw up to her mouth, so she could take as much as she wanted. When she finished, he asked, "Better?"

She licked her chapped lips and nodded. "What

happened?" she asked again. This time, it came out more coherently.

"What's the last thing you remember?"

She closed her eyes as she tried to remember. Suddenly, her eyes popped open. "Gerald."

"Dead. You made sure of that." Saxon wasn't proud of her for breaking the rules, but he was proud of the way she'd taken Gerald out.

She licked her lips again. "I remember going to meet Dante to get Gerald, but that's it."

"You and Dante decided to go rogue and take Gerald on your own. Apparently, he knew something was up, and he was waiting on the other side with his trusty ol' gun."

"And Dante was shot," Phoenix said, panicking as she remembered. She tried to sit up. "Oh my God, I have to see him."

Saxon leaped off his chair and pushed Phoenix back down. "You're not going anywhere."

"But I need to see if he's okay," she said as she tried to fight him.

"Shh...he's fine." Saxon said, trying to calm her. "At least he will be once he fully recovers. Besides, he's lying right next to you if you want to see him."

Phoenix whipped her head to look to her other side. Dante was lying on his side, facing Phoenix. He had dark circles under his eyes, and a small snore escaped from between his lips.

"What is he doing in my bed?" Phoenix said with a raised voice.

"Shh..." Saxon told her again. "Do not wake him up." He sat back down in the chair next to the bed. "He's been watching over you pretty much since you both got here. It was only after I promised not to leave your side, not even to take a piss, that he let himself sleep. And even then, he still refused to go to his own room. So, please, do not wake him up. The man is exhausted and weak, and he needs to rest."

"But what is he doing in my bed?" she asked in a hissed whisper.

"Do you remember anything else besides Dante getting shot?"

She squinted as she concentrated. "Lunging for Gerald and getting his neck…killing him…laying over Dante to try to stop his bleeding…calling you for help…giving Dante my blood…and then that's it."

"You saved Dante's life by giving him your blood, but you almost got yourself killed."

Phoenix grimaced. "I don't understand."

He couldn't believe she was serious. "Phoenix, you were shot and losing blood yourself. You didn't have any to spare, yet you fed Dante."

She looked down at herself. "I was shot?"

"Yes, dummy. You almost died on me."

She put her head back against the pillow and looked at him. "I'm sorry." She looked down again. "Why can't I feel anything?"

"Because you have more drugs in you than a crack house."

"Oh." She scrunched up her face. "I still don't understand why Dante is here."

Saxon faced the TV again as he explained, "Once he came to—which happened pretty fast, thanks to you feeding him—and found out what you did, he refused to leave your side. They had to give you a blood transfusion, and he went apeshit at anyone who volunteered, even me. Even though the doctor told Dante that he could not give up any of his blood after what had happened, he donated his blood to you. And since he's refused to leave your side, you've both been recovering in here ever since. That was two days ago."

When Phoenix didn't say anything in response, Saxon looked at her, only to find her sleeping again. He didn't even know if she had heard anything he'd said. But it didn't matter. She would hear the story again, and right now, she needed her rest.

Saxon smiled and shook his head at his two friends. Maybe one day they'd realize they were meant to be together.

(

Lexine stood outside the cat-shifter female's door, listening to the friend tell her what had happened, feeling sick to her stomach.

Lexine had rushed to the vampire clinic the moment she had heard Dante had been shot. Lexine had been hanging out with her new friends. Her phone had been shut off for the past couple of days since her battery died, and she hadn't bothered to charge it. Her brother's text was the first thing she had seen when she turned it back on, and she hadn't thought to do anything but come to the clinic, only to find Dante's room empty. When the nurse had told her that Dante was in Phoenix's room, Lexine had expected to find him sitting next to her bed. When she had seen that they were sleeping in bed together, her heart fell.

Lexine put her head back against the wall as her emotions transformed from heartbreak to rage.

Lexine liked her new friends a lot, but she had discovered early on that they had extreme views on vampires and shifters and the fact that they shouldn't mix. She usually tried to ignore their biased comments because she really had no hatred toward the shifters. Until now. If the stupid princess hadn't fucked the stupid cat-shifter, the two species would never have started to comingle. And if they had never started to comingle, Dante would not be lying in the slutty cat-shifter's bed.

Lexine's new friends had been careful to talk about certain things around her, but she wasn't stupid. She had caught on to the fact that they had some sort of plans to put a separation between the vampires and cat-shifters once again. She had been a little worried that they would go forth with their plans, especially since she didn't know the full extent of what they wanted to do.

But now, Lexine didn't care if what they planned to do was wrong. If it got the stupid cat-shifter's claws out of Dante so that he would be free to be with Lexine, she would do it. She was so occupied with hate and jealousy that she didn't even care if it was illegal.

She pushed herself away from the wall, filled with determination. Her phone rang as her brother's number came across it. Lexine let it go to voice mail, and instead of calling her brother back, she called her new friends to come and pick her up. She'd never thought it would happen, but betraying the Guardians would be easier than she'd ever thought possible.

EPILOGUE

TWO MONTHS LATER

KENZIE SHUT THE CAR DOOR, and she carried the bags of groceries into the house. She started unpacking them from the bags and putting them in the cupboards when she felt strong arms come around her and a large erection push at her back.

Sawyer nuzzled her neck and muttered, "I missed you, mate." His hand moved from her stomach up to her breast. "I'm so glad you're not working today."

She was, too, even though she loved her new job. The cat-shifters had really come through.

"I wasn't gone that long. I only went to check on Naya and then stopped at the grocery store." She laughed.

"I still missed you." Sawyer continued to caress her as she tried to concentrate on putting away all the food.

"I missed you, too."

"So, how are the parents-to-be?" Sawyer had wanted to

go with her, but he'd had prior obligations to his alpha that he had already committed to.

Kenzie paused. "Well…I guess I'd have to say they're both going nuts."

With Naya's due date just around the corner, she was miserable, and Vaughn's attempt to make it better by hovering only made Naya feel helpless.

"Naya hates being so huge, and Vaughn's constant attention only makes it worse. Hopefully, those babies will choose to be born soon."

Sawyer rubbed her belly. "If I promise to never do that to you, will you go to the doctor and get that thing out?"

Kenzie laughed. "Maybe soon."

Things had been good between the two of them, but Kenzie was being cautious not to move too fast. Technically, in the shifter world, they were already mates, but in the human world, they were just live-in boyfriend and girlfriend. She had talked to Sawyer a few times about getting married, and he'd seemed to be on board with it, but she hadn't pushed him because she wasn't quite ready yet. Truth be told, she was afraid of jinxing things, and she couldn't quite let go of her superstitious feeling that something was going to ruin everything for them.

She knew she wouldn't feel this way forever because, every morning, she'd wake up feeling better about their relationship. It was just that, right now, she was still worried that it would all be taken away from her. It seemed silly because Sawyer had continued to go to therapy, and he'd show and tell her every day how much he loved her, but the feeling was still the same.

Apparently, Sawyer was not the only one who had

changed. Kenzie used to be much more careless with her love life, or lack thereof, and now, she was much less reckless, whereas Sawyer had never been more open with his feelings in his life.

Sawyer continued to rub his nose across her skin when he suddenly turned stiff. He took the can out of her hand and turned her around to face him. He pushed all of her hair out of her face and stroked her cheeks with his thumbs, and he studied her.

She grabbed his wrist. "Is everything okay?"

He looked so serious. "You know I love you, right?"

"Yes."

"And that I would never force you into anything you weren't ready for or trick you into anything?"

Without a moment's hesitation, she answered, "Yes," again.

"I was teasing you just now, but…*shit*…there's something I need to tell you."

Kenzie put her hands on his chest as her throat tightened with fear. Immediately, her mind began to race with every bad scenario she could think of.

He loves me, but he needs to leave me. He thought he was ready for a relationship, but he isn't. He loves me, but it isn't enough. He's fallen in love with a shifter, and he realizes that is who he's supposed to be with.

"Sawyer, what is it?"

"I don't want you to hate me."

She took his fear as a good sign that he wasn't going to leave her, but until he told her what was wrong, she was going to think the worst.

"Baby, I told you I would never hate you. Now, will you

303

please tell me what is going on? I'm kind of starting to freak out."

Sawyer put one of his hands on her bicep and rubbed her arm. "It didn't work—or rather, it stopped working."

She didn't understand. "What are you talking about?"

He nodded down to her arm. "It doesn't work anymore."

She looked down at her arm, confused. Then, she suddenly realized what he was rubbing, and everything clicked. "Holy fuck, I'm pregnant."

Sawyer winced and nodded his head.

She dropped her hands from Sawyer's chest and leaned back against the kitchen counter in shock. "Oh my God. Oh my God."

Sawyer bent his knees to put himself more even with her line of sight. "I'm sorry, baby. I swear, I had no idea you were fertile. I would never get you pregnant without your knowledge. Please don't hate me."

Kenzie looked up at him. "Huh?"

"What's the point of being mated to a shifter if I can't even tell when you're ovulating? Listen, I know you're worried that I'm going to change my mind about being with you, and that's why you haven't wanted to get married yet, but I swear, I did not let this happen to trap you."

Kenzie looked up into Sawyer's handsome face. She loved this man so much, and now, she was going to have his baby. She knew they had a lot to work on and work out, but just like that, she knew everything was going to be okay.

She looked down as she put her hand on her flat stomach and whispered, "We're going to have a half Kenzie–half Sawyer."

"I'm sorry. What was that? I couldn't hear you."

She shrieked and threw her arms around her man. "Oh my God, we're going to have a half Kenzie–half Sawyer."

Sawyer picked her up, and she wrapped her legs around his waist.

"I know," he said with a laugh.

She leaned back far enough so that she could see his face. "Are you okay with this?"

"Are you kidding me? I'm fucking ecstatic." He brought her closer until their noses touched. "Are you okay with this?"

She grinned at him. "More than you could ever know."

FORBIDDEN ADDICTION SAMPLE

Phoenix Kaplan raised her hand to the Guardians' entrance, hesitating for a second before knocking. It was always the same. She shouldn't be here, yet here she stood.

She rubbed her hands over her arms. It was early April, and while it was spring, the nights were still cool, and she was wearing only a light sweater.

The door swung open to reveal Lexine Harlow. "Oh, it's you," she said with an air of disappointment and contempt. "He's in his office," she added, not even waiting for Phoenix to come in as she walked away.

One would think that, after the mating of the Guardians' vampire princess to the Minnesota Pride's alpha's son months ago and the birth of their babies around the corner, Lexine would be more cordial. A relationship had formed between the two species, and all the Guardians had been welcoming of Phoenix and her monthly visits, except for Lexine.

Not that Phoenix cared too much. It was more of an

annoyance than a concern. She really wasn't here to make friends anyway.

She was here for Dante.

Phoenix stepped over the threshold and closed the front door behind her before heading down the hall to Dante's office.

Phoenix had a somewhat complicated past with the vampire.

When Vaughn and Naya mated and someone tried to kidnap them along with Vaughn's sister, Phoenix was sent with Naya and Vaughn to stay at the Guardians' compound for safety. Phoenix didn't want to be there from the start. She wasn't prejudiced against the vampires; she just hated being on protective duty, on defense. She wanted to be out in the field, searching and fighting, on the offensive. She hated sitting around, waiting. And she hated her reaction to Dante.

Phoenix had a painful history when it came to the opposite gender and intimacy. She'd had a not-so-great childhood, and as she'd gotten older, she'd had a couple of sexual encounters that both ended in disasters. She wasn't able to be the kind of woman who men wanted in the bedroom. And, even with those couple of men—boys really because it had been years ago—she'd never felt attraction to them the way she did with Dante.

At first, she didn't know what she felt toward him, not recognizing her desire for what it was because she hadn't experienced it before. Her partners in the past had been good-looking with nice, gentle demeanors, and that was basically what had drawn her to them. But, with Dante, it was pure sexual magnetism. Pun intended because Phoenix's cat was very into him.

Good thing she had complete control over her cat since, no matter how much she was attracted to Dante, it wouldn't end well if she let herself go there. Because, now that she knew Dante better, Phoenix liked him. She would rather get in a fight with five to one odds than see that look of pity in his eyes that she'd seen from her past bedroom efforts. She might be damaged, but she still had her pride.

During her stay at the Guardians' manor, they discovered who was behind the abductions, and they were all planning to go out into the field when Vaughn brought up Dante's need to feed. Due to the male cat-shifter's new mate, he had recognized Dante's need, much to Dante's irritation.

Phoenix would do anything for her friends and fellow sentinels—they had proven their loyalty to her, and they were the only family she had—so she volunteered to be the metaphorical sacrificial lamb. It might not be a big thing to some, but for her to offer up her blood and therefore her body, it was a huge deal. The funny thing was, Dante promptly turned her down—informing her that, when he fed, he fucked—but she persisted, confronting him again a few days later.

He tried to intimidate her, which was easy at first. She caught him in his bedroom after coming out of the shower, so he was only wearing a towel, and he tried to use his near nakedness to get her to leave. She swallowed all her nerves and continued on with her mission to get Dante to feed. But, when she offered to have sex with him, most of the fight had left his body, and she was immediately relieved. It felt a little too close to prostitution, even with her unwanted attraction to Dante. Phoenix then thought he would feed from her wrist to maintain a good distance between them, but Dante fed from her neck instead. She didn't know if a part of him was still punishing her for pushing him into the situation or if he wanted to be close to her. Maybe both, but she didn't ask because she truly didn't know what she wanted the answer to be.

So, Dante pulled her close and held her against his bedroom door as he proceeded to sink his fangs into her neck. It scared her. Not because it hurt or because she was a coward, but because she was turned on. That frightened the shit out of her. And, somehow, Dante knew. Over the years, Phoenix had worked very hard to hide her feelings. Shifters and vampires could sense emotions, and she in no way wanted hers to be used against her again, so she had learned to cover hers. Yet Dante knew she was aroused, and he completely shocked her when he cut his thumb and stuck it in her mouth. She never tasted anything like it. Vampire blood was sweet. Not like sugary candy, but more like chili with loads of brown sugar in it. Rich, hearty, and saccharine.

But that wasn't even the biggest shocker.

What completely blew her mind was that, with the combination of Dante sucking on her neck, rubbing his erection between her legs, and putting his blood in her mouth, Phoenix orgasmed. Pathetically, the first one she'd ever had in her life. Not that she hadn't tried to get herself off before—she was a twenty-first century woman after all—but she just hadn't succeeded. Not only that, but her scent, the scent of her lust, filled the room. So ashamed and a little horrified that Dante had gotten her off and exposed her scent, she fled his bedroom as soon as he released her. It was only later she remembered that Dante had climaxed, too. It didn't ease her humiliation, but it was a relief to know she wasn't the only one affected.

Phoenix avoided Dante after that for a while. To this day, they still hadn't talked about it. And any thoughts of discussing it were pushed aside when she was kidnapped by her alpha's corrupt cousin and then rescued by Dante. She found out later that Dante had located her through the blood he'd consumed from her. She was shaken up from her ordeal, and she asked Dante to take her home with him. He hadn't even hesitated before agreeing. And, when Dante had discovered what Gerald had done to her while under his control, he was kind and gentle as he healed her with the enzymes in his saliva. After that encounter, she slept in his bed next to him for the next three weeks because she couldn't sleep alone with Gerald still on the loose. Something else they hadn't talked about because they went to bed and woke up at different times, and with the exception of Phoenix waking to find Dante sleeping on her hair, they hadn't touched.

Then, Dante was shot in the leg and asked Phoenix to feed him again while he was still in his hospital bed. Refusing him hadn't even crossed her mind. That time, she was the one who offered her neck, she was the one who cut Dante's finger and slipped it in her mouth so that she could suck on his blood, and she was the one who rubbed her groin over his. After they both came again, Dante seemed to have some regret, and she left the room before he could say the words out loud. She went back to the bunkhouse that night and ignored all of Dante's phone calls and texts.

Phoenix ran into him at Naya and Vaughn's New Year's party where she learned that him sleeping next to her and feeding from her had been no big deal to Dante. He wanted to make sure he hadn't hurt her since they were *friends*. While she hadn't slept next to another male and had experienced her most satisfying sexual experiences with him, it was "just sleeping and feeding, a form of nourishment" to him. It was way more than a big deal to her. The embarrassment still stung even if Dante had no idea how she felt. That was why she would not attempt a full-on sexual relationship with him. Anything she felt that night would be tenfold worse when he discovered how defective she was in bed.

She probably would have avoided Dante at all costs after that night, but when he later called three times in less than five minutes, she knew it had to be something important. And it was. Dante found Gerald, and instead of informing her alpha, Vance, he called her. She would forever remember that.

Dante and Phoenix went after Gerald, stupidly without backup. Phoenix was so angry at what he'd done to her that all she wanted was revenge. Dante must have known and didn't even attempt to stop her. And it almost got him killed. In their scuffle with Gerald, Phoenix was shot, and so was Dante, but this time, it hadn't been in the leg. Phoenix killed Gerald when she discovered Dante was hurt, and she finally used her brain and called for help before offering Dante her vein and passing out.

When she woke up in the hospital, she discovered that Dante had refused to leave her side and that she'd given him so much blood that she needed a blood transfusion, which Dante had provided because he wouldn't let anyone else do it. They spent the rest of their time in the hospital side by side—not touching, but reassuring each other with their presence. It was just one more thing the two of them hadn't discussed, and instead, since then, Phoenix would show up every month to feed Dante. Dante got blood, and she got skin-to-skin contact that satisfied her shifter DNA. They didn't talk about her coming—he didn't ask, and she didn't offer—but she always showed up, and he never refused her. One thing was for sure, Dante + Phoenix = Avoidance with a capital A.

Like she'd said, complicated.

She knew they couldn't go on like this forever, and she dreaded ending their time together, but she wasn't about to be the one to bring up the subject because it might end sooner if she said something. Nope, she was going to leave things exactly the way they were. She'd take what little she could get.

Phoenix reached Dante's office, raised her hand, and knocked.

(

Dante Leonidas raised his head from the map spread out on his desk from where he'd been studying it when he heard the rap at his door.

Phoenix.

Usually, he prepared himself before she arrived, but he'd been so lost in thought that he didn't notice her scent or her presence despite her blood in him. He cursed himself for not paying attention, but it didn't really matter. He'd never be truly equipped to see her.

"Enter," he called out.

The entrance to his office opened, and Phoenix slipped through before closing the door behind her.

Dante held his breath as the aroma of sunshine flooded the room, but it was too late. Her scent teased his nostrils, and suddenly, his pants were too tight as his cock hardened under his fly. He had to reach down and adjust himself under the desk before the painful position caused him to wince. Males always talked about having big dicks, but honestly, it wasn't that great. It could really be a pain in the ass sometimes. No pun intended.

"Hey," the beautiful cat-shifter said as she approached his desk.

She was sans makeup with her long red-and-black hair in a ponytail while she wore her usual outfit of shapeless clothing. Today, it was a sweater and jeans. But, despite her baggy attire, Dante could still make out her curves underneath. It didn't hurt that he'd seen her without her clothes in the past. Picturing her naked didn't help his hard-on.

She glanced down at the Minneapolis/St. Paul area map that he'd been reviewing before she entered. "What are you looking at?"

He pointed to the Xs he'd made in red. "I marked all the incidents on the list in hopes that maybe a pattern or something would jump out at me." Dante threw the pen he had been holding on top of the map as he leaned back in his chair and exhaled his frustration. "So far, it's been a bust."

Over the last few months, crimes had been happening to vampire and shifter residences and places of business. It wasn't like the paranormal community was immune to crime, but the unusual part about it was how they were all coming in pairs. Whatever happened to a vampire-owned place, the same thing would happen to a shifter-owned place. The first incident had been graffiti at a vampire-owned restaurant on the same night a shifter-owned restaurant was hit. It was an obvious message to both vampires and shifters. The latest incidents were fires started at vampire- and shifter-owned homes within an hour of each other. The worst part of the entire situation was that the human police were starting to notice.

Phoenix came around to his side of the desk and leaned over to read the map and his notes. Her baggy pants hung on her hips, but when she bent over, they stretched across her ass, and Dante had to fight not to ogle her. His erection got harder, if that was even possible, and he fought his desire to pull her into his lap, strip off her clothes, and bury himself inside her.

But that would never happen.

Despite the fact that she was there to feed him, they were not in a romantic or sexual relationship. Dante didn't know all the details about what had happened to Phoenix in her past, but he knew she had been traumatized. So, while he usually had sex with the females he fed from, the only thing he'd be sinking inside her were his fangs. His little head didn't get it, but his big head did, and he wasn't going to add to her issues. For now, feeding from her and being her friend was enough. But, damn, this celibacy thing just might kill him.

Maybe, someday, he would tell her how he felt about her, but today wasn't that day. She wasn't ready to hear it.

Turning his thoughts back to the task at hand, he asked her, "Have you guys come up with anything?"

She spun around and sat on the edge of the desk, the emerald green of her eyes filled with vexation. "No. Are you coming to the meeting tomorrow?"

"Yes, we'll all be there."

"That's good." She nodded her approval. "One of the wolf-shifter sentinels is an officer in the Minneapolis Police Department. Damien told Vance that the sentinel would fill us in on what the humans knew."

The wolf-shifter alpha was really proving himself to the cat-shifter alpha. Damien wasn't going to let the newly healed bond between the two subspecies get fractured again, it seemed.

Dante furrowed his brows. "You don't have any cat-shifters in the police force?"

"Yes, we do, but none of them are sentinels. They give us information, but we don't share what we know back with them. It's a good idea, what Damien did, having someone work both angles. I just hope Vance doesn't make one of us sign up for the police academy." She made a face of disgust. "At least, I hope it isn't me."

Dante chuckled. "Humans aren't that bad."

She looked at him like he was crazy. "Humans aren't that bad? The same species that traditionally comes at your species with a stake through the heart?"

"Pretty sure none of the members of the St. Paul Police Department are carrying stakes."

"No, just guns."

He laughed again. "I suppose you have a point."

"So, does that mean you have vampires on the force? How does that work with the sun thing?"

"Of course we do. They enter the academy before their conversion, and after, they work the night shift." Dante frowned. "Although I never thought to have one of the Guardians work for us and the police at the same time. It is smart."

The conversation stalled, and silence fell over the room. Their eyes met, but neither moved.

The knock at the door broke the quietness, and Dante looked at the bare skin on Phoenix's neck. "Come back later. I'm busy."

He swiveled his chair to face her and opened his legs. "Come here, Red."

Order Now!

ABOUT THE AUTHOR

R.L. Kenderson is two best friends writing under one name.

Renae has always loved reading, and in third grade, she wrote her first poem where she learned she might have a knack for this writing thing. Lara remembers sneaking her grandmother's Harlequin novels when she was probably too young to be reading them, and since then, she knew she wanted to write her own.

When they met in college, they bonded over their love of reading and the TV show *Charmed*. What really spiced up their friendship was when Lara introduced Renae to romance novels. When they discovered their first vampire romance, they knew there would always be a special place in their hearts for paranormal romance. After being unable to find certain storylines and characteristics they wanted to read about in the hundreds of books they consumed, they decided to write their own.

One lives in the Minneapolis-St. Paul area and the other in the Kansas City area where they're a sonographer/stay-at-home mom/wife and pharmacist/mother by day, and together they're a sexy author by night. They communicate through phone, email, and whole lot of messaging.

You can find them at http://www.rlkenderson.com, Facebook, Instagram, TikTok, Twitter, and Goodreads. Join their reader group! Or you can email them at rlkenderson@ rlkenderson.com, or sign up for their newsletter. They always love hearing from their readers.